CHILDREN OF THE SPIRITS

Guardians of the Circles:
Book Two

D J Eastwood

Copyright © 2021 by D J Eastwood

All rights reserved. This book or any portion thereof may not be reproduced or used in any manner whatsoever without the express written permission of the publisher except for the use of brief quotations in a book review.

First Printing, 2021

ISBN: 979-8706670726

www.apprenticetattoo.co.uk

Cover art by: Fay Lane

Map by: Dewi Hargreaves

THE GREAT ISLAND

Isle of Pigs
BRIDGE CLAN
High Island
Isle of Eagles
EAGLE TRIBE

The Long Islands
CLASSAC
Cheel People
BAY CLAN
CHEEL TOMBS
SHORE CLAN

Atay Clans
Doran Clans

Canna People

CRANAI TRIBE

Manu's Isle

The Great Forested Isle

Uru Tribe

ESTUARY CLAN
FOREST CLAN

Cambay Clans
Poan Lands
Ammen Tribe
GORGE CLAN
BRON'S CAVE

Yofa People

Danna Tribe
STANNA
BAY CLAN

Get your free book!

A prequel in the Guardians of the Circles series.

Albyn and Layne run away to avoid an arranged bonding with a man Layne doesn't love.
Heading for a new life on the Great Island, they are captured by the hostile Eagle Tribe and forced into slavery.
When their escape is thwarted, Albyn takes brutal revenge, and steals an artefact of great power, but how will he control the wrath of the spirit it holds?

Go to www.apprenticetattoo.co.uk for more details.

One.

"Lorev!"

She was here again.

He pulled the warm furs from over his head. The child's dark-rimmed eyes glared. A few rags were the only covering on her filthy, emaciated body.

Lorev rubbed at gritty eyes. "Why do you torment me, Verra?"

"Because you lived while I starved. You found parents, became protected-of-spirit, had siblings. I wander the earth, denied a place with my ancestors."

"I cannot help you, Sister. I don't know where your bones lie."

Hessa mumbled in her sleep nearby, turning over. Lorev glanced back at her.

"She will never be yours unless you free me," Verra whispered. "Avenge my death, lay my bones to rest, or you will never be worthy of her."

"But…" Lorev began, as the ghost of his sister faded. "Wait, how can I…"

She was gone.

Lorev lifted the furs and slipped from the bed. He pulled on his clothes and stuffed his few belongings into a bag. His travelling cloak was peppered with swan feathers, a cape of wolf-skin covered the shoulders. He fastened it around him and turned to look at the serene face of the sleeping girl.

"When I am worthy of you, Hessa, when I have avenged the death of my sister and laid her to rest, I will return," he whispered, stroking a stray hair from her face.

The door creaked as he crept outside and turned south. Silver starlight illuminated the thatched roofs of the silent village, and he almost left his skin when a voice came from the dark.

"What do I tell them, Lorev?" Albyn said, stepping out of the shadows, Lorev's small sister, Shilla, clutching his hand. Lorev knew better than to try to fool the spirit messenger.

"Tell them I have to go, so I may become worthy."

"Worthy of what?"

"Worthy to ask for Hessa's promise of bonding," Lorev said, stepping closer. He knelt before his sister, taking her free hand. "I have to go," he said. Shilla nodded. "Look after mother and father; take care of our siblings."

"Will you come back to us, Lorev?" Shilla asked, tears sliding down her cheeks.

"Yes, little one. As soon as I can." Lorev kissed her forehead and stood to embrace Albyn. "They won't understand," Lorev said.

"They may surprise you." Albyn felt for Lorev's hand and pressed a leather pouch into it. "These are talismans of power, they may be of use to you one day."

Lorev looked at the messenger's sightless eyes and patted his hand, then turned and walked away.

* * *

It had taken two days to reach the village of the Boat Clan. Lorev had neglected to take food with him, and his stomach rumbled as he traipsed down the hill towards the cluster of houses on the bay.

A pregnant woman stepped from a roundhouse as he approached. "Greetings, Apprentice Lorev," she said, holding out her hands, palms up.

Lorev grinned. "Greetings, Messenger Rolva. When is your young one due?"

"Soon. Very soon, I hope," she said, stretching and cradling her back. "Are you alone?"

Lorev nodded.

"Come in, we're about to eat. Did Col send you with a message?"

"No," he said. "I need to make a journey of my own."

"Where are you going?" she said, handing Lorev a bowl of stew. Her mate came in with their three children, and the conversation was forgotten.

* * *

"So, talk to me," Rolva said, pulling him aside. The meal had been cleared, and the children dispatched to bed.

"I am making my own journey," he said.

"Why?"

"To prove my worth."

Rolva studied his face for a moment. "What aren't you telling me?"

Lorev sighed. "My birth mother was a slave to outlaws. One of them fathered my sister and me."

"You have a sister?" she said.

"Had. When the villagers ran the outlaws off, my mother tried to return to her home. The clan leader refused to have my sister, Verra, and me in his village. He said our blood was tainted. Mother took us back to the cave, but there was no food. Verra died. She was just five summers old."

"Do you wish to find your birth mother?" Rolva said, "Col and Talla adopted you, didn't they?"

"Verra has haunted me for years," Lorev said, wiping a tear from his cheek. "I will never be worthy of Hessa until I lay my sister to rest and avenge her death."

"Does Hessa know you are doing this?" Lorev shook his head. "She loves you, you know."

"Hessa? She barely knows I'm there," he said.

"Spirits!" Rolva shouted. "Are you both blind? Stop this foolishness and go home, Lorev."

"No, I must do this," he said, "You will not change my mind."

Rolva glared at him and stood up. "Then sleep, Bek says you sail at first light."

* * *

Lorev was dying. He lay in the bottom of the boat, knees drawn up to his chest as he retched yet again. He'd never been in a boat on open water. His breakfast came up not long after they'd sailed, and now his belly was sore from dry heaving.

At last, the torture ended, and Bek helped him to the beach. He lay on the merciful sand for a long time, and the boat was unloaded and hauled by the time he struggled to his feet.

He refused food and crawled into the bed they gave him.

* * *

Lorev said his thanks to the Shore Clan next morning and took the path south.

He made good time that day, pulling the hide of his shelter over him to sleep in the warm night, then was away again at first light.

The rolling hills and broad green valleys were unlike his home on the island. He must have travelled this way after his adoption by Col and Talla but had no memory of it.

Travelling became slower when he reached the denser woodlands, but broad tracks led him further south, and half a moon had passed when Lorev reached a village one night that offered him shelter and food. He sat with the elderly messenger after they'd eaten; the fire casting writhing shadows on the wall behind them.

"How long before I reach the Poan lands?"

"This is the last clan of the Atay tribe," she said. "Two days' walk. Then you will be in Poan lands."

* * *

The wolf's fur was warm under his chin as he pulled his travelling cloak around him to sleep. He had set his little shelter on the edge of woodland, and was glad of it, for the night was cold.

He remembered the wolf, wounded by the hunters' arrows, lying whimpering, its breathing ragged. A lone wolf. Dangerous. His clan had tracked and trapped it.

"Wolf is your spirit animal," Col said, his foot holding the wounded animal's head down. "Take the kill, Lorev."

Lorev touched the fresh tattoos around his eye, took his flint blade and plunged it into the wolf's throat. Hot blood soaked his hand as the creature yelped and struggled its last.

"Take the skin," Col said, "Here, I'll help you."

The two of them stripped the hide, rolling it tight before following the hunting party home.

Lorev heard a low growl and turned over on the hard ground. Still dreaming, he thought. The noise came again, and he sat up, as a rasping snarl almost hid the scream of a man. Struggling free of his cloak, he crawled outside in the pre-dawn gloom. A grey wolf was tearing at a struggling form.

"Hey!" he shouted before he'd had time to think. The wolf turned, its muzzle dark and dripping, ravenous eyes glowing in the dying moonlight. It took only a moment to gather itself before leaping at Lorev. He pulled his flint knife as the beast hit him, crushing him to the ground. He held on to its neck as jaws snapped, and claws scrabbled at his belly and legs. Lorev rolled, getting behind the creature, his arms clutching its throat. He stabbed his blade under the animal's jaw, dragging downward. The yelp deafened him as he tried to hold on, while slick blood soaked his arms. He was losing his grip when the creature slumped to the ground, twitching. Lorev lay gasping for breath. He looked down to find himself covered in blood, unable to see if he was injured. He felt at his stinging belly but could find no wounds.

"Help me," a voice croaked. Lorev checked the carcass of the wolf, but it lay unmoving. He crawled towards the sound. The sky was lightening now, and he could make out a man, laying on his back, skin and flesh were torn from his shoulder. He groaned and reached a hand for Lorev.

"Help me. Please," he said, then passed out.

Lorev inspected the wound. The flesh was ripped away, the bone of his shoulder showing. Running to his shelter, he pulled a spare shirt from his pack, wrapping it around the bleeding joint. He checked the man but found no other wounds. He retrieved his cape, covered the body, and sat beside him.

Lorev didn't have the knowledge to treat the man. The wound needed sewing if it could be treated, and he did not know where he had come from.

"It hurts. It hurts so much," the man said, stirring.

"Where are you from?" Lorev asked, leaning down to hear.

"Village... West... Not far," he said, then lost consciousness again.

Lorev looked about. The only way to shift him would be a pole drag like those his clan used to carry game or move heavy loads. He searched the woodland, finding two fallen birches. Lashing the thin ends together with rawhide cord, he laid the shelter hide over the frame and tied it on. The man was dead weight as he dragged him onto the makeshift structure. Pulling on his cloak, Lorev picked up the pole drag, checked the rising sun for direction, and headed west.

Two.

Shilla sat on a rock, staring out across the water. She rubbed again at her reddened eyes.

"What's wrong?" Jeeha asked, taking her hand. The girls considered themselves sisters, both having six summers.

"Lorev's gone."

"He'll be back later. Come on, let's play in the sand."

"No, he's gone," Shilla repeated. "He left in the night."

"Shilla! Jeeha! Come and get your food," Hessa shouted from the door of the roundhouse.

"Coming," Jeeha called.

"Why the sad face," Hessa said, passing platters to the two girls, then feeding the smaller ones.

"Lorev's gone," Jeeha said.

Hessa turned. "Yes, where is he? I don't think I've seen him all morning."

"He has gone away," Albyn said, feeling his way to the hearth and settling in his usual place. He grasped the plate Hessa put on his lap.

"Cold meat and cheese," she told him, "The meat is nearest to you. When will he be back?"

"Many moons, I expect," Albyn said, finding a piece of beef and biting into it.

Hessa's face creased in confusion. "Moons? I knew nothing of a journey."

The old man finished chewing and swallowed. "He feels the need to prove himself worthy. He has gone to avenge his sister and lay her bones to rest."

"What do you know, Albyn?" Col said, joining the meal, "Where has he gone?"

"Across the water. He is haunted by his sister, Verra. He plans to put right the wrongs done to her."

Col set his platter aside. "I must go after him. That is no journey for a boy his age."

Albyn turned his blind eyes towards the sound of Col's voice and raised his hand. "No. He has fifteen summers, only a year less than you and Talla when you set off on your quest. He will not thank you for following him."

* * *

Albyn shuffled towards the sound of sniffling and felt for the edge of Hessa's bed, easing his frame down to sit beside her.

"Why, Albyn?" she asked. "I thought he might be ready to ask for my promise of bonding."

The messenger put his arm around her shoulders, pulling her head to him.

"Perhaps there are things he needs to do before he can ask that of you." He felt the wetness of her tears as she nodded. "Lorev promised Shilla he would return. He will not break that promise."

"But, what will I do without him?" she asked.

"Busy yourself. That is what I have always done when I need to put something – or someone out of my mind."

The girl wrapped her arms around the old man, and he held her while she cried.

* * *

"What can we do?" Talla asked, climbing into bed and laying her head on Col's chest.

"We should have laid the girl to rest when we found Lorev and his mother," Col said.

"But we didn't know she had not had the funeral rites."

Col shivered at the thought of wandering this plane eternally. "No."

"The Walking Spirits," Talla said, sitting up. "We must ask them."

"You're right. Lay with me, we'll travel together."

They lay side by side, holding hands, their breathing slowed as their minds went blank. They no longer needed the help of spirit mushrooms to take them to their walking spirits, just focusing and slipping into a trance state worked, especially together.

"Son of Fire, Daughter of the Winds," the two apparitions welcomed them.

"Greetings, Galvac, Dirva," Col said as he and Talla bowed. "We seek your help with something."

Dirva smiled. "The boy is well," she said. "He makes this journey for himself. Do not hinder him."

"He is young, we worry," Talla said.

"His Walking Spirit follows him," Galvac said. "He will get the help he needs."

"He has a Walking Spirit, already?" Col asked.

"Every human has a spirit that loves them, that watches over them, son of the Sun," Galvac said. "The only difference with spirit masters, such as yourselves, is that we can interact each with the other."

"Then he will return soon?" Talla asked.

"He has a special destiny, child of the air," Dirva smiled. "There are things he must discover about himself and his world. He will return when he is ready."

"There is one who waits for him," Talla said.

"The messenger, Hessa? She has much to learn before his return, too," Galvac said. "Begin her master's training soon."

Talla and Col bowed, thanking their guides.

"Back," Col said.

Talla stirred beside her mate.

"I shall still worry," she said.

"I know," Col said, pulling her close. "Sleep though, tomorrow we shall talk to Hessa."

* * *

"Master's training?" Hessa said, "But I've only just made it to messenger status."

"We have been told it is your destiny, Hessa," Talla said, taking the girl's hand. "Will you do it?"

Hessa nodded. "Yes, Spirit Master."

Three.

The sun was clear of the horizon when Lorev spotted smoke rising above the trees. His legs gave way just as the first houses came into view.

"Help me," he called, attracting the attention of a woman with a child. She stared, open-mouthed for a moment, then grabbed the child's hand and ran off, soon returning with a group of men.

"What has happened?" one asked, staring at Lorev's blood-soaked body.

"A wolf attacked him," Lorev said, nodding towards the pole drag.

"And you?"

"I killed it. I don't think the blood is mine."

"Take him to the messenger's house," the man said, taking the pole drag from Lorev. He breathed a sigh as two men pulled the body across the clearing towards a central house.

"I am Parlan," the man said, holding out his hands in a belated welcome. "I am Leader of the Forest Clan of the Poan people." He peered at Lorev's blood-streaked face. "Are you protected-of-spirit?"

"An apprentice," Lorev said. He rubbed dried blood from his tattoos, trying to catch his breath.

Parlan turned to the woman who'd raised the alarm. "Terra, take the apprentice to the stream to wash, then bring him to Messenger Govat's house."

She nodded, then led Lorev to the water's edge, helping him sit and bathe himself. She hissed when she spotted the gouges on the lad's legs and belly.

Lorev's finger traced a deep scratch, oozing blood, and he winced.

"Come," she said, taking his arm, "Messenger Govat will treat them. What is your name?"

"I am Lorev," he said, smiling. He saw the smile leave Terra's face for a moment.

"Come," she said, "Let's get you to the messenger."

* * *

A group of people were standing outside the messenger's house, peering through the doorway.

"Why bother with him?" one man said.

"He'd be more useful as food for the wolf," said a woman.

"Excuse me," Terra said, pulling a woman aside and dragging Lorev into the house.

"Who's he?" she asked.

"Mind your business and not mine," Terra snapped.

As Lorev's eyes became accustomed to the darkness in the house, he could see a man stooped over a bed. A young girl sat on the edge, a bowl of bloody water in her lap. Healing tools were laid out beside her. An awl, sinew, a blade and linen bandages. The man turned as Lorev approached.

"Sit. You look exhausted," he said. "We will talk after I deal with these wounds."

Terra led him to a spare bed and made him comfortable. "I am Parlan's mate," she said. "You are Lorev?"

"Yes. I am an apprentice of the Hill Clan of the Tribe of the West."

"You come from the islands, across the water," she said.

"You know the islands?" Lorev asked.

"Yes, I know who you are. Rest, I need to find someone."

Lorev wondered how this woman could know of his people, but the bed was soft and warm, and he soon closed his eyes.

* * *

Gentle fingers on his belly roused him. Lorev tried to sit up, but a small hand pushed him back.

"Keep still," the girl said, scooping ointment from a wooden bowl. Lorev peered down as she rubbed the green paste into his scratches.

It was the girl he'd seen sitting with the spirit messenger. "Are you an apprentice?" Lorev asked.

She nodded, turning her face so he could see the marks around her left eye. "I am Gianna," she said, "Govat is my father."

There was a commotion at the door, then a woman rushed in, looking about before coming to Lorev's bed.

"Lorev? Is it really you?" she asked, reaching to stroke his face.

Lorev flinched, inspecting the woman, wondering who she was, and how she knew him. It was when he looked into her eyes he saw it.

"Mother?" the word felt strange on his tongue. She was older, plumper than he remembered, but he would never forget the hazel of her eyes. Talla had been his mother for seven years, and Lorev wondered what his birth mother was to him now.

"Oh, Lorev. You came back to me." Her gaze fell to the wounds on his belly. "What happened to you? How did you get these scratches?"

"A wolf. It attacked the old man," Lorev said.

His mother turned to the spirit messenger as he washed the blood from his hands. "Who is hurt, Govat?"

"No friend of yours, Vinna. It is Arvan," the messenger said, walking over to Lorev's bed.

Lorev looked up at the name. "Arvan? The leader who killed my sister?"

"Killed?" Govat said.

Vinna pulled a bench closer and sat, motioning for Govat to join her.

"This was before you came here, Govat," she began, "Arvan was the leader then. He denied my children food and shelter. My daughter, Verra, died of starvation."

"But, what was he doing out in the woods at night?" Lorev asked, sitting on the edge of the bed.

"After you left with Col and Talla, the clan's fortunes worsened," she said. "Crops were poor, or failed, animals became sick and died, a boar injured two hunters. Our old spirit messenger consulted the ancestors. They said the spirits were angry at Arvan's treatment of you, that he was to blame. The village was desperate, so they made Arvan an outcast."

"Outcast? What does that mean?" Lorev said.

"He was no longer of the Forest Clan," Govat explained, "No longer even Poan. They threw him out of the village to fend for himself. No one could see him, no one spoke to him."

"Then why is he still here?" Lorev asked.

"He lives from the village midden, scavenging food, maybe finding wild food in season. I expect he was planning on stealing from you, but the wolf beat him to it."

Lorev sighed and buried his face in his hands. "I came here to kill him; to avenge Verra. Now you tell me I have saved his life?"

"He may live, it is true," Govat said, "But he is frail."

Lorev stood up and tried to fasten his ripped leggings and shirt. "Gianna, fetch some of my clothes for Lorev,"

Govat said. The girl scurried off, returning with clothing. Lorev thanked her and pulled them on.

"I must get my belongings," he said, "I left everything at my camp."

"Gianna will go with you," Govat said, "You are still tired and weak."

Lorev bid his mother goodbye and followed the girl outside. "This way," Lorev said, following the tracks of his pole drag out of the village.

"So, your father is a messenger, and you are an apprentice," Lorev said, "Is your mother protected-of-spirit too?"

Gianna slowed a little and looked at her feet. "She has crossed the death river," she said.

"I'm sorry."

Gianna sniffed. "There's just the two of us now."

They walked on in silence for a while, before Lorev spoke again.

"When did you apprentice? You have, what, eight summers?"

"Nine," she said, "I got my tattoos young, just seven summers."

"I have a sister of six summers…"

Gianna's hand shot out, stopping Lorev. He looked up, seeing the carcass of the wolf ahead.

"It's dead, Gianna. I slit its throat."

"It moved, Lorev. Watch."

They stood for a moment, then the dead wolf twitched. There was a snuffling sound, then silence.

"Rats?" Lorev asked.

Gianna drew a knife. "I don't think so."

They crept closer, eyes on the wolf. Lorev went right, Gianna left. There was a soft whine, then a small head appeared.

"It's a cub," Gianna said. "She had young. What do we do with it?"

"Wolf is my spirit animal," Lorev said, "I must take it with me." He knelt beside the cub, holding out his hand. The tiny animal bared its teeth as its ears flattened.

Gianna giggled. "He's a brave one."

Lorev scooped up the small wolf and found his pack lying not far away. He put the struggling cub into the bag, head protruding.

"Shall we take the skin?" Gianna said, kicking at the dead she-wolf.

Lorev took out his knife. "Yes, give me a hand." He muttered a prayer of thanks to the dead animal as Gianna slit open the belly.

* * *

The sun was overhead when they returned to the village. Lorev saw that someone had cleaned the blood from his shelter and hung it to dry in the sun. Gianna led him into the messenger's house, and they piled his belongings onto a bed.

"Lorev, a word with you, please," Govat said. Gianna took the struggling wolf-cub as her father led him outside. "I have done all I know to treat Arvan, but I cannot stop the bleeding," he said. "He will die."

"What then?" Lorev asked, "What becomes of his body, his spirit?"

"He has no clan, no people. I will not speak for him with the ancestors. He is an outcast."

"Then he will never cross the river?" Lorev said.

Govat shook his head. "No."

"Then, perhaps there is justice. Perhaps my sister's death will be avenged."

"Your sister demands this from beyond the river? Govat asked.

"She was never laid to rest. She walks this world still," Lorev said. "She haunts me."

Govat put up his hands, wrists crossed, palms out; the warding sign.

"No one sees her but me," Lorev said, "She will not trouble you."

"Go to the old man, before he dies," Govat said. "You may still find him conscious and say your piece to him."

* * *

Gianna pressed a cup of tea into his hand as he sat by the old man's bed. "Rosehip," she whispered, "Has he woken yet?"

Lorev shook his head. Gianna patted his arm and turned back towards the fire.

Arvan stirred, groaning as he moved his arm, blood staining the linen bandages. "Where am I?" he asked.

"The Forest Clan village," Lorev said.

"You… You saved me, didn't you?"

"I wish I hadn't."

"What do you mean?" Arvan asked.

"Do you know who I am? My name is Lorev, son of Vinna."

Arvan's eyes went wide.

"That's right. You remember, don't you? You banished my mother, my sister, and me to the caves in the hills. We lived like animals."

"I have paid for that, these last years," he said, "Living like a rat on the leavings of the village."

Lorev leaned closer. "My sister, Verra, starved to death because of you. She had no funeral rites. Her spirit walks this world yet."

"I… I'm sorry," Arvan said.

"You are dying, old man, and no one will speak for you. You will find out what it is like for your spirit to never rest."

"No! You must call the ancestors for me. I am Arvan of the…"

"Of what?" Lorev said. "Of no people. Of no clan."

The old man's breathing was fast and shallow now, his skin ash-grey. "Please," he whispered.

"Perhaps my sister will come to greet you," Lorev said, "To tell you what it has been like to find no rest for seven summers."

Lorev stood and turned towards the fire. He looked back over his shoulder. "I shall find her bones, and free her, but you will be trapped for all time."

Arvan sobbed with his last breaths, pleading to Lorev's retreating back. "Please. Stay with me. Speak for me. Please…"

"Has he gone?" Govat asked, as Lorev returned to the fire.

"If not yet, then soon," Lorev said.

Govat stood. "I should go to him."

"Let him suffer alone for his last moments," Lorev said.

Govat stared. "Is that necessary?"

"Almost every night I see Verra, every bone showing through her skin. She had five summers, Govat."

The messenger nodded and returned to his seat. "Very well."

* * *

Lorev heard whispering from the doorway as he finished the bread, and cheese, Gianna had brought him for breakfast. Three young girls shuffled in, standing in a line in front of him.

"I am Mai," said the tallest.

"I am Raya," said the middle girl. She nudged the smallest.

"Oh. I'm Debba."

"Devra," corrected Raya.

"Yes, Debba," she insisted.

Mai stepped forward, holding out her hands in greeting. "Mother sent us to meet you. We are your sisters."

Lorev stood, awkward with these strangers who claimed to be his blood. "Um, greetings. How old are you all?"

"I have six summers, Raya has five, and Devra has…"

"Three!" shouted the small girl, holding up four fingers. Lorev couldn't help but smile at the precocious child.

"Where is your mother today?" he asked.

"I'm here, Lorev," Vinna said, walking into the house and sitting on his bed. She touched his leg, and Lorev met her gaze. "I'm *your* mother too."

"No," Lorev said. "You gave me up. Col is my father and Talla, my mother. The ancestors agreed to my adoption."

"But you came back to see me."

Lorev glanced at the three girls. "Do the girls have tasks I am keeping them from?"

"Y… yes. Girls, help Joa with the ox hides."

The sisters scurried outside, giggling, as Vinna turned to her son.

"I came to avenge Verra," he said. "I came to find her bones and set her spirit free to go to those that love her. I never forgot you, Vinna, but I have another life now."

Vinna looked up at his use of her given name, a tear in her eye. "Then I have lost you? You are not the brother I have told my daughters about?"

"Brother? I don't know. I have a brother and two sisters at home, Vinna. I don't hate you. You had no choice but to give me up, but a brother to those girls?" He stared at the fire for a moment, fingers knotted in his lap. "I can only try."

Vinna nodded and sniffed. "I can see your parents have raised you to be an honourable man. I have cleaned your shelter, and I am repairing your clothing."

Lorev reached for her hand and squeezed it. "Thank you. Can we be friends?" he said.

"I'd like that," Vinna smiled.

Four.

Lorev watched as they carried the rigid body of Arvan out of the house.

"Where will you take him?" he asked Govat.

"The ridge to the south. The men will lay his body out, but there will be no ceremony. We will not inter the bones."

Lorev nodded. "Does Vinna have a mate, a father to the girls?"

"They cut the knot at the winter solstice. He returned to his home village," Govat said. "The children miss him, but all Vinna and he did was fight."

"May I stay awhile, Govat," Lorev asked. "Perhaps I should get to know Vinna's three girls."

"Stay as long as you wish, another apprentice is always useful."

* * *

The three girls sat on the grass, facing Lorev. He tipped the hazelnut-sized pebbles from the bag and turned to the eldest.

"Take four stones, Mai." The girl picked up four stones and looked at him. He nodded.

"Raya, take three." The girl picked up the pebbles, lips moving as she counted.

"Now, Devra. Can you count out three for me?"

"One… Two… Four… Three!" The delighted child held out the stones for Lorev to see. Mai and Raya giggled.

"You have the numbers mixed up, Devra," he smiled. "Let's do that again."

Lorev thought back to his own teacher, Albyn. The old blind man would sit for hours, feeling for the pebbles on the ground before him, arranging them in rows for Lorev to count. Once he was confident with the numbers, Lorev used to close his eyes, seeing the stones in his thoughts, just like Albyn.

He loved numbers and had exhausted his teacher's knowledge before he had ten summers. Numbers were constant. They were always right. Five and five always made ten, there was no doubt.

"One, two, three!" Devra chuckled, clinging to her stones. "Three, like me. Three summers." She looked at her siblings. "Three sisters!"

Lorev scooped up the stones and dropped them into the bag. "Enough for today," he said, standing. "Come, show me where to fill my water skin."

* * *

Lorev sat feeding strips of raw meat to the wolf-cub. Govat had told him he'd known several protected-of-spirit who had the wolf as a spirit animal, but none had ever kept a live wolf.

"How is he settling with you?" Gianna asked, stroking the cub's soft fur.

"He seems to have accepted me. What is your own animal?"

Gianna trilled a series of notes, and a robin flew in through the door, settling on her hand. The girl reached into a pouch, producing a few grass seeds for the bird. "Her name is Gliss. I have had her since I apprenticed," she said. "What will you call the wolf?"

Lorev picked up the cub. "Trav," he said, as the young wolf licked his face.

"Will you help me with the firewood?" Gianna asked.

Lorev set the cub on the ground and followed her outside, Trav bounding at his heel.

"How long will you stay?" Gianna said.

"Not long. I want to get to know Vinna's girls a little, though."

"Are they not your sisters?"

Lorev set down the load he was carrying and sighed. "My true sister, Verra, lies out there somewhere, her body and spirit trapped in our world." Gianna made the warding sign. "Until I free her spirit, I can't think about any other family."

* * *

In his dream, he had her at last. Hessa, the object of his affections, was his mate. He was cuddled up to her in bed. Warm. A smile on his face.

"No, Lorev," came the voice he knew so well. The vision of his love had vanished. He was alone in bed, Verra's ghost his only companion. "Not until you free me, will I allow you to have a mate. Until I am at rest, you will not rest."

"I have found my family here," Lorev said, "Our mother is here, we have sisters now."

"I am your sister!" the tiny child shouted. "Free me."

Lorev sat up in bed, rubbing at wet eyes.

"Are you all right?" Gianna asked, climbing from her own bed. She sat beside him. "You were talking in your sleep."

"She was here again. I have to find her, she will not wait any longer."

"Your sister?"

Lorev nodded. "I will leave tomorrow."

* * *

Lorev was lost. He'd set off from the Forest Clan village three days before, refusing Govat's offer of a guide. He'd walked the hills now for a day and a half, finding none of the landmarks he remembered from his childhood. Sitting on an exposed rock, he drank from his waterskin. The sun told him he was facing east. The outlaw cave had faced east. It had to be on this hillside. If this was the right hill.

The small wolf bounded off after some scent or another. Lorev got to his feet and followed, lacking any other idea of direction. He gasped as his foot caught a loose rock and he tumbled forward, pain shooting through his ankle.

"Curse this place!" he cried, rolling onto his back. He pulled his spare shirt from his pack, soaking it from his waterskin and wrapping it around the swelling foot. When he looked up, there it was. The exposed ledge where he and Verra had played as children was covered in scrubby trees. Bracken grew where once had been bare earth, but the black mouth of the cave showed through. Somewhere here, Verra's body lay.

He whistled for Trav and struggled to his feet. The cub bounced around him as he limped up the slope to the cavern he had once called home.

"Hello," he called, hobbling inside, though the place was deserted. Broken bed platforms lay strewn about, shredded, rotting furs clinging to the splintered wood. He had half expected to find some remnant of the outlaws themselves, but Vinna said they had all fled or died in the raid.

He sat on a rock shelf, examining his ankle. The joint was swelling, and it throbbed. Lorev pulled his sleeping fur from his pack and made a makeshift bed. He lowered himself to the floor and pulled out some of his travelling food. The hard bar of beef dripping, mixed with parched grains and dried berries was left from the previous winter, and the fat was becoming rancid. Lorev sighed and took a bite, chewing and swallowing as fast as he could, swigging water after each mouthful, washing away the stale taste.

He gathered up wood from the broken furnishings and got out his fire bow. Soon there was a small fire blazing in the hearth, and he stretched out, resting his leg, as the daylight faded.

* * *

Trav's playful yips woke him as the first rays of the sun speared into the cavern. He took a drink and checked his leg. The ankle throbbed, but he found it would bear a little weight. He hobbled outside, memories flooding back. He could almost hear the morning bustle of the outlaw camp, his mother lighting a fire to cook. If there was any food.

Lorev shook himself. The outlaws were gone, his mother was back at the village two days' walk away, but somewhere here, his sister's body lay. He forced down another bar of the travelling rations and explored the area.

Caves riddled the hillside, a few, like the one he'd slept in, were huge, others little more than burrows, just big enough to lie in. He started at the left-hand end and worked his way across the site. Some caves contained evidence of habitation, others were bare. He was almost at the end of the ledge when he found it. At the back of a tiny cave, laid out on a flat rock, were the bones of a child. Tears filled his eyes as he reached out, touching the small skull. The jaw bone shifted, clattering to the floor as Lorev leapt back, a cry escaping his lips.

"You can do this," he said aloud as his shaking fingers reached for the jawbone, setting it back in place. He put his right hand on her skull, the left amongst the jumble of rib bones.

"Ancestors that love us. This is Verra, a child of just five summers. She has been trapped here for seven years but wishes to join her ancestors across the river. Come for her, those of you who love her. Take her home." He withdrew his hands and waited. He needed to journey for her. As an apprentice, he'd tagged along on a few forays to the lower world, but he'd never led a journey, and he had no drum.

"Why didn't I think to bring a drum from the village," he whispered. He searched around, finding a stout stick and a hollow log that may once have been a pail. The wood made a satisfying 'thunk' when struck, so he sat next to his sister's bones, closed his eyes and began a steady rhythm.

Lorev felt like he was in a dense fog. The distant pounding of the makeshift drum sounded muffled somehow. He could see no distance in the grey landscape, could make out no figures. He shuffled forward, afraid of tripping in the gloom.

He heard it before he saw it — the splash and lap of water.

"Verra?" he called, hoping his sister was here, ready to cross to her kin. "Verra?"

Silence. Nothing but the sounds of the death river. Lorev stepped to the water's edge, raising his arms as he'd seen his father, Col, do.

"Ancestors that love us come for this little one. Take her home to her family."

Dark shapes moved on the far bank and the image of a man formed. "Who should we take, Apprentice? You are alone here."

"No. It's my sister. She needs to find peace."

"Then bring her to us," the spirit said.

"I... I spoke for her; laid hands on her and called her loved ones to her. I'm sure I did it right."

"She has not come to us. You have not brought her to us. Where is her spirit?" the figure asked.

"I don't know. Back!" Lorev shouted.

Lorev dropped the stick he was drumming with and crawled over to his sister's bones. He placed a hand on her skull and one on her ribs, repeating the prayer. Clambering back to his seat, he set up a rhythm again, descending into the dark world once more.

"Do you fail us again, Apprentice?" the spirit called. "Where is this girl you seek to send over the river?"

Lorev cast about, searching. "I spoke for her. She wants to cross... Verra? Verra?"

He was almost screaming the name when the form of his sister walked out of the gloom.

"There you are." He tried to reach for her, but she snatched her hand back.

"Would you touch a spirit of the dead, brother? Would you try to cross the river yourself?"

"No. You can cross now. I have freed you from this world. Go to your loved ones, Verra."

"I can't," she said, her wide eyes gazing into him.

"Yes, I have spoken for you. Go."

She shook her head. "The powers will not allow it. You have talismans, powerful magic, that do not belong to you. They must be returned."

Lorev clutched at the eagle talon necklace, unfastening it. He slipped the small stone tablet from his neck too and held them out to Verra. "Take them. They were a gift. I'd no idea they were stolen."

"You must return them, not I," she said, turning, "Their loss has caused much strife."

"Wait!" Lorev said, "I don't know who they belong to."

"Go north," the retreating ghost said. "Far to the north."

Five.

Hessa pulled the hood of her cloak tighter as the rain got heavier. She'd seen the storm coming, but had hoped to reach the Boat Clan village before it hit. She clattered in through the door of the messenger's roundhouse, pushing wet hair from her face.

"Thank you for coming, Hessa," the young apprentice girl said, rushing to hug her.

"I came as soon as the runner arrived, Dorlan," Hessa smiled, stripping off her wet cloak. "How is she?"

The girl led her towards the back of the house where Messenger Rolva lay, a tiny child asleep between her full breasts. Tired eyes opened, and Rolva attempted a smile.

"Hessa. Sorry to trouble you, this was a bad birth."

Hessa stroked the messenger's cheek. "It's fine. I will help all I can." She turned to the skinny apprentice. The ten-year-old had been with Rolva for just over a year. "What happened, Dorlan?"

"The baby was the wrong way up. Feet first," she said, "I had to get one of the village women to help me. I wasn't strong enough. Rolva bled a lot.".

"Has she stopped bleeding?" Hessa asked.

"Yes," Rolva said, moving the baby to her arm, "Dorlan was wonderful. She will make a great messenger in a few years."

Dorlan helped her mentor sit up. "Would you like tea? Some food perhaps?" she asked Rolva.

"A little, perhaps, but feed our guest. She must be tired from her journey."

"Let me help you, Dorlan," Hessa said, moving to the hearth with the girl. She remembered the first time she'd seen Dorlan. She'd been running around the village, naked, shouting at the top of her voice. Rolva had spoken to the girl's parents, explaining that the gifted girl could channel the ancestors and spirits. Her mother and father soon agreed to her to becoming a spirit apprentice.

"How long since the ancestors spoke through you?" Hessa asked.

Dorlan blushed. "A moon, perhaps a little more."

"Does it become easier?" Hessa asked.

"I never remember it," Dorlan said, giggling. "They tell me I insisted on being bonded to Jorn, the leader's son. I don't even have my moon blood yet. I couldn't join with anyone!"

Hessa stroked the girl's reddened cheek. "Do not be ashamed of your gift," she said, "You are a channel for spirit, your clan should honour you."

"They treat me well," she said, pulling hot stones from the fire. There was a knock, and Dorlan ran to open the door.

"Apprentice Dorlan," the young man said, his voice cold.

"Oh, Jorn, come in," Dorlan said.

Hessa smiled to herself. Jorn seemed not to have forgotten being asked to bond by a ten-year-old.

"Messenger Hessa," he said, stepping up to the hearth, "My father invites you to eat with us tonight."

"Thank you, Jorn. Tell Sarn that I'd be delighted if Rolva is well enough for me to leave her."

"Go," Rolva called. "Dorlan and I will be fine."

* * *

Hessa's belly was full. The food served by Sarn and his family was delicious, and, as a guest, they had piled her plate high.

"We thank you for coming to help Messenger Rolva," Sarn began as his mate collected the platters.

"It is my duty as protected-of-spirit, and my honour as her friend," Hessa said.

Sarn smiled. "Yes, of course. There is another matter, though. Our village is prosperous but grows too large. There is a suitable site in the next bay. We plan to build a new community there."

"A good idea," Hessa said, wondering how this concerned her.

"My son, Jorn, will take charge. He has nineteen summers and is an excellent farmer, hunter, and provider."

"An excellent choice, I'm sure," Hessa said.

Sarn's mate nudged him and nodded.

"Jorn would need a suitable partner, and the village would need a strong spirit messenger," Sarn said.

Hessa looked across at Jorn, who was concentrating on cleaning his wooden spoon with a thumbnail. Then she realised.

"Me? No, no. That is… I'm…"

"I'm sorry if I've spoken out of turn," Sarn said, "If you have made a promise to someone else, I apologise."

"No, it's just that Spirit Master Col has begun my master's training."

"Well, think on it," Sarn said, "You would be a great asset to the clan."

Hessa stood. "Thank you, Sarn. I'll think about your offer, but I should get back to Rolva, she's still frail."

"Thank you, Messenger," Sarn said, escorting her to the door, "Goodnight."

* * *

"He said what?" Rolva asked, struggling not to laugh.

Hessa sat on the edge of the bed. "He wants me to bond with Jorn; start a new village."

"But you and Lorev," Dorlan said.

Hessa's face fell. "Lorev went off on some quest to avenge his sister without even a word to me. I don't know if he wants me… If he ever wanted me."

"Well, that's easy," Rolva said, "Wait until he returns before you decide."

* * *

Hessa took on Rolva's duties for the next moon. She often saw Jorn, though they never said more than a brief hello. She breathed a sigh as she swung her pack onto her back and climbed the hill from the Boat Clan village. Rolva's colour had returned, along with her strength, and her mate and Dorlan could now cope with her, and the clan's needs.

The trek home took her two days, and she was glad to see the jagged stones of Classac on the horizon as she neared their village. Talla welcomed her home, and she fell back into her role in the Hill Clan hierarchy with ease.

She never mentioned Sarn's proposal, and she was a little offended that Jorn had not asked for her promise himself. But then, perhaps he was no keener on the idea than her.

Six.

Lorev sat in the tiny cave, staring at his sister's remains. He wondered how all his plans had gone so wrong. He'd vowed to kill the man that had caused his sister's death, then had almost saved his life. There had been no victory in Arvan's demise.

He had found the resting place of Verra's bones and tried to free her spirit, but she refused to go to her ancestors. Albyn's gift of the powerful talismans was just a curse in disguise. Now he had to return them if he could even find their owners. He sighed and collected his sister's bones, placing them in a pile at his feet. Long bones first, then skull and jaw, pelvis and backbones, ribs and shoulder blades.

He packed them in a small hide he carried and forced them into his backpack. It was only when he climbed out of the cave that he realised he still struggled to walk on the damaged ankle. He had almost exhausted his travelling supplies, just two of the rancid fat bars remained, and he was two days' walk from any village.

He returned to the main cavern and sat with a flint blade, fashioning a stick to help him walk, then called for Trav and headed away from the caves.

* * *

Lorev had no sooner set foot in the Forest Clan village when two squealing girls rushed him. He dropped to his knees as Mai and Raya hugged him.

"You came back. I knew you would," Mai said. Raya just clung to him.

"Where's Devra?" he asked.

"Having a nap," Raya said, as he stood and walked towards the roundhouse.

Govat looked up from his meal as Lorev entered. "Lorev. Have you eaten?" he asked.

Lorev shook his head. "No, not for a day or more."

"Gianna, fetch some stew for Lorev," he said. He noticed Lorev's limp. "What is wrong with your leg?"

"Twisted," he said, lowering himself to a bench. Gianna brought him food, and he smiled and thanked her.

"Have you succeeded?" Govat asked.

"No." Lorev spooning stew into his mouth, savouring the flavour. "She refuses to cross the river until I return these to their owner." He opened the neck of his tunic, showing the necklace and the stone tablet.

"Who do they belong to? May I see them?" Govat asked.

Lorev removed the talismans and passed them to the messenger. He explained how Albyn had given them to him when he began his journey.

"Eagle talons," Govat said, "They could be from anywhere. The stone is unique, though, it comes from the far north." He turned the thin stone flake over, inspecting the markings on it. "What do the marks mean?" he said.

"I don't know. I feel they have meaning, though. It's not just a pattern. Verra told me to go north when I last saw her. What you say confirms it."

"You're leaving us again?" Mai said.

"Soon. I will stay awhile, though."

Later, Govat and Lorev brought in stones, laying out Verra's bones and building a small cairn over them just inside the door. Vinna came and knelt at the shrine, tears dripping onto the temporary tomb, whispering to her lost daughter, while Lorev snoozed on his bed, three small girls piled around him.

* * *

Almost a moon had passed, and Lorev knew he couldn't delay any longer. Vinna held Devra in her arms as Mai and Raya clung to Lorev's leg. All were in tears as Gianna hugged him and Govat took his hands.

"Why do I always have to leave my family?" he said. "I left Vinna and my dead sister behind to go to the island, I left my brother and sisters of the Hill Clan behind to come here. Now I leave Vinna again, and my three new sisters."

"It seems the spirits have a destiny for you to follow," Govat said.

"Meddling, as they did with my father and mother, with Gren and Zoola," Lorev said. "Why do they interfere with the lives of humans so?"

"They are not of our world," Govat said. "They cannot do what we do."

"So they use us as playthings?"

Govat rubbed his chin. "Perhaps. Would you challenge them? Go against their will?"

Lorev sighed. "No. I just want them to be finished with me."

"Be careful what you wish for," Govat said, as Lorev hoisted the pack to his shoulders. Vinna stroked the decorated bundle that contained her daughter's remains.

"Lay your sister to rest for us, Lorev," she said. "Send word that you have done it if you can."

Lorev stroked his birth mother's face and kissed each of his sisters. Gianna smiled as he patted her shoulder, then he nodded to Govat and set out on the track north.

* * *

Lorev made excellent progress over the next moon, never staying more than one night at any of the villages he found. Travelling was common, and every clan welcomed those on a journey, as they expected their own to be received elsewhere.

The settlements had become further apart as his quest progressed and, as dusk fell one evening, he set up his shelter in a small valley beside a stream. He made a fire and heated water for tea, then ate cold meat and cheese gifted from his last hosts. Sated, he crawled into his shelter and rolled himself in his cloak.

* * *

The small voice calling his name woke him.

"Lorev!"

"What is it?" he asked. He knew her voice. Verra.

"I came to thank you," she said, "For finding me and taking me with you."

"It would have been better if you'd crossed the river," he said, opening his eyes. She looked different, somehow. Her eyes less sunken, her pallor gone.

"They would not allow it." She stepped closer, almost within his reach. "I bear you no ill, Lorev, but no one else could do this. Our mother did not see me. I showed myself to our sister, Mai, but she is too young, I terrified her. There is only you."

"I will do as you… as the spirits, ask," he said.

Verra smiled. Lorev had never seen the tiny ghost girl do that before. "I will help you, as I can," she said. "Sleep now."

Lorev watched her fade, then closed his eyes.

* * *

The grey stone mound stood stark against the rolling green hills — tombs of the dead. Cattle grazed nearby, and off to his right, Lorev saw smoke rising. He headed toward the fires, hoping to find the village that tended these burial cairns. A dozen houses clustered along a stream, people were fetching water, carry firewood, a woman scraped at a hide on a frame. He walked into the settlement.

"Greetings, traveller," came a voice. He turned, hands outstretched, finding a small man bearing tattoos he knew well.

Lorev bowed. "Greetings, Spirit Master." He gave his achievements as the man smiled and nodded. Lorev tried to guess his age. The hair was long, curly and ash-grey, yet the face was almost boyish.

"I am Golda." His voice was soft, the words almost a drawl. "I am the spirit master and guardian of the Tombs of the Cheel Tribe. Where does your journey take you?"

"I am bound for the islands to the north," Lorev told him. "The spirits have a quest for me to fulfil."

"Then come in, Apprentice," he said. His smile was warm as he led the way into the largest house, showing Lorev to a bench at the hearth. He crouched, raking stones from the fire, dropping them into a pot of water. Lorev looked around for an apprentice or a mate.

Golda never looked up from his task as he spoke. "I live alone, Lorev."

Did the spirit master know his thoughts?

"Sometimes I have had apprentices, but none for half a year or more. I never took a mate."

"I didn't... It's just that..."

Golda turned, his soft smile putting the tense lad at his ease. "Everyone asks the same thing," he said, "Why should I have someone do for me the things I can do for myself?"

Lorev smelled rose-hip and chamomile as he looked around at the trappings of the man's craft. Cloaks and masks, drums and rattles, carvings and painted hides adorned the walls and the support poles.

Golda sat and passed Lorev an ornate wooden cup. He reached over to a shelf, setting a loaf on the bench between them. Tearing off a chunk, he gave the bread to Lorev. "Eat," he said, filling his mouth.

Lorev broke off some bread and bit into it, tasting herbs and honey. "The bread is wonderful," he said, taking a second bite.

"What errand do the spirits expect of a young apprentice?" the spirit master asked.

Lorev took the talismans from his neck and passed the necklace to Golda. "I must return these," he said.

The flint-sharp claws were the length of Golda's fingers. "Sea eagle," he said. "Well made too." He looked at the leather cord Lorev passed him. The slim stone tablet, the length and breadth of two fingers, clattered to the floor as Golda dropped it. "Counting marks!" he gasped.

"What do you mean?"

Golda picked up the tablet as if it were a delicate flower, turning it over. "The marks on here are the sacred marks of the highest order of the protected-of-spirit."

"Spirit masters?"

"No. I am loath to even speak of them. Only those that have studied under them would recognise these signs. Where did you get it?"

"From an old spirit messenger called Albyn."

Golda shook his head. "I have never heard that name, but a messenger should not have this amulet. It should never have left the possession of the masters."

"This is from the islands to the north, isn't it?" Lorev asked.

Golda nodded. "I studied there many summers ago. I learned a little of the lore of numbers."

"Tell me," Lorev said.

"I... I shouldn't." The cheery smile had gone now. Worry creased Golda's brow.

"I am charged with the care of this – thing," Lorev said, "Tell me."

Golda pointed to a vertical line inscribed on the tablet, then held up a finger. "One," he said.

Lorev pointed to the next symbol, a sloping line rising from left to right. Golda held up a flat hand, edge-on, fingers closed, and held it at the same angle. He turned the hand, so the palm faced Lorev and opened the fingers. "Five."

"This," Lorev said, pointing to an X symbol. He held up the five symbol Golda had shown him, adding a second hand, crossing the first, "Must be ten."

Golda stared at him, mouth open. "How...?"

"I like numbers," Lorev said. He pointed to a four-sided symbol with points top and bottom. "What's this?"

Golda rubbed his forehead. "I was never good enough with the bigger numbers to learn more," he said. He pointed to the X again. "I think it is ten of these."

"One hundred?" Lorev asked. Golda's hands formed the warding sign, his mouth agape.

"You cannot know this! You say a messenger taught you this?"

"The numbers, yes, but these marks are new to me," Lorev said. He ran a finger along the row of marks, whispering under his breath. "Twenty-nine," he said. "A moon." He followed the next line and closed his eyes, seeing the numbers as he used to imagine Albyn did. "Three hundred, sixty, and five. A year!"

Golda shook his head, taking the tablet back from Lorev and staring at the marks, willing them to give up their information. He couldn't see it.

"You are going to the right place, Lorev. The islands to the north are the home of the teachers of this wisdom." He locked eyes with the young apprentice. "Do not admit the knowledge that you have," he advised. "It may be dangerous."

Seven.

Lorev had never intended to stay with the Tomb Guardians of the Cheel Tribe, but next morning Golda asked for help with his healing work. Lorev made infusions, under Golda's guidance, dressed wounds and tended the fire. The spirit master left him to cut lengths of rawhide thong after noon.

"Tell me the creation story," Golda said as they ate a meal together by the hearth.

"I… I'm not sure," Lorev said.

"Come on, you must know it."

Lorev began telling of the first warrior, Tarren. He could never remember the order of Tarren's exploits, and stopped several times, correcting himself. He blushed as he realised that his six-year-old sister, Shilla, could recite the story word for word as Albyn had taught her.

"I'm sorry, Master Golda, I do not remember stories well."

"You know you must remember all the old tales before you become a messenger, don't you?" Golda said.

Lorev bowed his head and nodded.

***

She stood by his bed again, whispering his name as the first grey light filtered in through the smoke hole.

"Lorev."

"What is it, Verra?" he asked, sitting up. She looked healthier, if the dead could ever look healthy. There was a shine to the eyes that were once sunken and dull.

"You must move on. The tribes you seek do not dwell here."

"Golda is helping me to learn the stories, the lore," he said.

"You are destined for greater things. Keep going north, Brother."

"You look different," he said.

She smiled. "You have given me access to the world below. Though I may not cross the river, I see my ancestors beyond. It feeds me, Lorev. Thank you."

"I will leave soon if it is important to you," he said.

"Before the next new moon," Verra said, as her form faded.

"Who were you speaking to?" Golda asked, raking at the ashes in the hearth.

"The spirit of my sister."

"Has she crossed the river?" Golda said, piling wood chips onto the glowing coals. His hands made the warding sign as Lorev shook his head.

"I must return the talismans before she can rest. She tells me I must move on, Golda. I must go before the new moon."

"I will direct you to the clan that sails across to the islands," Golda said.

* * *

Lorev stood on the shore, staring across the churning grey waters at the shadow of the islands beyond. He felt sick, just watching the waves crashing on the shingle at his feet.

"How long is the crossing?" he asked the boatman.

"Half a day, if the winds favour us," the sailor said, renewing a binding on the double-hulled boat.

"I... I suffer a sickness of boats," Lorev said. "The movement makes me ill."

The boatman snorted and pointed to the village. "See Yoth, the spirit messenger," he said, "She has a remedy for that."

Lorev had been at the village a day, waiting for the winds to drop. He knocked before stepping into the messenger's house.

"Messenger Yoth," he said. "I'm told you have a remedy for the sickness of boats."

The stocky woman looked up from trying to weave plaits into her daughter's hair. "Top shelf," she said, nodding towards the far wall. "The basket on the left."

Lorev smiled at the struggling child. Yoth and her mate appeared to be trying to populate a village on their own, with eight children, and Yoth's belly full again. Lorev reached for the basket and dropped a pinch of the herbs into a small pot, setting it on the bed he'd been using.

"When do you sail," Yoth asked, patting her child's head and turning to face Lorev.

"Tomorrow, weather permitting."

Yoth peered out through the door, watching the pattern of small white clouds against the blue. "The wind will turn tonight," she said, "to the south or west. Either will suit your trip well."

* * *

Lorev knelt in the boat, Trav at his side, as he and Bart, the boatman, paddled clear of the shore.

"That'll do," Bart shouted, dropping the paddle into the bottom of the craft. Lorev stowed his paddle and watched as the muscular sailor hauled the sail up the mast, tying the rope off then climbing back to the steering board. The taste of the peppermint tea lingered in his mouth, and he hoped it kept the sickness at bay. The craft scudded across the choppy sea in the fresh south-westerly breeze.

"A perfect wind for us," Bart said as he tacked the boat around. Lorev smiled as his fingers toyed with the eagle talon necklace. Maybe the island ahead would be the place he sought. The place where he could lay Verra to rest.

They'd been out half the morning, and the islands were taking shape ahead. He heard Bart curse and turned to see what was wrong. Thick black clouds were bearing down on them on the strengthening wind.

"Just a little longer, just a little longer," Bart chanted, leaning forward, urging the boat to greater speed. He glanced back, cursing again, his eyes wide with fear. Soon, thick drops of rain were splatting onto Lorev's head as the wind tore at the straining sail.

"We must land on the nearest island," Bart shouted, pointing to a grey shape visible through the murk. Lorev strained his eyes, staring at the land, his fingers grasping the edge of the boat as it hurtled onward.

"Bart, look out," Lorev shouted as black rock loomed out of the water just ahead.

"Curse the spirits," Bart shouted, dropping the steering board and leaping to release the sail. His foot slipped on the wet boards, and he grasped for the ropes. There was a jolt, and a clatter as the front of the flimsy craft reared up in the air. The sail rattled down the mast as Lorev watched Bart lose his grip and fall into the churning waters.

The craft righted itself and Lorev cast about, looking for some sign of the boatman. Trav whimpered at his feet as the boat turned side-on to the wind and rolled on the heavy swell.

The right side of the vessel lifted as white foam sprayed over Lorev's head. The boat tipped, and he grabbed for his pack as he slid off the seat and bumped into the side of the craft, toppling into the cold sea. Trav was beside him, nose stretched above the water, paddling for the shore. Lorev grabbed the thick fur at his neck and kicked his feet as he struggled to take a breath between the surging waves.

Lorev gasped in relief when he felt the shifting shingle beneath his feet. He dragged himself clear of the surf and looked back for his companion as Trav shook his wet coat.

"We're safe, Trav, we're safe," he said as his knees gave way and he dropped to the pebbled beach.

* * *

Lorev shivered as he rolled onto his back. The sun blinded him for a moment as he heard footsteps in the shingle. A shape cast a shadow over him, and he lowered his hand.

"This one's alive," a man's voice said. "Help me get him up."

Strong hands clutched his arms, pulling him to his feet. He tried to focus on the man holding his right arm. He was big and muscular; his hair shaved at the sides, but longer on top. His accent was strong, guttural, as he spoke. "Who are you? Where are you from?"

Lorev croaked, coughed and found his voice. "I am Lorev, a spirit apprentice from the Long Islands."

"Long Islands?"

The man to Lorev's left was smaller, older. "West of the Great Island. A long string of many islands. My father told of them." He turned to Lorev. "What are you doing on the Isle of the Eagles? We get few visitors."

"We made a run for shelter when the storm hit us," Lorev said. "Bart misjudged, and we hit a rock. Is Bart all right? Have you found him?"

The first man nodded to their right, and Lorev looked around for the first time. Bart's body lay on the shingle, hands folded across his chest, pale and still.

"And Trav? Did you find him?"

"We found no one else, nor did we find a boat," the tall man said.

"Trav is my spirit animal, a wolf."

"We chased a wolf away. Thought it was coming for your carcass. We found no boat, though."

"I expect he will find me," Lorev said, "He knows only me. He is not wild."

"Come, let's get you to the village," the bigger man said. "Can you walk?"

Lorev nodded.

* * *

They passed small fields of flax and barley as they walked towards the cluster of houses. Smoke issued from every roof, and there were many people, all busy. Some cut wood, another was chipping flint beside a house door. A group of women scraped at framed ox-hides, while a cluster of children played nearby. The two men led Lorev into a central dwelling, and he blinked as his eyes adjusted to the dark interior.

"Who is this?" a voice demanded. A figure stepped from the gloom, into the light from the hearth. He was tall and thin, perhaps thirty summers. His face was drawn into a scowl, and a livid red scar ran across his forehead and left cheek; the eye white and sightless.

"A spirit apprentice from the Long Islands," his captor said. Lorev stepped forward, hands extended.

"I am Lorev, spirit apprentice of the Hill Clan of the Tribe of the West," he said, smiling.

The man sneered. "I don't want your greetings, *Apprentice*. The Eagle Tribe has no allies."

"I meant no offence… Um.."

"I am Oshyn, Warrior King of the Eagle Tribe," he said, "And you are, no doubt, a spy from the Isle of Pigs."

"Spy? No," Lorev began.

Oshyn's eyes blazed, and he strode up to Lorev, ripping aside the collar of his tunic. "Where did you get this," he shouted, reaching for the intricate necklace around Lorev's throat.

"Majesty, no!" came a voice from the doorway. An old man stepped in as Oshyn snatched his hand back. Lorev breathed a sigh as he spotted spirit master's tattoos on the man's face. "You cannot touch it. You did not inherit it in the way our lore dictates."

"I am King!" Oshyn said. "You dare to tell me what I cannot do?"

"Blood to blood, King to King, no mortal man can hurt us. Break the line, shame the tribe, the power of Kya deserts us," the old man chanted.

Oshyn turned on him. "You think Kya, eagle spirit, has not already deserted us?" he shouted. His hand waved at a tattered collection of feathers and skin atop a wooden pole. "The last spirit eagle was my grandfather's." He gestured at Lorev's throat, "It died the day this talisman was stolen from us."

The spirit master moved to stand behind Oshyn, studying the necklace. "You cannot take it. It must be passed, father to son, or gifted to the true King," he said.

"Give it to me," Oshyn ordered, stepping up to Lorev.

Lorev caught the slight shake of the old spirit master's head. "Don't," he mouthed.

"How do I know you are the true heir?" Lorev asked. Spittle peppered his face as Oshyn screamed at him.

"I am King. Chief warrior of the Eagle Tribe. I have killed over thirty of our enemies." He pointed to his scar. "Do you think I got this picking daisies?"

Lorev stood his ground, though his legs trembled. "I will need to speak to my ancestors about this."

Oshyn turned to men who had brought Lorev to the village. "Tie him up." He stalked over to the spirit master.

"He's one of yours. You will guard him and find a way to get the talisman back," he said, storming out of the door.

Lorev struggled as they bound cords tight around his wrists, then dragged him from the dwelling.

Eight.

The two guards pushed Lorev onto a bed, throwing his pack beside him. They nodded to the old spirit master and left. Lorev looked around, taking in the trappings of one of the protected-of-spirit. Herbs hung in the roof timbers, and a lad of about ten years sat by the fire stretching wet rawhide over a drum frame.

"I am Sheryn," the spirit master said, pushing the door closed. "I will untie you later, Oshyn may yet return." He turned to the boy. "Make tea for us, Dryn."

Sheryn sat beside Lorev as Dryn busied himself at the fire. "Now, how do you come to have the talisman of kings?"

"It was a parting gift from the spirit messenger of my village," Lorev said, "But I think it's more of a curse than a charm."

"You meant to come here?"

"To the islands, yes." Lorev reached up with his tied hands and brushed his hair from his face. He told the story of his sister, Verra, and her refusal to cross the death river until he had returned the two talismans to their owners. He reached for his throat, and Sheryn put out a hand to stop him.

"Don't take it off," he warned.

"Yes, why wouldn't you let me return it when I had the chance," Lorev said.

"Because once Oshyn has it, he will kill you in a moment."

Sheryn reached for Lorev's neck and withdrew the stone tablet. He inspected it, tracing the series of lines engraved into the soft rock. "Do you know what this is?" Sheryn asked.

Lorev thought of Golda's warning and shook his head.

"It's a counting aid," Sheryn said, dropping the pendant back to Lorev's chest. "It comes from the Isle of Pigs, from a sacred place, the village between the worlds."

Lorev nodded. "And what did Oshyn mean about the Eagle Spirit?"

"The Eagle Spirit protects the Eagle Tribe. Every leader kept a sea eagle as his personal companion until the talisman was stolen. Since then, no king has kept a bird of their own. They die or fly away. Without the physical representation of the sea eagle, our leaders have become weak and quarrelsome."

"And he cannot just take it from me?" Lorev asked.

Sheryn shook his head. "It must be passed, father to son. If a king dies, the heir may take it. The legend says that if blood is spilt to get the necklace, it will lose its power forever."

"So, is Oshyn the true king?" Lorev asked.

"By blood, yes, but in spirit, no."

"Does he have offspring?" Lorev asked.

"Two, but he has banished them. They may both be dead by now."

"What do I do then," Lorev asked, "wait for him to kill me?"

Sheryn untied his wrists and passed him a cup of tea. "Let me think on it," he said.

* * *

When Lorev wakened, Sheryn was tying his wrists again. "Sorry. Oshyn is awake, I can hear him in the village," he said.

The door burst open, and Oshyn strode in. "Well, do you have a plan to get my talisman back," he asked Sheryn.

The spirit master walked over and talked in a hushed voice to the leader. Oshyn nodded, then his face twisted into something that may have been a smile.

"Good," he said. He beckoned in the two men that had brought Lorev from the shore. "Take him to the hill," he said, "Spirit Master Sheryn will follow."

Strong hands gripped Lorev's arms, propelling him out of the door and marching him away from the village. Lorev struggled to keep his balance, stumbling many times on the rough ground. He looked up as they stopped. Towering above him were two wooden structures, each flat on the top — Sky burial platforms.

"What are you doing?" he asked.

"What we're told to do," the taller man said, hoisting Lorev onto his shoulder and climbing the ladder. He threw him onto the platform, and Lorev struggled as the warrior untied his hands. The man was stronger, though, and strapped one hand to each side of the frame, then did the same with his feet. Without a word, he clambered back down the ladder.

* * *

Lorev lay still as the sun crept higher in the sky. He pulled at his bindings and peered over the edge of the platform. Bile rose in his throat as he saw the remains of the body laid out atop the other platform, not six paces from him. Ragged tatters of rotting flesh hung from the bones and, below the thin remains of hair, empty eye sockets glared at him. A raven alighted on the frame, eyeing Lorev with a tilt of its head before pecking at the stinking remains. Lorev turned away and closed his eyes.

He heard the scrabbling of clawed feet beside his head and turned to see the startled raven flapping away. He watched, sending each inquisitive bird away with a shout, though he could hear them squabbling over the corpse beside him.

The sun climbed as the day passed. Lorev's mouth was dry now, and his belly rumbled. He could feel his skin burning in the midday heat when a high, white cloud blocked the sun for a while. The birds still came. The braver ones now pecked at his arms and legs as he shouted and struggled to scare them off. It was none too soon when the sun sank towards the horizon, and the bickering birds flapped away to their roosts.

Sweat had soaked him in the day's height, but now the cold bit at his exposed body. He shivered as he closed his eyes and hoped for sleep.

* * *

"Hello, Lorev," she said.

"Verra?" Lorev strained his neck to find the ghost of his sister sitting on the edge of the platform.

She smiled. "You have a strange way of returning the talismans."

"If I can't find a way out, the birds will take me tomorrow," he said, tugging at the bindings.

"I will see what I can do," she said, her image fading.

"Wait, where are you going?"

"To get help," she said, as she disappeared.

* * *

The first grey light was seeping over the hill when Lorev opened his eyes, moving cold-stiffened joints. The faint sound of a drumbeat became louder as the drummer approached. Lorev struggled, pulling at his bonds, shouting.

"Sheryn? Sheryn? Let me free."

Sheryn's voice began a litany below. "Ancestors and spirits, come and take this brother, Lorev, back to those that love him. Carry him across the river to be with his family again. We bring offerings to the ancestors and ask for his safe passage to the spirit world."

"Sheryn, no. This is a mistake. Don't leave me here!" Lorev shouted.

There was a shuffling below, then the sound of the drum faded.

"Sheryn? SHERYN!"

Lorev lay wondering how he could ever escape death, now.

Then there was movement below, and he called out. "Hello? Who's there?"

There was a snuffling and a sharp 'yip'.

"Trav? Is that you?"

A few excited yaps came from below, but Lorev fell back onto the platform. How could a wolf help him when he was up this high?

There was a second sound now. Footsteps. Then a small snarl from Trav.

"Sheryn? Get me down from here."

"Who are you?" came a voice.

"I am Lorev, spirit apprentice of the Clan of the West. Can you help me?"

"You're not dead," the voice said.

"Not yet, but another day up here and the birds will take my eyes out."

Lorev heard the creak of footsteps on the ladder, then a face appeared. The dark hair was cropped at the sides in the Eagle Tribe warriors' style, yet the face was young with no sign of a beard. The young lad climbed onto the platform and pulled a knife. He was tall, and baggy clothes draped his thin body.

"Well, they've finally lost their senses," he said, smiling, "Burying folk that have yet to die. What did you do to deserve this?"

"I have something Oshyn wants," Lorev said, as the lad cut his hands free. He reached for the necklace.

"Is that what I think it is?" the boy asked.

"Talisman of kings, so I'm told. He needs me dead, so he can take it."

The lad looked puzzled, then the realisation dawned. "The prophecy," he said. "He can neither take it nor kill you for it."

Lorev nodded.

"I'm Jath," he said, cutting the last binding. "Come on, we need to get away from here."

They clambered down the ladder, Lorev's legs stiff from lack of use. Jath peered at Trav.

"Is the wolf with you?" Jath asked, shouldering a small pack.

"Yes, my animal spirit."

Jath tugged a pack from the platform frame. "Yours?"

Lorev nodded, glad, at least, that Sheryn had left that for him. Jath lifted another bag from the frame, peering inside. "Meat… Cheese…, Ooh, and some bread too. Offerings for the ancestors."

"Will you dare take them?" Lorev asked.

"Well now, since they don't have to take you across the river, why would they need offerings?" he said, slinging the bag over his other shoulder.

Jath led Lorev away from the hill, glancing around every so often.

"Where are you taking me?" Lorev asked.

"Somewhere safe," he grinned.

"Not the village?" Lorev asked.

"No, I'd be no more welcome there than you."

* * *

The sun was high when they reached the cliffs, Trav bounding back and forth between Lorev and Jath as they walked. Jath looked around once more.

"Do you think someone followed us?" Lorev asked.

"Unlikely, but you can't be too careful," he said. He cupped his hands to his mouth and gave a screeching call. "Keeeeya! Keeeeya!"

Lorev looked up in time to see the enormous bird spread its wings and drop to the ground a pace in front of Jath. The lad reached out and stroked the pale head as the eagle settled its feathers.

"A spirit animal? Are you protected-of-spirit?" Lorev asked.

Jath shook his head. "Her name is Kya," he said.

Lorev recognised the name at once. The tribe's eagle spirit. "You are one of Oshyn's children," he said, "Sheryn told me that there were two of you, banished by your father."

"I have… had, a brother. Our father made us outcast almost a year ago. Tobyn didn't make it through the winter."

"So how do you live? Where do you sleep?" Lorev asked.

"Come," Jath said, heading for the cliff.

They walked to the cliff edge, only spotting the narrow path at the last moment. Lorev leaned into the cliff face, grasping the coarse grass for balance. He was just wondering where Jath was taking him when a broad ledge appeared before them. A cave faced the sea, its mouth half-filled with a neat stone wall. Jath slipped inside, beckoning Lorev.

He stood in a cavern, almost the size of a roundhouse. A hearth sat a few paces inside the small doorway and a table and bench to one side. A large sleeping platform, covered in furs stood to the other. The place was in good order.

"You live well, Jath," Lorev said.

"I live as I can," he said. "The fire can only be lit at night, in case they see the smoke. I fish and hunt small game, Kya helps too."

"Do you have water? I'm so thirsty," Lorev said.

Jath unhooked a water skin from beside the door and passed it to him. "Come and sit," he said, pushing a wooden cup across the table to Lorev, then sitting on the bench.

Lorev set his pack down and joined Jath at the table. He downed three cups of water in quick succession and smacked his lips. "So, what brought you to the burial hill this morning?" he asked.

"Oh, I had a dream," Jath said. "A small girl came to me while I slept. She said that I would find something I needed at the hill this morning. Then I heard Sheryn's drum and followed the sound." He reached into the bag and pulled out a loaf of bread, tearing a lump off and passing it to Lorev. "I guess she meant the food. Eh?"

Nine.

Jath sat while Lorev recounted his story. He told of his journey to avenge Verra, finding Trav, then discovering his sister's bones. They finished the bread, each slipping pieces to Trav, then started on the cheese.

"We eat well today," Jath said, patting his belly.

"Are you often hungry?" Lorev asked.

"No. Winter is the worst. I can't fish or trap much then. Sheryn helps a little."

"Sheryn?" Lorev said. "He told me he wasn't sure if either of Oshyn's children were still alive."

Jath smiled. "He brings offerings for the ancestors to the Lookout Stone each seven-day. He drums and chants as he walks there and back. A blind man could find him."

"You take them?"

"Yes," Jath said. "He only started doing it after father banished Tobyn and me. I'm sure he means it for me. The Lookout Stone has no connection to the ancestors at all."

Trav sat beside Lorev, and he stroked his fingers through the soft fur. "Where does your brother lie?" he asked.

"His bones are there," Jath said, pointing to the back of the cave. "I have no way to help him cross the river, though."

"Do you have rawhide?" Lorev said.

"Plenty, why?"

"Because tomorrow, I will make a drum."

* * *

Lorev slept well. The bed was large enough for both of them, and he woke to find Jath pulling stones from last night's fire to make tea. They breakfasted on cold meat, then took spears to fish on the shore below the cave. They'd got six small fish by mid-morning and were about to head back when a screech sounded above them. Jath looked up, then gave his call for Kya. "Keeeeya!" The eagle dropped in front of them, a hare clasped in her talons. She relinquished the prize, then bobbed her head.

"She's saying that the hare is for us," Jath said, stroking the bird. He gutted the hare, leaving the entrails on a flat rock for Kya to eat. "This is food enough for two days," he said, "Come on, back to the cave, and I'll find the rawhide."

* * *

The drum frame only took until past noon, curving the finger-thick hazel rods to a circle and tying them with rawhide thongs. Lorev set it close to the cooling hearth to shrink the bindings. Jath had gone out to check snares, so he sat and cut rawhide strips, before putting the largest piece of hide in a pot of water to soak. He saw Trav's ears flick up as he raised his head. The young wolf stood, tail wagging, listening. Lorev stepped behind the shield wall at the cave mouth until Jath stepped through the door.

"Lorev?" he called before spotting him. "Oh, there you are. It's only me."

Lorev smiled. "We should have a signal, so we know it's one of us approaching."

"Do you know the curlew's call?" Jath asked. The rising whistle Lorev gave elicited a grin. "That's the one. We'll use that."

"No luck with the snares?" Lorev said.

"No, the cattle had been past and trampled everything. Still, we have food for today and tomorrow. Come, I know where there is good seaweed to go with our fish."

They walked along the rocky shore until Jath found the patch of weed he wanted. He pulled several handfuls and tucked it into a pouch at his waist. Lorev looked up at the distant cry of an eagle.

"Is that Kya?"

Jath shielded his eyes and smiled. "That's her, flying just for the fun of it." As he looked back down, something caught his eye. "Lorev. What's that?"

Lorev looked where Jath pointed. Upturned, and snagged on a rocky islet, was the hull of a boat. "I think it's the boat I came in, though it had an outrigger and a mast before."

"Do you think we could swim out and get it?" Jath said.

"Let's try."

They stripped off their clothing and splashed into the water, Lorev rushing to catch up with Jath. As he sank into the water, Lorev spotted the tattoo covering Jath's back. His awkward paddle was slow, compared to the lithe young warrior, and Jath reached the rock first, tugging at the bow of the big dugout boat. Lorev joined him, feet braced against the rock, hauling on one of the remaining ropes. The heavy craft slipped into the water, and Jath found another line, pulling it over his shoulder and kicking towards the beach.

They were both spluttering and laughing as their feet found purchase on the shingle, and they dragged the hull clear of the water.

"Your tattoo is amazing," Lorev said, watching Jath collapse, face down, in the coarse sand. "I've never…" His voice left him as Jath rolled over, giggling and panting at the same time. Rising from the smooth skin on Jath's chest were breasts. "You're a girl!"

Jath looked down at her naked body as if seeing it for the first time. "Why so I am," she laughed.

"But, you wear men's clothing… Your hair is in the style of a warrior."

Jath climbed to her feet, and Lorev couldn't tear his eyes from her. She'd never removed the baggy men's shirt, tunic and leggings in the entire time he'd been there.

"I'm cold," she said, wrapping her arms around her body. "Let's get dressed and haul the boat above the high tide mark."

Lorev nodded and picked up his clothing, pulling on his shirt and leggings. He fastened the tunic and slipped on his moccasins, finding Jath waiting with a rope in her hand.

They dragged the craft up the beach, wedging it behind some rocks, upside down to allow it to dry out.

"Come on," Jath said, retrieving the bag of seaweed, "Let's get something to eat."

* * *

Jath poured water into cups and set them on the small table, taking out the last of the cheese and some cold meat. She sat beside Lorev on the bench and sighed.

"Father — Oshyn, lives for his war. He devotes himself to fighting the people of the Isle of Pigs; thinks of nothing else. Three years ago, my mother was killed in a revenge raid, and I had to become a mother to Tobyn, my brother. For his thirteenth midsummer, Tobyn got his Eagle tattoo. Father was away fighting."

"Like your one?" Lorev asked.

"The same. I talked Sheryn into doing a tattoo for me too. Tobyn was a sickly child, he would never be a warrior or a king. I cut my hair so I could become the heir father needed."

"So, what happened?"

Jath blew out her cheeks, expelling a long breath. "He banished me. He said I was an abomination, and no woman would ever rule the Eagle Tribe. Tobyn came with me, and father searched for many days, but he never found us."

"So why keep it up?" Lorev asked. "The hair, the clothing."

"Because it's who I am." She looked into Lorev's eyes. "You're a man, in a man's body. You're happy that way?" Lorev nodded. "I'm a woman, but I want to be a warrior. I can't change my body, but I can dress and act like a warrior."

"So you want to be a man?" Lorev said.

"Yes… No. It's complicated."

"Do you prefer women as lovers?" he asked.

Jath buried her face in her hands. "I like both," she whispered. When Lorev went quiet, she looked up, finding him grinning.

"You know what they call that, don't you?"

Jath gave him a worried look. "What?"

"Greedy," he said, dissolving into a fit of laughter. Jath punched his arm.

"Shut up!" she said, laughing along with him.

* * *

As dusk fell, Lorev kindled the fire while Jath wrapped the small fishes in the seaweed, then in large dock leaves. She pushed them into the embers once they were hot enough. When they were cooked, she set them on the table, three apiece, and they sat to eat.

"S'good," Lorev mumbled through a hot mouthful. "The seaweed is tasty."

"Mother's recipe," Jath said, opening her second parcel of fish.

"Do you want to leave the island?" Lorev asked.

Jath finished chewing. "If I stay, eventually, my father will find me," she said. "If I go to the Isle of Pigs, they will treat me as an enemy, perhaps they will kill me."

"Together, though, they may accept us," Lorev said. "I am protected-of-spirit. I will make it clear that you have rebelled against your father. If they do not allow us to stay, we'll both travel further."

"You'd go with me?" she said.

Lorev nodded. He reached for the necklace around his throat, unfastening it. "You are the true heir to the rule of the Eagle Tribe," he said, "So this belongs to you." He leant over and fastened the eagle talon talisman around Jath's neck. When he pulled back and straightened it, he saw tears running down her face.

"I may never rule the Eagle Tribe," she said.

Lorev smiled. "Believe, Jath, believe that one day, you will."

They cleared their meal and banked the fire, preparing to sleep. "May I see your tattoo?" Lorev asked.

Jath pulled off her tunic and unfastened her shirt, baring her back in the firelight. Lorev stared in awe. The wings of the eagle stretched the width of her back, the head turned to one side, beak agape. Its tail spread just above the cleft of her backside. The outline was filled with intricate spirals and whorls. Lorev winced. He remembered the pain from his own apprentice tattoos.

"It must have been sore," he said.

"It was. I lay for almost the whole day while Sheryn cut it. It took a moon to heal."

"It's beautiful," Lorev said, pulling off his moccasins and climbing into bed. Jath slipped on her shirt and followed.

* * *

The drum had hung over the hearth for two days, the skin tight and hard now. Lorev took charcoal and drew the image of his spirit animal, the wolf, on the inside of the taut hide, blessing its use with prayers to the ancestors. He took the beater he'd fashioned from driftwood and struck the skin for the first time. He saw Jath shiver at the high, bright tone it made. Lorev stepped over to the laid-out bones of Tobyn, arranged on the cave floor. He placed a hand on the skull, the other on the ribs, as he spoke the verse for the dead.

"Will you travel with me?" Lorev asked, settling himself close to the fire.

"Is that allowed?" Jath said, taking her place beside him.

"Let's find out," he said. "Close your eyes, keep your breathing slow, and feel the drumbeat in your body."

Lorev set a slow cadence, increasing speed as he closed his eyes and was pulled down to the world below.

His eyes became accustomed to the gloom of the lower world, and he turned to find Jath close behind him. She looked scared.

He pointed across the river. "It's alright, Jath. The land of the dead is over there, we're safe here."

A skinny boy stood beside the river, his back to them.

"Tobyn?" Jath called. The boy turned. "Tobyn, it's you," she cried, rushing towards him. Lorev grabbed at her sleeve, stopping her just in time.

"You cannot touch him. He is a spirit, ready to pass over," Lorev warned.

"Thank you, Jath," the boy said.

"For what? I let you die."

"No," he said, smiling, "I was never destined to live a long life. Those last months with you were the best of my life."

Jath's tears flowed as Lorev raised his arms and called across the river. "Ancestors of our brother, Tobyn. Come and take one of your own back to those that love him."

Two figures materialised out of the gloom. "We are here spirit apprentice."

"Grandfather. Grandmother," Jath whispered, clinging now to Lorev's arm. The ghost of Tobyn turned one last time, smiled at his sister, and stepped into the water. Welcoming arms pulled him from the river, hugging the lad as they turned and disappeared.

Lorev clasped Jath's hand as they made their way back from the riverside.

"Hello, Brother," Verra said. Lorev looked up to find his sister's ghost, not ten paces in front of them. "Jath is a worthy recipient of the eagle talisman, it pleases the spirits. When you find the owner of the stone tablet, I will be free to cross the river too."

"I hope it will be soon, Verra," he said.

"So keen to see me gone?" Verra said, smiling as her form faded away.

Lorev turned to Jath. "Keep hold of me," he said, "Back!"

Lorev opened his eyes and laid down the drum and beater. Jath was still clinging to him, tears streaking her face.

"He is with his loved ones now," Lorev said.

"He thanked me," she said. "I always thought I'd taken him away from his family, made his life miserable."

"He saw it differently," Lorev said, "Now, let's gather up Tobyn's bones and lay him to rest."

They collected the remains, placing them in a small niche at the cave's back. Lorev laid the skull on top of the pile last of all. Jath bowed and placed a kiss on her brother's forehead.

Ten.

Trav struggled as Lorev lifted him into the boat. The wolf-cub made straight for Jath, laying at her feet.

"I think he's as much yours as mine now," Lorev said, shoving the boat off from the beach and leaping aboard. He grabbed the makeshift oar, fashioned from driftwood and an ox shoulder blade, and began paddling.

They had spent many days packing belongings and tidying the boat for their journey. The new moon's lesser tides coincided with a period of calm, sunny weather, and they decided it was time they left the Isle of Eagles. Jath knelt at the front, Lorev at the back, each paddling the boat's bare hull towards the gap between the two closest islands.

"Are the small islands inhabited?" Lorev asked.

Jath glanced over her shoulder. "They used to be. The people became victims of Oshyn's war and moved to the Isle of Pigs."

They paddled on, passing between the small islands, then heading for the closest point of the bigger land-mass ahead. It was noon when the boat ploughed into the soft sand, and Lorev, Jath, and Trav jumped ashore. The wolf-cub seemed excited to be on dry land again, and danced around them, yipping, while they dragged the boat up the beach, clear of the high tide mark.

"We'd better turn it over," Lorev said. "We've no way of knowing if we'll need it again." Jath joined him as they heaved the vessel over to protect it from the weather, then they sat in the sand beside it and rested.

"We have visitors," Jath said, nodding to the right. Three men were making their way along the beach, each carrying a spear. She chuckled as they got closer. The man in the centre was short and stocky. His body rocked back and forth, like a willow tree in a storm, from some injury or another. The other two were struggling to keep up, both were well past their fortieth year, and were wheezing as they drew to a halt twenty paces away.

"Who are you? What do you want here?" called the crippled man.

Lorev stood, helping Jath to her feet. "We are travellers escaping the Isle of Eagles, we are seeking refuge."

The man on the left regained his breath a little and pointed at Jath. "He is an Eagle Warrior," he said.

Lorev smiled. "*She* is an outcast from her people, banished by Oshyn, the same man who tried to have me killed." Lorev stepped forward. "Do you not recognise the marks of a spirit apprentice?"

The man at the centre waddled forward, peering at Lorev's face. He bowed his head. "Apologies, spirit apprentice. I did not recognise your status."

"No matter," Lorev said, smiling, "Do you have a spirit messenger or master we can talk to?"

The second old man shook his head. "There are few of us left here. The Chief takes all the young men as warriors. Those that remain are old people, some women, and a handful of children."

"Come, though," said the crippled man, "We will take you to the village and decide what we must do with you" Trav chose that moment to return, loping out of the tall seagrass towards Lorev. "Look out!" the man cried, raising his spear. "A wolf."

"Put up your weapons," Jath said, reaching for Trav and petting his fur, "He is Lorev's spirit animal."

The men stood aghast as the warrior woman stroked an almost full-grown wolf. "Shall we go?" Lorev asked.

"Oh, yes. Come on."

"What is your name?" Jath said, as they lifted their packs and set off along the beach.

"I am Kern," the limping man said. "These two are brothers, Kemay, and Ravay." The men nodded as Kern introduced them. The village was beyond the shore, and Lorev smelled the wood-smoke as they waded through the tall sea-grasses and came out in a small field system. Kern led them to a ramshackle hut, larger than the rest. He pushed the groaning door open and led them into the dank interior. There was a whispered conversation, then Kemay turned to them.

"I apologise, Spirit Apprentice. We intended to honour you by giving you the messenger's house. None of us realised how much it had deteriorated in the year since our messenger died. Please, come and be guests at my home."

Lorev bowed. "Thank you, Kemay. We would be honoured."

* * *

Kemay's mate, Jen, made them welcome, soon becoming used to having Trav in the house. They were well-fed, though every person in the village seemed to visit that day, the women to stare at the warrior girl, the children to play dare with Trav.

"Tomorrow, we must take you to the Bridge Clan, to the village between the worlds," Kemay said. "You must speak with our chief there."

"The village between the worlds?" Lorev asked.

"Our main settlement, the home of our Chief and the protected-of-spirit. It lies on a spit of land between two lakes. To one end is the stone circle of the living, to the other, the stone circle of the dead."

"Then we shall follow you there tomorrow," Lorev said. Their hosts showed them to a spare bed, piled high with soft furs, and Kemay and Jen wished them a good night.

* * *

Kemay was flagging when they spotted the Circle of the Living in the distance. It took the entire day to walk from the south coast of the island, and the old man was relying on his stick now. The circle of stones lay deserted when they passed, though the remains of a fire smouldered in the central hearth. The walled village stood on a narrow strip of land, bordered on both sides by vast lakes. Two warriors ran out as soon as they spotted the travellers, spears at the ready. One aimed a shot at Trav, though the wolf was far too fast for him.

"Leave the wolf," Kemay said, "It is the spirit animal of this apprentice."

The guard eyed Trav as he retrieved his spear. "Inside the gate, all of you," he shouted, prodding Kemay with his spear butt. They walked into the village, to the front of an imposing building with great standing stones on either side of the entrance.

"Wait there," one warrior said. He headed inside while the second stood guard. When the warrior returned, a trio of men followed him. One was dressed in thick leather armour, a polished stone mace in his hand. Behind him came two older men, both with facial tattoos, though Lorev didn't recognise their significance.

The armoured man glanced at the trio. "You are a Souther?" he asked Kemay.

"Yes, Chief Norlyn."

Norlyn turned to the guards. "Give him food for his trouble and send him on his way." He glanced at Jath.

"Take the prisoner and tie him up with the others. The Spirit Apprentice and I will discuss the bounty for bringing him in."

One guard prodded Kemay with his spear butt, while the other grabbed Jath's hands and bound them behind her back.

"Wait," Lorev said, "What do you think you are doing?"

"Quiet," Norlyn said, "You'll get your bounty. What do you want? Food? Tools?" He looked Jath up and down. "He's not worth a cattle beast if that's what you're after."

"Is this how the Chief Norlyn greets visitors?" Lorev said. He stood tall, arms outstretched to the front, palms up. "I am Lorev, Spirit Apprentice of the Hill Clan of the Tribe of the West, from the Long Islands. This *woman* and I came of our own free will. She is not my prisoner. We are seeking refuge from the Isle of Eagles."

"You are a woman?" Norlyn asked.

Jath glared at him. "Yes."

"And you both came from the Isle of Eagles?"

"Yes," Lorev said.

"Tie them both up and throw them in with the other prisoners," Norlyn said, turning to walk away. His two attendants rushed to stop him, and there was a brief heated discussion. "Very well," he said, "against my better judgement, hold them in the temple." He turned to the remaining warrior. "You will guard the door," he said, before stalking off.

The guard pushed them into the grand building, though he came no further, taking up his post outside. One man untied their bindings while the other spoke.

"I am Brode," he said, holding out his hands in greeting, "Star Master of the Bridge Clan of the Drogga people. I apologise for your treatment. The war has been hard on our tribe."

Jath rubbed at her wrists, then held out her hands. "Jath, of the Eagle Tribe," she said.

"And I am Urdan," said the second man, "star keeper, and pupil of Brode."

Brode looked at Jath, and Lorev saw his gaze settle on the eagle talon necklace. "You are of Oshyn's blood?" he asked.

Jath glanced at Lorev before nodding. "His daughter, though he has disowned me."

"You wear the talisman," Brode said, "I know of it. Why is it in your possession?"

"Lorev returned it to our people," she said, "He seems to think I have more right to it than my father. It is one of two talismans he was charged with returning."

"What is the other?" Urdan asked.

Lorev reached into his shirt, slipping the pendant off and passing it to Brode.

"The lost tablet!" he said, holding it up for Urdan to see. "This has been missing for thirty years." He turned to Lorev. "Losing this, and the fire beads, was one cause of the war between the Drogga and the Eagle Tribe." He looked at Jath. "The other was the loss of the Talisman of Kya, was it not?" Jath nodded. "Where did you get these, Lorev?"

Lorev sighed. "The fire beads? Were they a string of polished amber stones?"

"Yes," Brode said, "you have seen them?"

"I know of them," Lorev said, looking at Jath. "Is it possible for us to get food and drink? There is a story to tell tonight."

Urdan turned to a woman cleaning a stone altar at the far side of the building. "Dreena, will you arrange extra food for our two guests? We will eat when you are ready."

The woman smiled and hurried away. "My mate," said Urdan, "She is also our temple keeper."

Brode and Urdan had no sooner finished arranging benches and a table near to the hearth, when Dreena returned with a young woman, each carrying platters of food. They made two journeys, then joined the others. Urdan introduced the young woman as his daughter, Kimmi, and they sat for their meal.

* * *

Kimmi cleared the remains of the meal while Dreena stoked the fire. They arranged benches around the hearth, then all eyes turned to Lorev.

"I do not tell, or remember, stories well," Lorev began, "But this is the story of my adoptive parents, Col, and Talla, and their friends Gren and Zoola." He told of the threat to his parents' lives, their flight south, and their adventures. Brode and Urdan leaned forward in their seats when he got to the part about the fire mountain and the amber beads' effects.

"The fire beads have been destroyed, then?" Brode asked.

"To break the hold of the old Fire Spirit, yes," Lorev said.

He closed his eyes, searching his memory for the details of his parents' return, telling of his adoption and the struggle to rid their clan of the corrupt leader.

It was when he got to the part where the four heroes claimed their places as spirits of the elements, that his audience's eyes widened.

"You are the son of Fire and Air?" Urdan asked.

"Yes," Lorev said, "I suppose I am."

"But we have seen Lorev's parents, Urdan," Brode said, "In ceremony. You remember when we felt that the spirits of the elements had become, somehow, more human? That must have been when they took their power."

Urdan looked pensive. "Norlyn has imprisoned the son of the fire spirit and the air spirit. This is bad, Brode."

Brode turned to the girl. "Kimmi, fetch Spirit Master Gelyn for us, please." She ran from the house as Brode turned back to Lorev. "So, the talismans?" he said.

"Our messenger gave them to me when I left home," Lorev said. "He told me they were tokens of great power, though they have been nothing but a curse to me."

"Does this messenger have a name?" Brode asked.

"Yes. He is the guardian of the stones of Classac. His name is Albyn."

"Who speaks that name?" came a voice from the doorway. A wizened little man entered, a staff clutched in his left hand while his right squeezed Kimmi's elbow. Lorev smiled, reminded of his sister, Shilla, and her relationship to her mentor, Albyn.

"Sit here, by the hearth, Master Gelyn," Kimmi said, easing the frail man onto the bench. He muttered a word of thanks and patted her arm as she went back to her seat.

"Now, who speaks of Albyn, the thief?" he said.

Lorev stared, open-mouthed, as the spirit master caught his gaze. "Thief?"

"What do you call a man who takes what is not his?" Gelyn asked. "A man whose actions began a war that has lasted two generations?"

Eleven.

Brode recounted the story of Col and Talla for the spirit master, Lorev correcting minor details. It amazed him that the star master could remember so much from just one telling.

"The fire beads have been destroyed, then?" Gelyn asked.

"It was necessary," Brode said.

"And what of the other talismans? Have you recovered the stone tablet or the talisman of Kya?"

Urdan held up the tablet on its leather thong, then nodded towards Jath. "Lorev has returned the talisman of Kya to the heir of the Eagle Tribe," he said, "Jath will, in time, rule the Isle of Eagles."

Gelyn leant forward, peering across the fire to where Jath sat. "Jath? A woman's name?" Jath nodded. "You are twin-spirited, then?"

"Twin-spirited? I don't know what that means," she said.

"You wear the clothing and manner of a warrior, yet have the body of a woman," Gelyn said. "Two spirits were joined at your birth, they share your body for this lifetime."

"You know of this?" she said, "I am not the only one afflicted?"

Gelyn's laugh was little more than a dry croak. "It is not an affliction! There are many like you, whose spirit is at variance with their body. Most become servants of the ancestors. There is nothing wrong with you, girl, you are honouring both of your spirits. It is an honest expression of who you are."

Jath relaxed a little, a smile creasing the corners of her mouth.

"Do you need me further?" Gelyn asked.

"Norlyn has imprisoned them here," Brode said. "I am worried we will anger Lorev's parents, the spirits of air and fire."

"I will speak to the spirits tonight," Gelyn said, struggling to his feet, "Then I will speak to Norlyn tomorrow. Kimmi, would you help me?"

Kimmi rushed to his side, taking his arm as he turned from the hearth. "Will you assist me?" he asked her.

"With the drum?"

Gelyn nodded. "It would be easier if you apprenticed."

Kimmi smiled. "I'm still thinking on it," she said, as the heavy leather curtain closed behind them.

* * *

The small bed in the temple was built for occasional use, and was far from the hearth, so both Lorev and Jath woke cold and stiff. He waited for Jath to finish, then stepped behind the curtain to relieve himself in the pot placed there. It felt odd — wrong to be peeing indoors, under a roof. They made their way to the hearth, and Lorev stirred life into the few coals still glowing amongst the ashes. Jath fed the fire while he looked for water to drink.

"Good morning, Apprentice Lorev. Good morning, Princess Jath," said Kimmi, setting a tray of meat and bread on the table. She unhooked a water skin from her shoulder and hung it from a peg. "Spirit Master Gelyn and Star Master Brode are speaking to Chief Norlyn, but they asked me to bring you breakfast," she said.

"Will you join us?" Jath asked.

Kimmi smiled. "Thank you," she said, sitting on the end of the bench.

"The meat is good," Jath said, stuffing her mouth.

"The Drogga have the best cattle on all the islands," Kimmi said, nibbling at a slice of beef.

"Were there two women here, twins?" Lorev asked.

"Arva and Atta?" Kimmi said. "They were so much fun. It's them that suggested I should apprentice to Master Gelyn. A vision came to me last night. I'm going to do it."

"Have they left the island?" he asked.

"Yes, a moon ago. You know them?"

"They are good friends of my parents," Lorev said, "My friends too, I suppose."

Brode pulled aside the drape at the temple door and led Gelyn in. He sat him at the hearth and smiled at Lorev and Jath. "May we have tea, Kimmi?" he asked.

The girl set aside her food and raked hot stones from the fire, dropping them into a pot of water. "What would you like, Masters?" she asked.

"Meadowsweet," Gelyn replied, "Run to my house, you know where I keep the basket."

"We have spoken to Norlyn," Brode said. "He will release you, on conditions."

"Which are?" Jath asked.

"You, Lorev, are to work with Spirit Master Gelyn, or with myself and Urdan. Jath is to be with you, or us, at all times. I'm sorry, but I cannot get him to trust you, Jath."

She gave a tight smile. "I suppose I should expect that," she said. "To him, I am an enemy."

"We might help you escape if you want to return to your island," Brode said.

"I lived alone, in a cave, in fear of my life," Jath said. "I'll stay."

* * *

The day was hot and clammy, and Jath sat in the shade of one of the great megaliths outside the temple. Lorev was working with the star master. Numbers, or some such thing.

"Would you like to help me milk the cattle, Princess Jath?" Kimmi said, setting down a pot and bowl.

"Why do you call me that? I am nobody's princess," Jath said, "My father disowned me."

"But Brode says you will, one day, rule the Eagle Tribe."

Jath got to her feet. "Then we will have to see if he is right. Shall we check with Brode?"

"Oh, I did. He says it's all right if you're with me."

Jath took the pot, and Kimmi the bowl as they made their way through the village gate, towards the lush grass nearby where the cattle grazed. At first, Jath watched, but soon Kimmi was instructing her in milking.

"Squeeze at the top. That's it. Now close your fingers — no, one at a time." Milk squirted out, some hitting the bowl. "That's it. Just keep practising," Kimmi said.

They had almost finished with the last cow when a voice startled them.

"What are you doing away from the village? You are my prisoner," Chief Norlyn shouted.

"Star Master Brode said he permitted it," Kimmi said.

"I did not say I permitted it," Norlyn said, stepping towards the girl.

Jath came between them. "She has done nothing wrong," she said. The blow took her by surprise, the back of Norlyn's hand slamming into her face. Jath felt her lip split as her head whipped around and she lost her footing. She staggered back, tipping the full pot of milk onto the grass.

Lorev came running towards them, Urdan and Brode close behind.

"You hit Jath," Lorev shouted. "Is this the honour of a chief, to strike down a woman?"

Norlyn turned on Lorev, a flint blade appearing in his hand as his arm came around. There was a flash of grey, a snarl, and Norlyn's hand dropped the weapon as sharp, white teeth clamped onto his arm.

"Get it off!" Norlyn screamed as Trav worried at him.

"Trav, stop," Lorev ordered. The wolf dropped the chief's arm and slunk to his side. Lorev stroked the ruff of soft fur at Trav's neck as he glared at Norlyn.

"I will have you both put to death, and that damned wolf's head on a pole," Norlyn said, struggling to his feet.

Brode stepped forward, his eyes fixed on the chief. His face was pale, his words only a whisper. "You will do no such thing," he said. "Lorev, take Jath and care for her wound. Kimmi, take the milk pot and go to Chief Norlyn's mate. Tell her she must replace the milk that was spilt."

The three left, Trav trailing at Lorev's heel. Urdan stood beside Brode, nodding towards the west as a sudden icy wind whipped at his white beard. Black clouds clustered over the lake's dark waters, as shards of lightning danced around the distant hills. Moments later, the low grumble of thunder rolled around them.

"See what you have wrought?" Brode said, his voice rising above the freshening breeze. "See how the spirits of fire and air repay you for your threats to their son?"

"It's nothing but a story," the chief said, though there was fear in his eyes.

Brode pulled back Norlyn's sleeve, inspecting the deep gouges in his forearm. "Go to Gelyn and get that treated," he said, turning towards the village. Norlyn opened his mouth to speak, but Urdan shook his head before following the star master.

* * *

Norlyn winced at Gelyn tightened the last stitch. "You have angered the spirits, Norlyn," Gelyn said. Lightning crackled, and thunder roared as the rain flooded down the flagstone roof.

"You spoke to them for me — last night," Norlyn replied.

"I guaranteed Lorev's safety here. What did you do?"

Norlyn mumbled.

"What?"

"I threatened him," the chief said.

"With what?"

"Death," he whispered.

Gelyn finished binding the honey-smeared wound and pulled Norlyn's sleeve down. "Go home. Burn herbs. Say prayers at your ancestor shrine. Send your mate and children to a neighbour. You must make your own peace with the spirits this night."

Norlyn was soaked to the bone before he had taken a handful of paces. The rain stung his skin as his shadow writhed on the ground before him in the flash of the fire spirit's anger. He burst into his house, slamming the door behind him. Someone had banked the fire, and a platter of food sat on the table. There was no sign of his family.

He ran to the corner, kneeling before the ancestor shrine. A mace head glittered in the firelight, polished green with veins of blood-red through it. He touched it, then ran trembling fingers over the bones: past chiefs, his father, grandfather. Most were leg bones, taken from the tomb to hold their spirits with him.

"Speak for me ancestors. You that love me, speak to the spirits I have angered."

He stood and spun around as the storm crashed through his roof. A hail of stone and dust fell. A rock hit his head, and he dropped to his knees. The wind swirled through the gaping rent in the roof, tearing at the tables and benches, strewing the fire across the floor.

"I am sorry!" he cried, raising his arms towards the ragged hole in his roof. "Tell me what I must do."

The voice startled him. "You threatened my eldest son." He turned, meeting a violet gaze in an ice-white face.

"Shall I take your eldest, Chief Norlyn? Shall I take your heir?" he twisted to the second voice. Black-ringed eyes glared from a blood-red visage.

"No! Take me. It was I who threatened him. Leave my son. I beg you."

"Stand, warrior," said the air spirit.

"We will take what you value above all else," said the spirit of fire.

Norlyn sobbed. He closed his eyes in defeat as rain poured through the roof. Lightning shattered the night as the house shook with the thunder's blast.

Even through closed eyelids, the glare of light blinded him. Pain exploded in his body as he fell to the floor, jerking and writhing.

Then, all he could hear was his own scream.

Twelve.

Kimmi ran to the door as the storm raged over the village, her eye pressed to the gap at the edge of the flapping leather curtain. She shrank back as a flash seared into a nearby house.

"Father, Chief Norlyn's house has been struck," she said, rubbing at the shadows on her eyelids.

Brode got to his feet. "I must check on him," he said. Urdan held him back.

"You do not know if the spirits are finished with him," he said. "Wait until the storm abates."

Brode sat stiff and uneasy as the flashes and roars of the storm shook the grand temple. Another crash sounded overhead, and they all heard the scream of a man in agony. Brode jumped up, striding to the door and flinging the curtain aside.

"Urdan, come with me," he called. Lorev, Jath and Kimmi all followed the star keeper outside. The rain had eased a little, but they were soaked before they reached Norlyn's house. They caught up with Brode as he pushed the door open and stepped inside. Remnants of the fire were scattered around, brands of wood burning on the floor. Furniture was smashed. Face down on the ground, smoke still rising from his scorched clothing, lay Norlyn.

"Help me," Brode said, trying to turn the body over. Urdan joined him, getting the chief onto his back. Brode took a blade, cutting away the smouldering sleeve of Norlyn's tunic.

"Lorev, Jath, help us carry him. We must get him to Gelyn," he said.

The four of them lifted the limp body, head lolling back, mouth gaping in silent agony. They carried him to the spirit master's house, setting him on the floor as Gelyn struggled to his feet.

"So, he has paid the price for his threats," Gelyn said. His voice showed no surprise at the body on the floor.

Lorev pressed his ear to the chief's chest. He held up a hand to quieten them. "He breathes, and I hear his heart."

Gelyn turned to the girl standing just inside the threshold. "Close the door, Kimmi, and bring me light," he said. He turned to Brode. "Lift him onto the bed here."

Gelyn worked fast, stripping away Norlyn's remaining clothes, cutting what was not easily removed. Kimmi held a shell lamp close by, handing a second one to Jath.

As the flames illuminated the naked man, Urdan gasped, and his hand came to his mouth. "They have marked him," he said.

Gelyn's fingers traced the fine red lines that drew patterns from Norlyn's right wrist to his ear. Twisting, swirling designs, like angry ferns. He reached for his pouch, taking out a small pot of lamp-black.

"What are you doing?" Brode asked.

Gelyn filled his fingertip with the greasy dye and began smoothing it into the vivid patterns. "The spirits have scarred him. Should he live, I do not want him to forget this night."

"Will he live?" Urdan asked.

"I will not decide that," Gelyn said, glancing upwards. "They will."

* * *

Lorev and Jath slept late, despite the uncomfortable bed in the temple. The night's drama had exhausted them both.

Kimmi shook them awake and made them tea while they dressed and relieved themselves.

"Does he live still?" Jath asked, nodding towards the spirit master's house.

"Norlyn? Yes," Kimmi said. "Gelyn says he is asking for you both. When you have eaten, you are to go to him."

They breakfasted on bread and milk, then made their way across the muddy yard. Jath looked up at the split and broken flagstones of the chief's roof.

"Your mother and father did that?" she asked.

"So it seems," he said.

Trav followed them into Gelyn's home, taking a seat by the hearth. Lorev looked across to the bed where Norlyn lay. His face was grey and pinched with pain. His family sat on a bench beside him. The woman, Lorev remembered her name was Keer, turned to him, a weak smile on her lips.

"He still does not believe he will survive," she said. "He needs to make his peace with you." She stood, chivvying the children outside, leaving the bench for Jath and Lorev. Norlyn's face had aged ten years since his ordeal.

"Chief Norlyn," Lorev said.

His eyes opened, red-rimmed and watery, struggling to focus on Lorev's face.

"I want to give you my sincere apology, both of you," he said. "My temper has often got the better of me. Sometimes, as a warrior, that is a good thing, but mostly it is not. I had no right to threaten you, and the spirits ensured I have paid the price."

"But you will recover," Jath said.

Norlyn reached across his body, wincing as he lifted his scarred right arm with his left. He dropped it, and it fell to the bed, unmoving. "They said they would take from me what I valued most. I feared for my mate, my children, but the spirits know me better than I know myself. They have taken my strength and my spear arm. I will never go into battle again."

Lorev looked down at his feet. "My parents were harsh with you, Chief Norlyn."

"As I would be if someone threatened my children. Do not feel bad for me. In my rage, I may have killed you and your woman."

"Jath is not…" Lorev began, glancing at the eagle warrior. She gave a shy smile, almost girlish, before her hand covered her mouth and her shoulders shook. "We are friends," he said.

"You are free," Norlyn said. "You may stay here or leave. I will understand either way. Ask Keer to come back in for me, would you?"

Jath ran to the door, finding Keer waiting outside.

"I bear you no ill will," Keer said, squeezing Jath's arm. "He brought this on himself. I love him, but he can be such a fool." She slipped back into the house as Lorev came out.

"What do you want to do?" Lorev asked.

"Come, let's ask Brode for his advice," Jath said.

* * *

Brode had settled them beside the fire with cups of rose-hip tea. Urdan, Dreena and Kimmi joined them, for the old star master shared a home with them.

"Do you wish to stay here?" Brode asked.

"Perhaps, there is much to learn, but I would like to return home one day," Lorev said.

"How long until the new moon?" Urdan asked him.

"Eleven days," he said, without pause.

"And the winter solstice?" Brode said.

This time Lorev shut his eyes. Brode watched them moving beneath the closed lids as if dreaming. "Two moons from the next new moon, but the solstice is a day or two after that," he muttered. His brow wrinkled. "Sixty and eight days, perhaps sixty and nine. I cannot be sure," he said.

"That calculation would have taken me much longer, Lorev, and I would have been no more sure that you. You have exceptional skill with numbers. I wish you would stay and let me develop it."

"The one who taught me to count, to add and subtract, was Albyn," he said.

Brode nodded. "Life moves in circles, and every circle has to close on itself. Has it occurred to you that this Albyn knew the one place you could learn more about numbers was the village between the worlds, and that the talismans would bring you here?"

"Why, that devious old weasel!" Lorev said.

Brode turned to Jath. "And you, my dear. What do you want to do?"

"I seem to have thrown in my lot with Lorev," she said. "I see no reason to change that."

"We worry about Gelyn," Kimmi chipped in. "He becomes stiffer and more infirm with each passing moon. Would you consider moving into his house? He lives there alone."

"Wouldn't he have to ask us?" Lorev said.

Kimmi smiled. "I think I can arrange for him to think it's a good idea. Perhaps you might like to learn some healing skills from him, Jath."

* * *

Lorev laid out Verra's bones on the hide he'd used to carry them. Skull and shoulders, back and ribs. He worked his way down her small body, tears dripping onto the dry, yellowed bones.

"It is time to lay you to rest, little sister," he whispered. "The man responsible for your death is dead, I have returned the talismans, you can sleep now."

Jath helped Gelyn to kneel beside Lorev and watched as he wafted burning herbs over the tiny skeleton. He placed a hand on her skull, another amongst the rows of rib bones. "Ancestors of this child, Verra. Take her across the river to be with her loved ones again. We have met the conditions the spirits imposed, and we hand her into your care now."

Lorev packed the bones back into a neat parcel as Gelyn leant on Jath's arm and stood.

"Take a token of her," Gelyn said. "A memory of her, to keep."

"I shall never forget her," Lorev said.

"Nevertheless, take a small bone, to hold her close." Lorev selected a finger bone, tucking it into the pouch at his waist.

"You know what you must do," Gelyn said. "Take her to the tomb, sit the night with her, drum her across the river. I am too old to do it now."

* * *

Lorev stacked Verra's bones into the niche in the tomb and sat, Jath at his side, on the chamber's damp floor. It had taken a while to convince Gelyn to allow the uninitiated girl to enter the tomb and travel to the lower world. Lorev described his laying to rest of her brother, and he relented.

"Put out the lamp," he said. "We must be in darkness until the dawn."

Jath blew out the tiny flame as Lorev picked up the drum. He smiled as he felt her hand creep onto his leg, fingers gripping. Even warriors had their fears.

He began a slow heartbeat, closing his eyes as the tempo increased, and he felt himself dropping through the floor to the world below.

The grey of the lower world was familiar now. Jath was at his side as he stood close to the river and called out.

"Ancestors of mine, ancestors of my sister, Verra. Come."

Shifting mists on the far bank coalesced into human shapes. One stepped forward. "You return, Apprentice," the spirit said.

From his left, the small shape of his sister walked to the river. She turned to Lorev.

"Thank you, brother. You have done all that the spirits asked, I am free now."

"I will miss you, Verra," Lorev said, wiping a tear from his cheek. "I will not see you again until I join you in the land of the dead."

"Perhaps," she said, a smile on her lips. "Jath, I charge you with his care now, as long as you are together."

Jath nodded as the tiny girl stepped into the shallow water.

"But…" Lorev said. Verra turned, her finger to her lips, then waded to the far bank. The spirit reached for her hand and led her away from the water as their forms drifted away.

* * *

Lorev stirred as the first shafts of dawn light crept along the passage wall. He straightened his stiff legs, smiling at the head laid on his shoulder.

"Jath. It is dawn, we can go now."

She opened her eyes, stretching the ache from her bones as Lorev crawled out of the cold stone tomb. Scrambling behind him, they both emerged into the sunrise. Jath reached for his hand, leading him towards the village. "I need to sleep in our bed and get warm," she said, pulling her cloak tighter around her.

They could hear Gelyn's snores from the back of the house as they stripped off their damp clothes and climbed under the warm furs. Jath laid her head on his chest, her arm wrapped around his waist.

"Jath, you are twin-spirited. Should we be close, like this?"

"I have the body-spirit of a woman, and the warrior-spirit of a man," she said. "Perhaps I want to honour my body-spirit for a while."

Her bare leg hooked over his as her head settled onto his chest again. Lorev hesitated for a moment, then wrapped his arm around her, pulling her chilled body closer.

Thirteen.

Lorev's fingers ached from holding the stick of charcoal. The marks on the flat stone altar would have meant nothing to him a year ago: full moon, new moon, sunrise, sunset. He consulted the painted hide Brode had given him to study. Rows of the counting marks spread across the chart. He inspected one section again.

"A new moon," he muttered. "Symbol for the sun… one, two, three, four," his mouth gaped. "Over four hundreds of years?" He ran to the temple door, searching for Brode or Urdan. "Master Brode?" he called, "Do you have a moment?"

Brode walked over to him, smiling, "Another new symbol you need me to explain?" he asked.

"Yes. Well, no… Come and see."

Brode pored over the charcoal marks on the altar stone. "These are good, Lorev. What is your question?"

Lorev pulled the hide closer to his calculations. "This mark," he said, pointing, "What does it mean?"

"Ah. That is an eclipse. The moon steps between us and the sun, a battle ensues, and she shows her power by turning day to night. I have never witnessed it, but it is both an auspicious and frightening time."

"Count," Lorev said, his voice trembling.

Brode's finger ran across the old hide, lips moving as he traced the numbers. "One, two, three, four hundred, ten and five… Spirits! Lorev, it is near to the time for another eclipse."

"The hides are true? They are accurate?" Lorev asked.

"Yes, each star keeper must copy his predecessor's charts in exact detail before he becomes a master. My mentor checked every scrap of this, and all the others, when I made them. His master would have done the same."

"Can you tell which moon it will be?" Lorev said.

"No," Brode said, taking the charcoal and adding to Lorev's marks. "Before the winter solstice as close as I can tell."

* * *

Jath stirred the pot of warm milk with her hand. It had been sitting since the early milking, close to the hearth. She had cut a small piece of the salted calf stomach, dropping it into a cup of water that morning, and now she poured the golden liquid into the milk. A few more stirs and she took her hand from the pot. It would set in a short while, and she could hang it in a linen cloth to drain overnight.

"I have something for you," said Kimmi, placing a bundle on the bed.

"What is it?"

Kimmi unfolded some pale tan leather, holding up a beautifully tooled jerkin. She passed it to Jath, then shook out some matching leggings.

"What are these?" Jath asked.

"A present," Kimmi said, "Try them on."

"For me?" Jath stripped off the baggy, worn, eagle tribe leathers. The leggings fitted well, and she tied the waist cord, securing them. The jerkin went over her linen undershirt, leaving her arms bare. She laced the front tight at the waist, tapering out at her chest.

"It shows off my breasts," she said.

"Do you not like it?" Kimmi asked. "I meant it to compliment your twin spirits, woman and warrior. It is Drogga men's style, but tailored just for you."

Jath saw the doubt in her new friend's eyes and hugged her. "It is perfect," she said. "I hid my body for so long, afraid that there was something wrong with me. No, this is a perfect honouring of my two spirits." She kissed Kimmi's cheek. "Thank you."

"Jath. I have discovered something in the old record hides. There's going to be…" Lorev's voice tapered off as he took in the sleek form of his friend, wrapped in fitted leather. "You look beautiful!" he said.

"You don't call warriors beautiful, Lorev," Kimmi said.

Jath walked over to him, wrapping her arms around his neck, kissing him. "Seeing it's you, I'll settle for beautiful," she said. "Now, what were you going to tell me?" Lorev explained about the eclipse. "When will this happen?" she asked.

"A new moon, before the winter solstice, but we don't know which one. I will study further tomorrow to see if I can make a better guess."

"You and your numbers," she said, folding her old clothes. "Supper will be ready soon. See if you can find Gelyn."

* * *

"An eclipse?" Gelyn said, draining the last of the stew from his bowl, "The legends tell of this. We will have to warn the other tribes. It is a frightening experience to have day turn to night."

"How can we do that?" Lorev said.

"A runner, for the Isle of Pigs," he said, "But someone will have to make a journey south."

"Who?" said Jath, offering him more stew.

Gelyn held out his bowl. "You?" he said, looking from Jath to Lorev.

"No, no," Lorev said, "The sea makes me ill."

"Seasickness?" Gelyn laughed. "Oh, we'll cure you of that."

* * *

Lorev lay on his side. Gelyn, kneeling beside him, placed the thick leather pad under his earlobe. The awl pricked Lorev's ear as the old spirit master pressed it into place. The small wooden club fell, and Lorev screamed.

"One done, now hush," Gelyn said, pulling out the awl. Lorev hissed as he pushed a tapered bone crescent into the hole, then he felt honey being smeared over the stinging skin.

"Turn over," Gelyn said.

Lorev winced. "Perhaps one will be enough, spirit master."

"Turn over," Gelyn said, cleaning blood from the awl.

The second piercing was worse, only because Lorev knew what was coming. He sighed with relief as Gelyn fitted the ornament and applied the honey.

"Turn them often," Gelyn instructed, "More so when the seasickness threatens."

"May I have my ears pierced too?" Jath asked.

"You suffer from the sickness as well?" Gelyn said.

"No, but they look good, don't they?"

"It was popular when my grandmother was alive," Gelyn said, wiping the awl clean.

Jath lay down. "Then perhaps we should revive it."

It surprised Lorev to hear just a faint squeak from her as Gelyn punched the awl through her lobe, and she smiled as she turned over.

Gelyn reached into his pouch, pulling out two leather bands, each with rawhide laces. "Fix these to your wrists when you sail," he instructed, passing them to Lorev. "They will help too."

Later, Lorev sat with a bone comb and a flint blade, shaving the sides of Jath's head. He marvelled at how easy it was to get close, using the comb to avoid cutting the skin. Jath instructed him in shortening the crest of longer hair on top of her head, then they swapped places as she trimmed Lorev's hair and beard.

"How long until the new moon," she asked.

"Seventeen days," he said.

"So, we sail soon?"

"Yes, west to begin with, then south. We will call at my home village if we can." His eyes took on a distant look.

"What's her name?" Jath said.

"Who?"

"The girl you're thinking of."

Lorev sighed. "Hessa."

"Pretty name," Jath said, tidying away the grooming tools.

* * *

The warm body rolled on top of him as he opened his eyes. He could make out Jath's grin in the fire's dying glow.

"Jath, I…" he started.

"Shh," she said, straddling his hips.

"But Hessa…"

"Will enjoy your greater experience," she chuckled, reaching between them, before lowering her body onto his. "You and me? This is just for fun, Lorev."

His hands found her waist. "Just for fun?" he asked, as her hips rocked.

Lorev felt as if he was betraying Hessa, sharing himself with Jath, yet he had made no promise to the girl from the Hill Clan. Though he hadn't initiated their love-making, he didn't refuse Jath's advances, discovering a woman's body for the first time. Though she said she was honouring her body-spirit in their coupling, it was apparent to Lorev that the warrior was in charge here, too.

* * *

"The boat will be ready soon," Jath said, coming into the temple a few days later. "She's a double hull with a good-sized sail."

"I'll leave the sailing to the boatman and you," Lorev said, making for the door. "The first time I was in a boat, I thought I would die. The second time, I almost did."

Jath smiled, crossing the temple to sit with Kimmi who was weaving offering baskets in a corner.

"You weave so fast," Jath said, laying her hand on Kimmi's leg.

"Thank you," the girl smiled. "I… I like your hair. It's lovely."

Jath ran her fingers through the thick crest. "Not as pretty as yours, though," she said, stroking Kimmi's cheek.

"I… It's… I didn't mean…" she started.

"What did you mean?" Jath said, leaning forward and pressing her lips to the blushing girl's mouth.

"Oh, Spirits!" Kimmi gasped.

"Did you like that?" Jath asked. Kimmi's wide eyes never left Jath's face as she nodded. Jath kissed her again.

* * *

Lorev wakened as Jath climbed over him, settling in her regular place beside the wall. It was full dark, and the fire was out.

"Where have you been?" he asked.

"At the temple."

"Until the middle of the night?" Lorev said.

"Mmm-hmm. I was keeping Kimmi company."

"You… and Kimmi?" he asked. "But…"

"I'm not your mate, Lorev. I'm not looking for a promise of bonding. We had some fun, same as you and I do." She slipped an arm around his waist, and he froze, feeling her head lay on his chest. His arm hovered for a few moments before he sighed and wrapped it around her shoulder.

* * *

They had carried their packs around the great west lake to the seashore, loading everything into the boat.

"Take these charts," Brode said, handing Lorev the rolled skins. "Since the war with the eagle tribe, we have neglected our travelling. I do not know if you will encounter any surviving star masters on your journey."

"Are they few in number, then?" Lorev asked.

"There were once twenty that I knew of, three on the coast you will travel. Show them the proof of the charts, if you find them."

Lorev nodded and clasped Brode's hand. He looked across at Jath, whispering into the ear of Kimmi. The girl clung to the eagle warrior, sobbing. Urdan looked on with disapproval, though her mother, Dreena, had a smile on her face as Jath peeled the girl from herself and climbed into the boat.

"Farewell," Urdan shouted, as Keld, the boatman, pushed the vessel clear of the beach and jumped aboard.

Fourteen.

Albyn sat beside the roundhouse door. The warm sun on his face told him he was facing south. He could hear his two small charges whispering as they played a game of their own invention on the grass beside him.

"Visitors," hissed the voice in his head. In his last years, he was sure that this was the entity that would have been his walking spirit, had he become a spirit master.

"How many, and from where?" he asked.

"From the south, a leader, and a messenger amongst them."

"Thank you, spirit," he said, pushing himself to his feet.

"Can we help you, Messenger Albyn?" came Shilla's voice from his left.

"My swan's feather cloak," he said, reaching out his hand. He felt the familiar grip of his lore apprentice and guide, leading him into the house.

"Jeeha? Tell Master Col to expect guests," he called, knowing Shilla's friend would be close by.

"Yes, Messenger," came the voice, as feet scampered away.

* * *

Col and Talla smiled as the party entered the village, each one acknowledging the bull's skull on the boundary post. Zoola and Gren stood beside them, Albyn, Hessa and the apprentices at their backs.

"Greetings, Sarn. Greetings, Spirit Messenger Rolva," Col said, hands held out in welcome. He dispensed with the formal statements for these friends and allies. Sarn clasped Col's hands in his.

"Good to see you, Col," he said. Rolva went straight to Talla, drawing her into a hug before greeting each of the others.

"How is the little one?" Hessa asked, peering into the sling on Rolva's back. "What have you named him?"

Rolva chuckled, untying the sling and passing the wriggling bundle to Hessa. "His name is Dass, and he has the appetite of a pig."

Hessa cooed over the baby while Rolva greeted the younger ones, even Shilla, who had yet to take her apprentice marks.

"Come," said Col, leading the way into the large roundhouse, "I think we can all fit inside."

The young ones busied themselves with making tea as the leaders and protected-of-spirit drew up stools and benches.

"We have flint to spare this autumn," Sarn said, starting the trading as leader of the boat clan. "There is quality pottery and some fine linens."

Col listened to what Sarn had not said. There was no mention of food, and he knew the boat clan was constructing a new village. They had many mouths to feed over the coming winter.

"We have need of flint, Sarn, and linen too. Would you accept an offer of grain and good cattle for slaughter in exchange?"

Sarn smiled. Col and his mate, Talla, were excellent leaders. He had read Sarn's offer well, saving the leader from having to ask for what they needed.

"We would accept that," he said, taking a cup of tea from an apprentice. He stood. "Come, let us walk and discuss terms."

Col turned to Talla, receiving a nod to conduct the trade. They were true partners in leadership.

"Is there any word of Lorev, your older boy?" Sarn asked when the trade was agreed.

"He is on the Isle of Pigs," Col said, sitting on a bench in the sun. "In our spirit form, we have stepped in to help him. His life was threatened."

Sarn sat beside him. "He is safe now?"

"Yes. I do not understand the nature of his quest, but he is safe, at least."

"There is another matter," Sarn said. "Jorn, my son, will be the leader of the new village. A good spirit messenger would make an ideal mate for him."

"Hessa?" Col asked. Sarn nodded. "I am not her father, Sarn. I will not suggest who she bonds with."

"Oh, I don't mean you should influence her," Sarn protested, "I wish to make sure you have no objection to Jorn asking her for a promise."

Col smiled. "None, but she will make her own decision. Now, come and eat with us. You'll stay the night? The apprentices will make beds ready for you all."

* * *

It was late morning when Hessa finished her chores and sat with Talla for a cup of nettle tea.

"We will take you to meet your walking spirit at the full moon," said Talla.

"I'm excited but nervous," Hessa said. She spotted Jorn coming towards them and glanced at Talla. She smiled and nodded.

"Spirit Master Talla," he said, bowing his head. He turned to Hessa. "Spirit Messenger Hessa. I wondered if you would like to take a walk with me beside the shore."

"Oh. I still have to take care of the children," she said, turning to Talla.

"Go," Talla said, "I'll manage the children. It's a pleasant day for a walk."

She watched them stroll away. Col had told her of his conversation with Sarn, and she wondered if Hessa would wait to see if Lorev returned before deciding.

* * *

"We have five houses almost ready," Jorn said, "The main roundhouse will be thatched before the full moon. It will be a suitable home for my mate and me."

Hessa looked up, smiling. "Then you have found a mate? Oh, I'm glad for you, Jorn."

"Um, no," he said, shuffling from foot to foot. "I was hoping to ask you for your promise of bonding." He looked up, meeting her gaze. "You are a healthy woman, Hessa. You are skilled with both spirit work and healing, a hard worker and pretty too."

Hessa gave a weak smile. His attraction to her seemed a long way down that list of her attributes. "I am sorry, Jorn. I am not promised, but there is someone I am waiting for."

"Lorev?" he asked, "Who knows when he will return, if ever. The Bay Clan needs a spirit messenger now, Hessa."

She turned back along the beach, Jorn pacing to keep up. "Perhaps you had better look elsewhere then," she said.

* * *

"Well, did he ask you?" Talla said as Hessa stepped into the house.

"He did."

"And? What did you say?" Zoola asked.

"I said no. I told him I wanted to wait for Lorev to return before I decided."

"A new house, in a new village," Zoola said. "Bonded to a clan leader. He's good looking, Hessa."

Hessa knelt to pile more wood on the fire. "It's a shame he doesn't think the same about me then," she said.

Hessa avoided the Boat Clan party when they left, not wanting to deal with further advances from Jorn. Talla said the refusal had disappointed him, but he had instructed her to tell Hessa that his offer stood.

"Do you think Lorev will return?" she asked.

"You will see him again, Hessa. Do not fear," Talla said.

* * *

Hessa had woken early. She had not slept well since the visit from the Boat Clan. Thoughts of Lorev and of Jorn, and doubts about her future, dogged her. She walked along the shore, cutting the coarse grasses for basket-making.

The clatter of a sail being dropped made her jump, and she crouched down in the thick grass, peering at the approaching vessel. Its double hull and yellow sail were foreign to her. There were three figures on board. The one at the steering board would be the boat master. The other two jumped from the bow, into the shallow water, hauling on ropes to get the boat clear of the surf. The sailor joined them, getting the vessel well up the beach.

Hessa could see the other two now. One had a warrior's dress and bearing; short hair, leather leggings, and a heavy cloak. The other was... Lorev? As if to confirm it, a huge grey wolf leapt from the beached vessel. Hessa almost jumped from her hiding place; almost ran down the bank to greet him. Then the warrior took Lorev's hand and led him further along the beach.

Hessa watched as Lorev walked, deep in conversation, with the second man. She felt knots in her stomach as they turned, face to face. The warrior wrapped his arms around Lorev's neck, and their lips met.

"No," she whispered. She dropped the bundle of grasses and ran. Up the bank towards the village, past the boundary post, her fingers grazing the sacred skull. This was why he showed no interest in her. This was why he'd blushed at her nakedness, run from her advances. He liked men.

Hessa ran to the apprentice house, the others all still sleeping. She pulled her pack from under her bed and began thrusting her few personal possessions into it: her healing tools, spare clothing, some herbs.

Hessa couldn't stay here and watch Lorev with another. She had to get away. Pulling on her cloak, she grabbed her drum and staff.

"Where are you going?" Shilla asked, stirring from sleep.

"To the women's circle, then I must go on an errand to the south," she said, hurrying out of the door.

Hessa almost ran to the smaller circle of stones, across the valley, to the east. She bowed her head as she entered, placing her hand on the mother stone, then sitting at the centre of the ring of megaliths.

Facing west, she slowed her breathing and tried to calm herself. She set up a steady rhythm with her drum, closing her eyes, dropping to the grey world below.

The river was low, trickling over black rocks, marking the boundary between life and death. Hessa raised her arms, almost sobbing now.

"Ancestors who love me, come. I am Hessa, Spirit Messenger of the Hill Clan of the Tribe of the West. Come to me."

A black shadow, across the water, coalesced into form. A woman stepped forward, smiling at the girl — arms out in greeting.

"You honour us with a visit, Messenger. What is your wish?"

Hessa stared at the figure. "Song Master Geth? Is it you?"

The spirit stepped to the water's edge. The old woman had carried the songs, and history, of the tribe for so many years, Albyn's sister, Geth.

"It is I. Why do you summon me, Messenger Hessa?"

"I don't know what to do. Lorev... he is with a man. He... he doesn't like me at all."

"Have you spoken to him?" Geth asked.

"No. I cannot face him. I thought... I hoped he wanted to be with me."

"Lorev may not be what he seems, Hessa," Geth said.

"I know that." The tears flowed again. "I have seen with my own eyes."

"What do you wish?" the spirit asked, "A prophecy?"

Hessa looked up, wiping tears from her face, hope in her eyes again. "Yes!"

Geth folded her arms. "You know the cost of prophecy may be the very knowledge it brings?"

"Yes, yes, tell me," Hessa begged.

"You will be bonded," she said, "but this is not the time or the place. You will bear a son first, then a daughter. You will make your home elsewhere, not at Classac. In time, you will be happy."

"His name?" Hessa asked.

"You know his name, child."

Hessa sobbed again. "No," she whispered. "No." She turned from the river without another word. "Back," she called.

Snatching up her pack and drum, Hessa ran from the stone circle, not even stopping to offer thanks to the mother stone in her haste. She shouldered the bag and set off south, jaw set, tears streaming, towards her destiny.

Fifteen.

Lorev twisted the bone ornaments in his earlobes, feeling the nausea in his belly recede. He watched the coast, eyes trained on dry land, wishing he were there. Jath smiled as she ducked under the sail and settled beside him. She was a seasoned sailor, never remembering a time when boat journeys were not part of her life.

"We leave the coast here and continue west," she said, "Keld says we'll see the Long Islands soon, then we can turn south along the far side."

"He is sure he can find Classac?" Lorev asked.

"Yes, his father entrusted him with his charts."

Lorev looked back at the receding coastline. "Will we get there today?"

"Perhaps not," she said. "We may lie up tonight and sail in tomorrow morning."

Lorev swallowed. Another night at sea.

"Bring the sail around," Keld shouted. Jath jumped from her seat as the boat heeled over to one side, the left hull almost lifting out of the water as they turned. She hauled the sail around, tying off the rope with a flick of her wrist.

"Have you sailed this route before, Keld?" she asked, climbing back to the seat beside Lorev.

"No. My father did, before the war with the Eagle Tribe. Since then there has been almost no trade to the west."

"Should we have brought trade goods?" Lorev asked.

Keld shrugged. "We don't know what they might need," he said. "What would we bring?"

Lorev nodded. There were small gifts: Stone orbs, mace heads, things to confirm the truth of their journey and their message. The cliff clan of the Cheel Tribe, on the mainland, had received them graciously when they had explained their mission, their chief accepting a schist axe along with news of the coming eclipse.

As the mainland hills became shadows on the horizon, Keld shouted and pointed to the left. The bank of cloud hugged a black line that must be land, must be the Long Islands.

* * *

The rub of rope against the edge of the hull roused him, and Lorev sat up. Keld hauled the anchor stone into the boat and raised the sail. Grey light changed to crimson over the island as they turned into the broad inlet. Soon after, Lorev spotted the jagged outline of the Classac stones silhouetted against the red clouds.

As they neared the shore, Jath clambered over to the right-hand hull, waiting with a rope in hand. Lorev climbed forward, picking up his own line. The sail clattered down as the vessel nosed the beach, and both jumped into the shallow water, dragging the bow clear of the lapping tide. Trav leapt from the boat, still nervous of sailing, but willing to follow Lorev anywhere.

Jath glanced back at Keld, then took Lorev's hand and led him along the shore.

"You need to find out if she is still waiting for you, Lorev," Jath said.

"Hessa? She is a Spirit Messenger. I am an Apprentice."

"You still keep a lamp lit for her, though," Jath said, patting her chest. "In here."

"You and me…" Lorev began. Jath stopped and turned to him, her arms going around his neck.

"You and I had a little fun," she said, kissing him. "It sounds like your feelings for this Hessa are far more than that. Find her, Lorev. I claim no hold over you, nor you over me. Go."

* * *

The scream startled him as he entered the village.

"Lorev!" He turned to find his little sister, Shilla, charging towards him. Scooping her up in his arms, he clutched her tight.

"You came back. I knew you would come back. Oh, I've missed you," she chattered, her face buried in his shoulder.

"I missed you too," he said, peeling her from his chest and setting her down. "You've grown so much."

"I don't think anyone is awake yet," she said, tugging him towards the main house. "Come on, we must wake mother and father."

A tousle-headed Talla was raking hot stones from the glowing embers as they entered. She turned at Shilla's excited chatter.

"Lorev? Oh, Lorev, it's you, you came back."

"Hello, Mother," he said, smiling.

"Col. Get up, Lorev is home," Talla called.

Soon all the protected-of-spirit were gathered around the hearth, talking over each other to get Lorev's news.

"Please," said Lorev, raising his arms to silence them, "Boat master Keld and my friend Jath are still at the shore. There is a boat to haul."

Volunteers soon made their way to the beach, making simple work of getting the craft above the high tide mark. Trav slunk behind Jath's legs, unnerved by the crowd of people.

Lorev crouched and called him, running his fingers through the thick ruff of fur at his neck.

"You have your spirit animal," Col said.

"Yes," Lorev said. "This is Trav. I have had him since he was a cub. He will harm no one."

Lorev carried his small brother, Glev, back towards the village as Shilla dragged him along by the hand. As soon as he sat beside the roundhouse fire, she jumped into his lap, wrapping her arms around his chest.

"Are you back to stay?" Shilla asked as everyone quietened to hear his reply.

"No, little one. I come with a message from the star masters on the Isle of Pigs. I must travel on soon. Every tribe needs to hear the prophecy they have made."

"Star Masters?" Albyn said.

"Yes, Messenger Albyn. It seems they remember your name still," Lorev said.

"Indeed. Perhaps you and I can talk of it later," he replied.

"Yes, later."

"What is this prophecy?" Zoola asked.

Lorev stood, looking around at the faces. Looking for one in particular. "Before the winter solstice, at the new moon, there will be a battle between the moon and the sun. The star masters call this an eclipse. The moon will try to take the sun's light away from us."

"But what if she succeeds?" asked an apprentice.

"I am told that she fights this battle on rare occasions," Lorev said. "The sun is stronger, of course, but the battle is frightening. This is why they sent me."

"Which new moon," Col asked. "We must prepare."

"We... They do not know," Lorev said. "Only that it must be a new moon before mid-winter."

* * *

Breakfast was finished, and most of the crowd had set off to take care of morning chores. Lorev sat with Glev and Shilla still on his knee.

"Introduce us to your friends," Col said, smiling at Jath and Keld.

"I'm sorry," Lorev said, setting the children down, "Everyone was so loud before. Please, Mother, Father."

Col and Talla stood, each reciting their status and bowing to the visitors.

"I am Keld, Boat Master of the Drogga Tribe, from the Isle of Pigs," the sailor said, hands extended.

"I am Jath, of the Eagle Tribe," she said.

Albyn stood, turning to the sound of her voice. "Come to me, girl," he said, holding his arms out. Jath walked over, taking his hands.

"You are mistaken, Albyn," Talla said, "Jath is a young warrior, not a girl."

Albyn's hands slid up Jath's cloaked arms, feeling for her shoulders, then her neck. Fingers closed around the eagle talon necklace, tracing the rows of sharp claws.

"Are you the heir, the princess?" he asked.

"I apologise for our messenger," Col said, moving over to take Albyn's shaking hands from the warrior's throat.

"Are you a princess of the Eagle Tribe?" Albyn almost shouted.

Jath took his hands, pulling them away from the talisman and holding them in front of her. "I am Jath, daughter of Oshyn, King of the Eagle Tribe. Heir to the throne of Kya," she recited. "The talisman has been returned, Messenger Albyn."

Col looked puzzled until Jath shrugged off her cloak, showing the fitted leather jerkin and tight leggings. "Apologies, Princess," he said. "You wear the garb of a warrior."

Jath grinned. "It confuses many people, though not Albyn."

The way she said the name seemed odd to Col. It sounded like 'Albyin' from her lips. Lorev recognised it though, the way the Drogga spoke that name ending was unique.

Trav whined at Lorev's heel, and he knew the young wolf was asking to relieve himself. "Sorry," he said, "Trav needs to go outside, and I don't want to scare those who have yet to meet him. I'll be back soon."

"You are Lorev's sister, Shilla?" Jath said, smiling at the girl.

"Yes," Shilla said, taking Glev's hand and marching out of the door. Jath looked to Col and Talla, but they both shook their heads at their daughter's behaviour.

* * *

Talla showed Jath and Keld to one of the guest houses, setting an apprentice to light a fire for them. She sat awhile with Jath, learning of the war between the Drogga and the Eagle Tribe, telling something of Lorev's history. She had just got back to her own house when Lorev returned. He poured a cup of water, then sat at the hearth.

"May we talk with you?" Col asked, sitting beside him. Talla joined them.

"What about?" Lorev asked.

"It worries us that you have not yet tried to become a messenger," Talla said.

"We hoped your journey would allow you to find your next achievement," Col added.

Lorev sighed. "Perhaps I am not destined to be a messenger," he said. "I seem to have failed at every other thing I have tried."

"Failed, how?" Talla said.

"I set out to avenge my sister's death, yet I almost saved her killer."

"Arvan lives?" Col said.

"He died of his injuries, not at my hands," Lorev said. "I tried to set my sister's spirit free. This time it was the spirits who prevented it. It seems the talismans Albyn gave me came with their own consequences. I could not lay her to rest until I had satisfied the conditions set on me. I was captured by the Eagle Tribe, rescued by Jath, then threatened by the Drogga."

"At least we could help you there," Col said.

Lorev's nostrils flared. "Did it not occur to you that I might need to fight my own battles?"

Col looked at Talla, surprised by the outburst. "They threatened your life, we wanted to help you," he said.

Lorev stood, glaring at his parents. "Do you intend to wrap me in a blanket of your weaving my entire life?" he shouted, storming out of the door, Trav at his heel.

* * *

Shilla found him by the shore, sitting on a rock. She sat close beside him, and his arm wrapped around her shoulder.

"Mother was crying," she said, "Were you mean to her?"

Lorev sighed. "I suppose I was, but I am not a child any more, Shilla." He turned to his sister. "Where is Hessa?"

"She left early this morning. She means to be away for some time, all her things have gone."

"Where did she go?" Lorev asked.

"An errand, she said, but no one knows what it is. Perhaps she has gone to the Boat Clan in the south."

"Why would she go there?"

Shilla glanced up at him. "She has had an offer of bonding, from Jorn, the leader's son."

Lorev stared out to sea. "An offer? Has she given him her promise?"

Shilla shook her head, then turned to Lorev. "Why are you with *her*?" she said, nodding towards the guest house.

"Jath? We are friends. Nothing more."

"Then perhaps you should go after Hessa," Shilla said. "You may catch her yet."

He palmed his face, rubbing at tired eyes. "I can't. We must leave on the morning tide. We must deliver the star master's message."

Shilla stood. "I will come with you," she said, hands on hips. "I miss you too much to let you go again."

Lorev reached for her and pulled her into a hug. "No. It is a long and dangerous journey. You must stay here."

Her face creased into a frown. "Will you return then? Promise it. Promise you'll return to me."

"I promise," he said.

* * *

Lorev sat in the falling dusk, staring at the orange horizon. He glanced around at Shilla's voice.

"The bench is to your right, Messenger," she said, steering the blind man to Lorev's side. Albyn sat, groaning as his knees clicked. "Send for me when you two have talked," she said, running off.

"Why?" Lorev said.

Albyn turned at his voice. "They needed to find their rightful owners."

"Yes, but why take them?"

"You know?" Albyn asked.

"That you stole the Talisman of Kya, the fire beads, the stone tablet? Yes. A war has raged ever since. Many hundreds have died for your greed."

"It was not greed," he said, "I had my reasons to hate both the Drogga and the Eagle Tribe."

"What could justify thirty years of fighting and killing, Albyn?"

"It is too painful to tell," Albyn said. "Many times, I thought to go back. Many times, I told myself to face their wrath and return the talismans. Then the spirits told me your father needed the fire beads." His fingers traced the empty sockets where his eyes had been. "Then it was too late for me to do it. I will not live much longer. You were the last chance to send them back."

"They almost got me killed," Lorev said. "If not for Jath, I would be dead."

Albyn's voice was a whisper, now. "I am sorry, Lorev. So sorry."

Sixteen.

Keld leapt aboard the boat as the lapping waves floated the stern. Jath and Lorev pushed the heavy vessel clear of the shore and clambered in. Lorev looked back at the beach, empty but for the tiny figure of Shilla. He waved, but she turned, walking away, her shoulders heaving with her sobs.

"After our journey, you can come home to her," Jath said, reaching for the rope and hauling the sail up.

"I don't know if this is still my home, Jath," Lorev said, "I don't know if anywhere is."

* * *

They made good speed down the west coast, calling at islands and peninsulas along the way. The Great Forested Island was the first place where they met resistance.

"Who are you to make such prophesies," the Tribe Chief said, handing back the beautiful stone orb Lorev had gifted him. Refusing a gift was almost an act of hostility in their culture.

"The star masters of the Isle of Pigs have sent us. We are only to warn you of the eclipse," Jath said. "We have done as they asked. Thank you for your welcome."

The welcome had been almost non-existent, but Jath didn't want to aggravate the leader further.

"Star master? Why we have our own star master. If this were true, we would know of it," the chief said.

"May we speak with him?" Lorev said.

"Fetch Dorbna," the chief called.

Soon, two men arrived, carrying a seat with a back. An ancient man sat on the contraption, his brown skin wrinkled and creased. Hands, like clawed bird's feet, clutched to his belly. They set the seat beside the chief.

"These upstarts think to bring us news from some distant star masters, Dorbna."

"Well, Sandur, once there were many of us." He turned to Lorev, squinting at the tattoo around his eye. "A spirit apprentice," he said. "Tell me where these star masters hail from."

"Star Master Dorbna," Lorev said, bowing. "We have travelled from the Isle of Pigs with this message. There will be an eclipse before the winter solstice. It was our task to spread the word to save people from becoming alarmed."

"The Isle of Pigs? That was where I trained in my youth," Dorbna said.

"Do you have the star charts?" Lorev asked.

"Destroyed years ago in a fire," Dorbna said. Lorev reached into his pack, pulling out a rolled hide. He spread it before the old man. A crooked finger traced its way across the leather, dirty, broken nail scratching on the painted surface.

"Here?" he said, pointing at the eclipse symbol.

Lorev crouched beside him, pointing out the row of number symbols. "And here," he said.

Dorbna muttered as he followed the counting marks. "Spirits!" the old man said. "You're right — either this new moon or the next. Sandur, make the apprentice and his party welcome. They have saved me a great embarrassment."

Sandur bowed, shouting orders for tea and food, leading the way into a large rectangular hall. "My apologies Apprentice Lorev," he said. "Please sit."

"These are my companions," Lorev said. "Boat Master Keld, and The Princess Jath."

Sandur bowed to each and ordered two men to bring Dorbna to the hearth. Lorev once again proffered the stone orb. Sandur took it with a smile. He clutched it to his chest, then scrutinised it.

"It is a unique gift, Apprentice Lorev. Thank you," he said, showing the proper appreciation for the offering. He reached for a pouch on the table, extracting a polished stone disc on a leather thong. "May I offer this trinket for your generous information?" he asked.

Lorev saw Dorbna nodding. "The disc is a woman's adornment," the star master said. "Perhaps the princess would accept it on your behalf, Lorev?"

Jath stepped forward, bowing as Sandur slipped the cord around her neck. She admired the disc, then turned to Dorbna.

"It is beautiful. Thank you."

Food and drink arrived, and the party was soon chatting like friends to the tribe's people. Sandur offered them beds, and Lorev agreed they should stay the night.

* * *

Keld had fallen into conversation with the tribe's boat master and elected to take a bed with his family. Lorev and Jath took a spare bed in the house Dorbna shared with a young spirit messenger.

Lorev slipped in beside Jath, feeling her warm body wrap around him. She seemed to sense his apprehension and smiled. "Just a cuddle, Lorev. That's all," she said.

"I think I've lost her," he said.

"Hessa? You must ask her that, Lorev."

"She has an offer of bonding from a village leader," he said, "I think that's where she has gone... why she was not at Classac."

"Time will tell," Jath said, stretching up to kiss him.

* * *

Jath's body was on top of him when he woke, eyes shining as she rolled her hips.

"Good morning," he said, reaching for her slim waist.

"It is now," she said, her lips finding his.

"We should try to catch the tide, Lorev," said Keld, walking into the house.

"A moment more," Jath said, making no effort to cover herself.

The boat master chuckled. "A moment then… or maybe two."

They found the boat already afloat when they got to the shore, Keld at the steering board. "About time," he yelled, as Lorev blushed and threw his pack aboard. He helped Jath and Trav, then clambered in.

"Thank you," called Sandur. "We will welcome you again, I hope."

They waved a farewell as the wind cracked in the sail, and they were underway again.

* * *

Time was getting short. They had pored over Keld's charts the previous evening, anchored in a small bay.

"This big inlet," Lorev said, pointing to the chart, "You can navigate it?"

"Yes, to this mark here, at least."

"Drop me there," Lorev said. "I will go overland to Stanna. Jath, will you travel on to the Frass Tribe across the water?"

"It makes sense," she said. "Keld and I are the sailors, and you can travel overland. How will we meet up?"

"We will need to overwinter," Lorev said. "I will stay at Stanna. Come, if you can, or join me in the spring."

"I'll miss you," she said, stroking his cheek.

"Just a few moons, that's all," Lorev replied.

* * *

Lorev stood on the shore, a pack and staff in his hand; Trav at his side. He waved to the retreating boat, long out of shouting range, and turned east.

Heavy clouds loomed above the sea, a frigid wind driving them onshore. Pulling his cloak tighter, Lorev set off into the unfamiliar, wooded country. He was used to the islands' open lands, and the dense forest seemed to crowd him. Rustling, and sharp bird cries, snapped his head back and forth. He was glad, before dusk, to smell wood-smoke on the air. The village was tiny, and a young messenger greeted him along with her mate, the clan leader. He warned of the upcoming eclipse, and they asked him to stay the night.

Over the following days, he needed his shelter only once and, one morning, he walked out of the edge of the woodland to find a great earthwork ahead. A circular ditch enclosed a ring of standing stones. This could only be Stanna.

"Greetings," came a voice as he approached the sizeable village. Lorev knew, from his parents' stories, that they used it only at the solstice.

"Greetings," he said, holding out his hands to the couple bearing Spirit Master tattoos. "I am Lorev, Spirit Apprentice of the…"

"Hill Clan of the Tribe of the West," said the man, smiling. "We know your tribe affiliations, and your parents, it seems. I am Tooev, and this is my mate, Yalta. No doubt you have heard our names."

Lorev breathed a sigh. "I am happy to see you, Master Tooev, Master Yalta." He glanced down at the wolf, sat close behind his leg. "This is my spirit animal, Trav. He will not harm you."

"You have a powerful creature, Lorev. It bodes well for your own strength, perhaps?" Yalta said.

Lorev looked uncertain for the first time. "Perhaps."

"Come in," Tooev said, ushering him into the meeting house. A stout woman looked up and smiled, raking stones from the fire.

"Tea, excellent," Yalta said. "Shola, this is Lorev, son of Col and Talla."

"The twins have spoken of you," she said.

"Are Arva and Atta here?" Lorev asked.

Yalta laughed. "No. Away on their travels again. Classac, The Isle of Pigs, and now, off across the seas to another island."

They settled with drinks, other protected-of-spirit filling the seats around the hearth. "What brings you here, Lorev?" Yalta asked.

"I come from the Isle of Pigs," he said. "I spent some time with the star master there. He sent me to warn of an eclipse."

"An eclipse?" Tooev said. "A sky battle?"

"Yes. Star Master Brode predicts the moon will challenge the sun, either in three days or at the new moon at the solstice."

Tooev glanced at Yalta. "We must send out runners," he said. "This will frighten people if we do not foretell it."

"I have come from the great estuary on the west coast," Lorev said. "I have warned the clans I met on my way here."

"Just to the north, east and south, then. Thank you, Lorev," Yalta said.

Shola served food, and the conversation turned to the winter's activities.

"Will you spend the winter with us?" Yalta asked. "The weather grows colder now."

"If I may," he said. "My companions have sailed on to the Frass people. They may make it here before the winter sets in. If not, they will winter across the water."

"Excellent," Tooev said. "And while you're here, we can get you trained as a spirit messenger."

Lorev bowed. "If you wish, Masters," he said.

Seventeen.

By noon, Hessa was high in the hills between her home and the Tribe of the South's lands. She sat beside a stream, dipping her cup to drink. In her haste to get away, she'd forgotten to take any food, but her journey would take only two days.

Her thoughts still swirled round and round. How had she not noticed that Lorev liked men? Why had he not said? There was no shame in it. Some people, both men and women, were born to the wrong body, or with twin spirits. The tribes all honoured a free person's choice of mate.

A man, though. A warrior. When she had thought he wanted her. She felt such a fool.

She thought back to the prophecy of the spirit of Geth. That Lorev was not what he seemed. That she would be bonded, and live somewhere else, not at Classac. That she knew her mate's name.

Yes, she knew his name. Jorn.

***

It was dusk when she walked into the Boat Clan village. It was a familiar place, and she headed straight for Rolva's house. She didn't bother to knock, stepping in to find Rolva and Dorlan trying to serve food and feed Rolva's hungry brood all at once.

"Hessa!" Dorlan said, hugging her tight. "It's good to see you." She passed a toddler to Hessa, then a bowl and spoon. "Feed him. I'll make you tea."

"Hello, Hessa," Rolva said, filling bowls of stew for her mate and remaining children. "What brings you here?"

"Later," Hessa said, feeding the small boy.

* * *

"So. Have you come for a visit?" Rolva asked as she tucked the baby into its crib.

"I have thought again about the offer Jorn made," she said.

Rolva stared at her. "What has happened?" she asked. "You had made your mind up. What has changed it?"

Hessa opened her mouth to speak, but the words didn't come. "I... I wanted to wait for Lorev," she managed.

"And?"

"He returned two days ago. He has found someone else." She was sobbing now, and Dorlan rushed to her.

Hessa clutched the young apprentice. "I saw him as he landed at the shore. He was with a warrior from some distant tribe. They... they kissed."

"He likes men? I didn't know," Rolva said.

"I lived with him half my life, Rolva. Why did I not know this about him?"

Rolva sighed. "Sometimes it takes time to find out these things, Hessa. Maybe he just discovered it."

"I couldn't stay," Hessa said. "I want him to be happy, but I couldn't watch him with someone else every day. It would kill me."

"You and I will be neighbours," Dorlan said, wiping a tear from Hessa's face. "Perhaps I can assist you too. Be a joint apprentice."

"I would like that," Hessa said, trying to smile for the excitable girl.

* * *

"Good morning, Jorn," Hessa said.

Jorn peered down from his perch, high in the roof timbers of a new house. "Hessa? Wait there, I'll be right down."

He stood, unsure of how to greet the spirit messenger. Hessa smiled at his awkwardness. "Does your offer of bonding still stand?" she asked.

"The offer... Yes, yes, it does. You have reconsidered?"

Hessa opened her arms, accepting a hug from the young clan leader. "Yes, I have."

"We will make such a wonderful couple, Hessa. A leader needs a strong mate, and a spirit messenger needs a steady partner."

"Your question?" she said, smiling.

Jorn released her from his arms and took her hands. "Hessa, spirit messenger of the Hill Clan of the Tribe of the West, will you be my bonded mate?"

"Yes, Jorn, Leader of the Bay Clan of the Tribe of the South. Yes, I will."

Hessa might have expected a kiss, but Jorn grabbed her hand and pulled her toward the path leading to the Boat Clan village. "Come on, we must tell my father and mother," he said.

* * *

Hessa stood waiting. Rolva smiled at her, Dorlan at her side, assisting. "I'm sure he will be here soon," Rolva said.

"It's usual for both people to turn up to a bonding," Hessa said, forcing a smile to her lips.

"Sorry. Sorry," Jorn said, running up. "I wanted to get the roof on that last house this morning." His matted hair was filled with bits of straw, his clothes dusty.

"Shall we begin?" Rolva asked.

Hessa looked at Jorn, sighed, and nodded.

"Members of the Boat Clan and the Bay Clan, you are gathered to witness the bonding of this man and this woman."

Hessa listened to the familiar ceremony. She had performed it herself three times now. She liked to look at the young couples as they made their promises and watch the love in their eyes. What did the villagers see as they looked at Jorn and her? Then Jorn was making his vows.

"I, Jorn, leader of the Bay Clan of the Tribe of the South, promise to be a powerful chief to this clan. I take this woman as my mate. I will be a support and an ally to her in her work as our clan's spirit messenger. I honour you, Hessa."

Hessa stood, mouth open for a moment. There had been no mention of love, of caring, of a future, just talk of their responsibilities. A tear came to her eye. It was too late to go back now. Anyway, what would she go back to?

"I, Hessa, spirit messenger of the Hill…" She stopped, correcting herself. "I, Hessa, spirit messenger of the Bay Clan of the Tribe of the South, promise to support this man as our Chief. I promise to help and heal our people and provide the spiritual support they need. I honour you, Jorn."

She felt she had given what she had received, a statement of their duties. But if her vows disappointed Jorn, he never showed it. He smiled at the assembled people as Dorlan stepped forward, tying the ribbon around their joined wrists, and made the prayer to the ancestors for them.

There was cheering as Rolva led them to the table to begin their bonding feast.

* * *

"So, bonded, and a leader's mate," said Dorlan, raking out the ashes from the hearth. "Are you happy?"

"Of course," Hessa said. Dorlan looked up at the flat tone of Hessa's voice.

"Of course," she echoed.

"So, no bonding night with your mate?" Rolva said, lifting Dass to her breast.

"The house was not ready. Jorn wanted to finish the last village house before he completed ours."

"He is an excellent leader," Rolva said.

Hessa nodded. "Yes, an excellent leader."

Eighteen.

A cold northerly wind tugged at the sail as Keld and Jath turned for the shore. They had been lucky with the winds, and Jath was sure they had a few days before the new moon. There were figures on the beach now, and smoke rose from the cluster of houses behind.

"Hello, the boat!" called a voice.

"Hello," Jath shouted. "Are you Frass people?"

"Yes, welcome strangers, come ashore," came the reply.

They dropped the sail, riding the surf onto the shallow slope of the sand. Two men and a woman ran forward to help them as they jumped into the water, ropes in hand, and soon hauled the vessel.

"I am Jath of the Eagle Tribe, far to the north," she said, "And this is Boat Master Keld, of the Drogga Tribe from the Isle of Pigs."

"Welcome," said the oldest man. Jath glanced at the tattoos around his eye as he smiled and extended his hands in greeting. "I am Carg, Spirit Messenger of the Beach Clan of the Frass people. You honour us with your visit from so far away. Are you traders?"

"We have been charged with delivering a message," Jath said. "We had a spirit apprentice with us, but he has gone on to Stanna with our message. You will, perhaps, be familiar with his parents, Col and Talla."

"It was years ago that they were here, but we have heard their story repeated many times. Please, come to the village for refreshment."

They grabbed their packs, Jath taking the bag with the last of the trust-gifts. She listened to the talk as they walked the path to the Frass village, understanding little. Jath realised that Carg had changed his speech, using Great Island inflexions when talking to her.

They were taken to the spirit messenger's house, and a child set about providing food and drinks while Carg sat them at the hearth. A man entered, his clothing and bearing said he was a warrior – an important one. Jath stood, and Carg smiled at her manners.

"Jath, Keld, this is our clan chief," Carg said. The warrior smiled and held out his hands in greeting.

"I am Waldon, Chief of the Beach Clan of the Frass people. Thank you for honouring us with a visit, you are most welcome."

Jath extended her own hands. Though his accent was heavy, the greeting had been elaborate, Waldon was keen to impress. "I am Jath, Princess of the Eagle Tribe, heir to the rule of the Isle of Eagles." She turned to Keld. "This is Boat Master Keld, a sailor of exceptional skill who has sailed our vessel the length of the Great Island to bring us here."

Waldon turned first to Keld, bowing his head. "Boat Master. Our own sailors will be keen to meet you, and talk about your journey when you have eaten."

"It would be an honour," he smiled. The sensitive nature of the meeting was not lost on the sailor.

"And Princess Jath," Waldon said, a deeper bow this time. "Please, enjoy our hospitality, and we will talk later."

Jath reached for the leather bag, taking the last engraved stone orb. She cupped it in both hands and presented it to Waldon. "It would give me pleasure if you would accept this trust-gift from our people."

Waldon took the orb, clutching it to his heart before inspecting it. "It is a gift of great value, Jath. I am honoured."

The last gift was an eagle talon necklace — a small copy of her own badge of office. "Carg, this is a gift for the protected-of-spirit. It is suited to a woman. Do you have a mate?"

"I never took a mate, Jath, but I am sure that we would be pleased to accept your gift. Nuru, will you receive this offering for our clan?"

Jath had been aware of the others in the house but had not noticed the woman until she stepped forward. She was tall, skin as black as obsidian. Jath looked into the deep brown eyes as she smiled and bowed her head.

"Please accept this trust-gift from our people," she said, placing the necklace around the woman's neck.

Their eyes met again. "I am Nuru, Spirit Messenger of the Beach Clan of the Frass people. I am honoured by your gift, Princess Jath." Nuru reached in and placed a kiss on Jath's cheek.

Her face reddened as she struggled to tear her gaze away from those beautiful eyes.

"Princess Jath," Waldon said, drawing her attention. "This is a token from our tribe to yours. Please accept it." He passed her a polished stone mace, the head shaped almost like a flower, the handle carved with symbols she didn't recognise. Jath took it, holding it to her heart before admiring it.

"It is beautiful, Waldon. Thank you."

Nuru slipped a stone bangle from her own wrist, and Jath saw her glance at Carg and receive a nod.

Her deep voice and exotic accent sent a shiver through Jath as Nuru took her hand in strong fingers, and slipped the bracelet onto her wrist.

"Please accept this gift from the protected-of-spirit, of the Frass people," Nuru said.

Jath gripped Nuru's hand as she kissed her cheek. "Thank you," she whispered.

Carg's voice pulled her back as she tore her eyes away from Nuru's. "Please, let us sit. Tell us of your message, Jath," he said.

Jath settled by the hearth, surprised when Nuru sat beside her, and told the story of the upcoming eclipse. Both Carg and Waldon had questions, and she answered them as best she could.

"We will send out runners tomorrow," Waldon said, "We must inform the neighbouring tribes. When is the next new moon, Carg?"

"Just two days away. We must prepare." He turned to Keld. "You will stay with us a while, our own Boat Master will be pleased to have you lodge with his family," he said. "Princess Jath, you would honour us if you would stay here. Nuru will make you comfortable."

* * *

When Jath awoke the next day, the northerly wind had strengthened and brought snow. A team went to the shore, hauling Keld's boat to the top of the beach for safety as foam-topped waves pounded the coast.

Jath sat weaving grass cords by the hearth with Nuru. They traded stories, Jath telling of her brother, her banishment and her escape from the Isle of Eagles with Lorev. Nuru told of her life with the Frass, and a sister called Ivarra who was wintering at Stanna, across the water, hoping to become a messenger.

They were growing closer, and Jath wondered if Nuru felt the same as she did.

Nineteen.

They assigned Lorev a house. It was cold, unused for six moons. He said a silent thank you to whoever had left fire-starting materials by the hearth and got out his fire bow. The words of the prayer to the fire spirits came to him as he spun the stick, and before long, a glowing coal formed. He soon had a blaze and hunched over it as the breath steamed from his mouth.

Yalta had said that others would start arriving soon for the winter teachings, but he was alone for now. He pushed together some straw on the floor to make a bed for Trav and settled on his own platform, furs piled over him.

* * *

He spent his first day getting to know people, and by evening a few apprentices had arrived. Lorev showed the first five to the house where he'd spent the night. He supposed they would be housemates for the winter now.

Of the three boys and two girls, one stood out. She was small, with sky-blue eyes and barley-straw hair. Her name was Ivarra.

"So, you are here to try for messenger status," she said. "I hope to improve my status this winter too."

"I came to deliver a message," he said, "but Yalta thinks I should learn while I am here. The weather has turned, and I will not get home before spring."

"Where is home?"

"Far to the north," he said. "The Hill Clan of the Tribe of the West."

"The Long Islands?" Ivarra asked. "Do you know Col and Talla?"

"They are my parents, they adopted me seven years ago."

The girl flung herself at him; her hug stronger than she seemed capable of giving. "Then we shall be friends, Lorev."

* * *

Two days later, the learning began. Their teachers were senior spirit messengers, drawn from those attending to become masters. The knowledge they had seemed limitless to Lorev, as he tried to absorb the prayers and chants, medicines and treatments, stories and legends.

Lorev had spent his life around plants and treatments. He knew how to sew a wound, and the uses of the herbs and remedies were almost second nature. But the names... Show him a plant, and he could reel off its properties and benefits, but he never remembered what they called it.

It was the same with the prayers. He could name all the outcomes and reasons for the petition to the spirits, but not the correct words.

The thing he was worst at were stories. Every child knew the creation story, but Lorev struggled with the order of things. He wanted to shrink into the ground when, on their second day, they asked him to recite the creation tale for the group. He had paused and stuttered for a long time, listening to the sniggers of his peers, before the spirit messenger stopped him and asked someone else to continue.

"What is it that makes stories difficult for you, Lorev?" Ivarra asked when they were walking back to their house.

"I can't remember them. It's like I jumble all the events in the story up, and I can't separate them. If only they were like numbers. Numbers make sense."

Ivarra gasped. "Numbers? Numbers are so hard, Lorev. Could you help me with numbers, and I'll help you with stories?"

So their little pact began. Each evening they would sit together, each learning from the other. Lorev sat with pebbles, teaching Ivarra to count, add, and subtract. He coached her in the bigger numbers and the moon cycles.

"My turn to teach tonight," Ivarra said, sitting beside him. "Now, the creation story."

"It's no use, Ivarra, I can't make sense of it at all."

The little blonde girl took his hand. "Close your eyes," she said, "We will go for a walk."

"What? A walk?"

"Keep them closed! Now you walk out of your house. It's dark, before dawn. You can see a tree by moonlight. What is it?"

"Acorn tree."

"Oak," Ivarra said. "At the foot of the tree is a flint. Pick it up."

"Ivarra, what are we doing?" Lorev asked.

"So, Tarren's story begins in a bleak world with only moonlight. So you walk in the dark. The first thing he discovers is how to make a blade, so you find that by the first tree."

Ivarra went on, walking Lorev through the story, finding prompts at each new landmark.

"Tell me the landmarks," she said.

"Dark, moonlight, oak tree, flint, ash tree, spear..." Lorev reeled off the walk he took for the creation tale.

"Remember that," she said, "Two days from now I'll ask you for the list again."

* * *

Just as Ivarra had said, two days later, Lorev remembered the stages of the first hero's journey. He could put them in order on his walk.

It took over a moon, but the time came when he sat and told the group the creation tale from beginning to end.

"Why are his eyes closed," the spirit messenger asked Ivarra as he finished.

"Remembering is hard for him. It's just his way," she said.

Ivarra's numbers came along too, and soon she was adding sums larger than she could count on her fingers.

It was coming near to the solstice, and Yalta had sent them all out to hunt small game for the visitors. Each clan brought pigs, perhaps an ox, but it was better to have too much. Lorev was adept with a spear, Ivarra with a bow, and the two friends set off together that morning into the thick woodland.

Ivarra spotted deer droppings, picking them up, bringing them to her nose, feeling the texture. "Fresh, no older than this morning," she said, pulling an arrow from her quiver and nocking it to the string. They crept ahead, hearing a soft rustle in the foliage. Ivarra, by far the more experienced, pointed left and waved Lorev to circle around.

Lorev slipped off, spear at the ready, through the undergrowth. He had walked quite a distance, never taking his eyes off the small spinney where they'd heard the noise when there was a rustle above him. He looked up as something dropped from the trees; then there was pain and darkness.

* * *

Ivarra lost sight of Lorev in the thick growth and advanced on the dense patch ahead. The silhouette of the hind stiffened as she approached, and she drew back on the heavy bowstring. A crash from her left spooked the deer, just as Ivarra's arrow flew, the flint head sinking into a tree where the animal had stood.

"Lorev!" she shouted. "I almost had her. Why did you make so much noise?" There was no reply.

* * *

The pain in his head struck him first. Lorev opened his eyes, trying to raise his hands to his throbbing temples, but they were tied behind his back. He looked around. The shelter was constructed from rotting branches and the lower limbs of spruce trees. Pine needles littered the muddy floor, and there was no hearth. Stripped bones lay rotting outside the doorway.

Lorev tensed at movement outside the rough shelter. Ragged leggings appeared, then the figure crouched to crawl inside. His hair and beard were filthy, and a stench of decay swept over Lorev as the man spoke.

"Not much to show for an apprentice," he said, tipping out Lorev's pouch. He picked up a blade, inspecting the edge. "Not bad," he said, "and the spear is excellent quality. Lost my last one to a boar. Who are you?"

Lorev stared at the man. He knew what the solid black tattoo under his eye meant. "I am Lorev, Spirit Apprentice of the Hill Clan of the Tribe of the West."

The outlaw's head snapped around. "The white-haired woman, with the violet eyes?" he said.

"Talla? She is my mother."

The rough hand gripped Lorev's hair as the outlaw's stinking breath enveloped him. "Oh, I will have fun with you."

The hand in his hair tightened as Lorev fought to shake free. He saw the blade, his own knife, in the man's hand. He struggled as it came closer and closer to his right eye. A squeak escaped his lips as the keen edge sliced into his cheek.

"She made me an outlaw," the man hissed, "Had that pig Yalta believing her instead of me. Let's see how she likes it when her son comes home with an outlaw mark."

The blade bit again and again, far deeper than tattoo cuts. He felt the blood running down his face now. He tried to kick out, but his feet were tied. The outlaw reached for a crude lamp in a blackened seashell. The grimy finger swiped the soot towards his wounds. Then there was a 'thunk' from outside.

"Who's there," the outlaw shouted, dropping the lamp. He grabbed Lorev's spear and crawled out of the opening in the shelter. "Come out. Show yourself. I have a hostage, I'll kill him."

Lorev heard the hiss of an arrow. There was a gasp as the outlaw's body crumpled to the ground, the head faced him, mouth working like a landed fish. Blood spurted around the arrow shaft embedded in his throat.

"Lorev!" Ivarra's voice. "Lorev, I'm coming." Small hands dragged the twitching body from the doorway, and the girl's face appeared. "Oh, Lorev. What has he done to you?"

* * *

Yalta bathed the mess of slashes under Lorev's eye, and he smelled lavender from the warm infusion she trickled into the fresh cuts. He remembered little of his journey back to Stanna village, Ivarra half leading, half dragging him as his heart pounded in his chest, and blood-soaked his tunic. He shivered now from the cold and fear.

"The cuts are deep, Lorev, but he didn't get any lamp-black into the wounds. You will have scars, but you will heal." Yalta patted the cheek dry, and the smell of honey filled his nose. "I'll bandage it, and Ivarra has promised to nurse you until it heals," the spirit master said.

"Ivarra is not injured, is she?" he asked.

"No," Yalta said. "She feels guilty for letting you get hurt, though. I sent her to wash off your blood. She will be back soon." They placed a cup in his trembling hands. "Drink it, it's willow bark, then rest, Lorev."

* * *

When he woke, Ivarra was there, worried blue eyes searching his.

"I'm so sorry, Lorev," she whispered. "I let you get hurt."

"It's all right, Ivarra. You saved me."

"I took too long to find you," she said. "I panicked. Missed the tracks I should have seen." The girl reached for his face, stopping short of the bandages, afraid to hurt him.

"Yalta says it will scar, but it is not a tattoo."

"It will have damaged your apprentice tattoo," Ivarra said.

"Yes. Perhaps the spirits are trying to tell me something," Lorev said.

Twenty.

"You know I can't pass you, Lorev," Yalta said. The apprentices had been filing in to see her all morning, receiving good or bad news. "I will give you the healer's tattoo when your face has healed, but the names of plants are still beyond you, and you struggle too much with the legends to get your lore tattoo."

"I am sorry I failed you, Spirit Master. My parents were excellent pupils," he said.

"You haven't failed, Lorev, you have not succeeded yet." If she expected a smile at that, she didn't get one. Lorev looked up, meeting her gaze.

"I must accept that I may never be a spirit messenger," he said. "I do not have the memory, the organised mind that it takes."

"You have other skills, Lorev. You are a fire keeper, and now a healer. Your grasp of numbers and the cycles of the heavens is exceptional."

"My parents wish me to be a messenger, though," he said, standing.

"You can return in the summer," Yalta said as he turned to leave.

Lorev didn't look back. "I don't know where I'll be by summer," he said.

* * *

The ground was cold beneath him. Huddled in his cloak, Lorev lay staring at the countless stars. He twisted his head to the east; the moon would rise soon, spoiling his view a little. He heard footsteps, and a figure laid beside him.

"They are beautiful, aren't they," Ivarra said.

"Yes."

"They appear to turn in the sky."

"It is us that are turning, though," Lorev said. "They stay in the same pattern, for the most part. This one here, though, is different.

Ivarra followed his finger in the dim light. "It's brighter, glitters more," she said. "It looks almost red."

"The red star is its name," he said. "Its movements are distinct."

"Can you not sleep?" Ivarra asked.

"No, not tonight. I am thinking too much," Lorev said.

"You didn't pass, did you?"

Lorev sighed. "No. I don't expect I ever will."

Her hand felt for his, squeezing. "Don't say that. There will be other years, other chances."

"And in the meantime?" Lorev said. "I fell out with my parents. They expect me to be like them. I am not. If I go home, I'll be an embarrassment — the failed son. My sister has seven summers and can recite every tale and legend she has ever been told. It took you a whole moon to teach me the creation story."

"This woman you speak of, the one you travelled with, can you not go to her people?" Ivarra asked.

"Jath? She is in exile. She cannot return to her home, either."

"Come home with me," she said. "The Frass Tribe are very welcoming. Carg, our spirit messenger would love for you join us."

"Thank you," Lorev said, sitting up. "You are a wonderful friend, Ivarra, and I owe you my life, but I must make my own way, somehow."

The girl climbed to her feet. "The offer stands," she said, "Don't stay up too long."

Lorev watched her dark silhouette move towards the village, then stood and followed.

* * *

The messengers ceremony held no joy for Lorev. He stood with the group of apprentices that had not completed their training that winter, all younger than him. The successful students claimed their status and joined the group in the great circle. Lorev led the apprentices back to the village.

He built fires for the feast, gathered wood, and helped with all the solstice tasks, but felt he would never be part of this elite.

"Will you help to build a fire-walk?" Tooev asked.

"Yes, Spirit Master," he said, taking one of the antler rakes and heading for the embers of the cooking fires. He, and another apprentice, dragged the coals into a long rectangle, finishing just as Tooev returned.

"Would you like to walk the fire tonight?" the spirit master asked.

"No, thank you, there are new fire keepers here. They should have the honours," Lorev said.

Tooev nodded. "As you wish."

* * *

It was the day of the new moon – the day of the solstice. This had to be the time of the eclipse. Lorev searched the sky for the disc, judging its distance from the sun.

"It will be in the afternoon, won't it?" Yalta said, sitting on the bench beside him.

"Yes. Just past noon."

"Thank you for bringing the news to us, Lorev," Yalta said.

"It was the task they charged me with. I'm glad I could carry it out well."

"Was it you who made the discovery?" Yalta asked. "My ancestors say you are more than the bearer of a message."

"I saw something in the charts," he said. "I'm sure the star master would have seen it too, given time."

"Don't underestimate your gifts, Lorev. You have skills that few others possess."

Lorev fixed her with a stare. "Spirit Master, I have failed in my attempt to become a messenger. Please don't pretend that I can compensate for that because I can count."

"It's more than just counting, Lorev."

He stood up. "Thank you, Spirit Master."

Yalta watched him walk away. She seldom failed, prodding and goading her students to succeed, bit by bit. This one, though, she feared she was losing.

* * *

The moon's disc edged its way over the sun. The light left the earth as if night were upon them. As the sky darkened, Lorev heard the evening songs of the birds all around him. An almost naked figure danced into the sacred circle, spinning and swooping. Vola was known for her powers of prediction and premonition. Her painted skin glistened with sweat, despite the cold air. She muttered to herself as she danced, lunging at first one person, then another.

"Our time is passing!" she yelled at Yalta. "Others will walk in our footsteps soon." She gyrated, lurching towards Lorev. "Master yourself, if you would master others, star boy," she shouted.

"What do you know of me?" Lorev said, grabbing her arm. The reeling woman slipped from his grasp.

"Heed me," she said, crouching, eyes flicking back and forth. "Know what you want, know what you need, and decide which you will have." She spun off across the circle of people, collapsing at the centre, unmoving as the sky went dark.

"Help her," Yalta said. "The prophecies are hard on her as she ages."

Two men ran out, gathering the limp body and carrying her clear of the crowd. The people gazed in awe as the sun forced his triumph over the moon, peering out from behind her back, bringing back the daylight.

A voice came from the edge of the circle where they had taken the dancing woman. "Spirit Master Yalta. Vola is dead."

* * *

"What did she mean?" Lorev asked. Yalta had taken him aside as soon as they'd got back to the village. "I will never be a master, I cannot even qualify as a messenger."

"She said, master yourself. That is something we must all do," Yalta said. "Who knows in what sense you may master others."

"But I have no desire to be master over anyone."

"Do you think I did?" she said. "I love this role I have, but it was not my wish. They thrust it upon me. I was too young, had too little experience, but the spirits gave it to me, anyway. I struggled, so they brought me Tooev as a mate. When we could not have children of our own, they gave me Arva and Atta. This was not what I wanted, but I never gave in. It was what I needed."

"And me?" Lorev asked.

"What do you want, Lorev?" she said, "What do you think will make you happy?"

Lorev thought a moment. "To be a messenger and achieve what my parents want for me. To find a mate, a home, a family of my own."

Yalta looked into his eyes. "What if being a spirit messenger is not your destiny?" she said. "What if the things Col and Talla want are not what you need? Perhaps the mate you desire will come, perhaps not. The home you seek may not be in the place you imagine. Our lives are not carved into stone, Lorev. We cut our own marks with our choices."

He sat, staring at the fire for a moment, and Yalta wondered if she'd pushed too hard.

"If not a messenger, what?" he said. "If not Classac, where?"

Yalta laid her hand on his shoulder. "I don't have the answers, but opportunities will come. You must take them or reject them, as you see fit. Think about it. I must go back to the gathering."

He sat for a long time, watching the fire consume the logs, watching the embers crumble and dim to ash. Ivarra found him as the festivities ended. She sat beside him, pulling him from his thoughts.

"You missed everything," she said. "What were you doing?"

"Thinking about my future," he said. "What to do. Where to go."

She grabbed his arm, tugging him to his feet. "Come, help me bank the fire. It's time to sleep."

They passed Yalta in the doorway. "Are you alright?" she said.

"Yes. I've just been considering things," Lorev replied.

Yalta squeezed his arm. "Go to bed. We'll talk more tomorrow."

* * *

The next day, most people left Stanna for their homes. Lorev and Ivarra helped to clear the site, piling any waste onto the midden. It was long past noon when Yalta found them.

"Thank you both," she said, smiling. "Come and eat with us."

"Me too?" Ivarra asked.

"Yes, Messenger, you too."

The meal was leisurely, and when they had finished eating, Yalta sat with Lorev and Ivarra. "Where will you go?" Yalta asked.

"North," Lorev said. "I must see my parents, then return to the Isle of Pigs to let them know of my journey and return the star charts."

"I will wait for my sister," Ivarra said. "She will come to collect me soon."

"Perhaps my companions will come with her," Lorev said, "They must have wintered with the Frass Tribe."

"After we leave, I know I will see you again, Lorev," the girl said. "You are my friend. Our paths will cross. I will make sure of it."

Lorev gave her a rare smile. "Thank you. I look forward to it."

* * *

It was four days later that they spotted the visitors coming towards the village. Two men led, then a tall black woman beside Keld, the boat master. At the rear was a warrior woman, clad in leather. She spotted Lorev and ran forward, hugging him, lips finding his.

"Hello, Jath," he said grinning.

Twenty-one.

"What happened to your face?" Jath asked, stroking a finger across the scabbed wounds under his eye.

"An outlaw captured me. He tried to mark me like himself, but Ivarra saved me."

"Ivarra?" she said, "This is Nuru, Ivarra's sister."

The tall black woman stepped forward, hands out in greeting. "I am Nuru, Spirit Messenger of the Beach Clan of the Frass people, Plant Keeper, Lore Keeper, Fire Keeper and healer," she said.

"I am Lorev," he replied, "Spirit Apprentice of the Hill Clan of the Tribe of the West, Plant apprentice, Lore apprentice, Fire Keeper and healer. It is an honour to meet you. I owe my life to your sister." He inspected her left eye, the tattoo little more than raised scars on the dark skin.

"Has she been playing the hero again?" Nuru asked. "An arrow, no doubt."

"How did you know?" Lorev asked.

"At fourteen summers, she is the best archer in our clan, perhaps the whole tribe." Jath stood beside Nuru and took her hand. Lorev noticed it then. A bonding ribbon. He was just about to ask when he spotted its twin around Nuru's wrist.

"You… you're bonded?" he said.

Jath smiled. "Yes, Nuru and I have tied the knot." She reached up and kissed her lover's cheek. "We have found each other, Lorev. Be happy for us."

Lorev's jaw clenched. Nothing was ever as it seemed. Nothing he wanted was possible. "I congratulate you, Jath, Nuru," he said, bowing.

Ivarra spotted her sister then and came running. She leapt into her arms, wrapping her in a hug. "It's so good to see you, Nuru," she squealed.

Nuru laughed, setting down the excited girl. Ivarra spotted the bonding ribbon straight away.

"You have a mate? Who? Who?" she asked, looking around.

"Jath," her sister said.

"I knew it would be a woman," the girl giggled. "Greetings, sister," she said, hugging Jath. She looked around for Lorev, but he was already walking away.

* * *

"Does it offend you, Lorev, the bonding of one woman with another?" Yalta asked.

"What? No. Jath has twin-spirits."

"It seems that Nuru has too. You are unhappy, though," she said.

"Jath and I… I thought we had something together."

"Had she made a promise to you? The protected-of-spirit take a dim view of those who disregard a promise."

Lorev sighed. "No. Jath said it was just fun between us."

"There is no harm in that, Lorev. Did you think there was more? Did you feel more?"

He nodded. "My first love left our village because she had a better offer. Now Jath leaves me for another. Why, Spirit Master? Why?"

"The ancestors follow their own plan," she said. "We cannot know it, we just take what they give us."

Lorev's eyes were red now. "What have they given me?" he shouted. "They took my sister, took my mother, sent me on a fool's errand with curses disguised as gifts. They took my Hessa. Oh, yes, they gave me Jath, only to take her away again." His fingers went to his scarred eye. "They gave me an apprentice tattoo, then denied me the skills to become a messenger. I disappoint my parents, I disappoint you, and now I am not good enough for Jath."

He began stuffing his few belongings into his pack as Yalta placed her hand on his shoulder. Lorev shook her off, retrieving the star maps and rolling them up.

"It seems you have had many setbacks, Lorev," she said. "The spirits are not always kind to those they wish to serve them. They tested your own father many times, but he triumphed."

"I am not my father!" Lorev yelled, marching towards the door.

"How will you travel, if not by boat?" Yalta asked.

Lorev turned, eyes glaring. "I will walk."

* * *

Ivarra brought the visitors to the meeting house, making the introductions. Yalta and Tooev seated the guests at the hearth.

"Where is Lorev?" Jath asked.

"Gone," Yalta said. "He is... disturbed by your bonding."

"Gone? We had no promise, Yalta. He knew that."

Yalta held up her hand, silencing Jath's defence. "I know. Lorev knows it too. He feels the spirits and the ancestors have cheated him. He says he will walk home."

"I will go after him, he is my friend," Ivarra said, making for the door.

Yalta caught her sleeve. "If he is your friend, Ivarra, perhaps you should let him go. He needs time to think. The long walk home may give him what he needs."

* * *

It was half a moon later that Jath, Nuru and Keld left the Circle of Stanna. They walked to the coast where they had left their boat. Keld wanted to get back, and the weather was fit for coastal sailing. They dropped Ivarra at the Beach Clan, then headed north. They stopped less often, coming ashore when they needed supplies, and the south-westerly winds made their journey go all the quicker. Following the coast of the Great Island, they bypassed the Long Islands. Less than a moon after they left Stanna, they were approaching the Isle of the Eagles.

"We can get to the head of the sea-lake," Keld said, hauling the sail over. Jath took the rope, tying it off as Nuru, a natural sailor it seemed, held the steering board over. A party of people were gathering on the shore, and Keld turned to Jath.

"Can you guarantee our safety?" he asked. "I am close to home, and I would like to see my family again."

Jath grinned, bow in hand, an arrow nocked to the string. "We will see what our welcome is before we land," she said, eyeing the crowd.

As they came closer, Jath noticed that most of the assembled tribes-people were women. "We are friends," she called, "May we land?"

One of the few warriors came forward. "We will not harm you. Come ashore."

Eager hands grabbed at the ropes as the boat crunched on the shingle. Jath leapt ashore, standing at the water's edge, waiting.

"Jath? Is it you?" came a voice. She turned to find a slight girl in a blood-streaked linen dress.

"Brinn? Oh, it's good to see you. What has happened?" she said, lowering her bow.

"Get your boat hauled, bring your friends to the village. There is much to tell," the girl said.

"But my father…" Jath said.

Brinn shook her head. "Gone," she said. "Come."

* * *

Smoke and the stench of death met them as they entered the village. Half of the houses were in ruins, smoke still rising from the charred poles. There were bodies in the square at the village centre. The warriors led them into the king's house, bowing before allowing Brinn to come forward. The girl was thin, black rings under her eyes. She had been Jath's childhood friend before her banishment.

"Who did this?" Jath asked.

"The Drogga. Your father mounted an attack on their village. They must have had the same idea. While the king was away, they attacked. We were defenceless. They killed many, but we took a toll on our attackers. Only a handful went back."

"And our attack on them?" Jath asked.

One warrior came forward, Coryn, she remembered. "We did considerable damage to their village, but at a high cost. There are four able warriors left, a few wounded that may survive. Your father died in battle. I carried his body home myself.

"Take me to the wounded," said Nuru, coming forward. "Did your spirit messenger or master survive?"

Jath looked about, then realised they had not understood Nuru's accent. "Nuru is a spirit messenger, take her to the wounded," she said. The warrior led the way, and Nuru followed.

"Spirit Master Sheryn?" Jath asked. Brinn shook her head. "We must organise ourselves, Brinn. Get anyone that is able. As soon as Nuru has helped the living, we will deal with the dead."

* * *

Nuru lay close on the bed, Jath's arm around her. The spirit messenger had worked long after dark, treating wounds and burns, sending the dead on their journey. The next day would see them laid out on the hilltop. There were two sky burial platforms they had reserved for Spirit Master Sheryn and Jath's father. They would lay the rest out on the rocky peak. There were twenty, most were Eagle Tribe, some were Drogga warriors. Jath had asked that all receive full rites for the dead.

"They need a leader," Nuru said.

Jath turned to look at her in the flickering firelight. "Me?"

"Who better? The king's daughter." She ran a finger down Jath's back, "You even have the tattoo."

"They may not accept me, Nuru."

"If you ask, if they say yes, I'll stay here with you. They need a messenger too," she smiled.

* * *

Jath and Nuru worked alongside the remaining villagers, salvaging belongings from ruined houses. By late afternoon they had done all they could. Rebuilding would take years, but life could go on. Nuru smiled at her mate as Jath jumped onto a rescued table.

"This has been a blow to the Eagle Tribe, but we have healed our injured and honoured our dead." She pushed a shaking hand through her hair. "You need a leader. The king, my father, has no living son. I am the only heir."

"You are a woman. The Eagle Tribe has always had a king," called a warrior.

"Yes, we do not even have Spirit Master Sheryn to ask for his advice," a woman said.

Jath looked to Nuru, receiving a nod. She unfastened her tunic, handing it to her mate. She lifted her undershirt over her head, standing topless in front of the village.

"This talisman was taken from our people," she said. "When it was returned, they returned it to me, and this pleased the spirits." She spun around, flinging her arms wide, displaying the eagle tattoo that covered her back.

"Sheryn gave me this tattoo, so I could be the leader that my brother could not."

She turned to face them again, ready to ask for their support. The screech made her pause and look upwards. Circling high above was the unmistakable silhouette of a sea eagle, wing-tips outstretched like fingers as it rode the air currents. It was a gamble, for she hadn't seen her friend in many moons. Jath cupped her hands and called.

"Keeeya! Keeeya!"

The bird circled lower, dropping fast now, levelling out in a swoop towards her outstretched arm. She staggered as the bird gripped her, sharp talons piercing her skin as Kya settled her feathers. Jath reached up to stroke the smooth head, whispering thanks to the bird.

She turned to her audience again, finding them staring in awe. She felt her warm blood trickling along her arm. "This is the gift from the Eagle Spirit. This is the embodiment of Kya." She smiled, clambering down from the table. She hooked her spare arm into Nuru's. "Tell me when you have reached a decision," she called, walking towards her father's house.

She threw Kya into the air with the last of her strength, and the eagle flapped up to perch on the stone slated roof.

"Let me wash that and dress it," Nuru said, inspecting the arm.

"It's not too bad," Jath said.

Nuru glared at her. "You may be the chief, but I am the healer," she said.

"I am not their chief yet."

Nuru poured water into a bowl, soaking a cloth and washing the rows of punctures in Jath's forearm. "No, but you will be before sunset," she said.

* * *

It was late afternoon when the knock came at the door. Brinn poked her head in.

"Can I talk to you, Jath?" she said.

"Come in, Brinn. Would you like tea?" her friend said.

They sat at the hearth while Nuru pulled stones from the fire and boiled water. Once they were all seated with cups, Brinn began.

"They want you to be the chief," she said.

"I will rule with my bonded mate," Jath said, taking Nuru's hand.

"That was assumed and agreed."

"Are there terms they wish me to meet?" Jath asked.

"No. You have the talisman from the spirits, the tattoo from Sheryn, and the first real eagle since the war began. They accept you and Nuru as their leaders."

"Were there any dissenters," Nuru asked.

"One, he was told he could stay or leave, but the village has picked you."

"And you, Brinn, are you happy?" Jath asked.

"I just want my friend back," she said, hugging Jath. Nuru coughed.

"Oh, I'm sorry spirit messenger," Brinn said, pulling back from her friend, "I meant no disrespect."

Nuru grinned and spread her arms. "I was wondering where my hug was," she said.

Twenty-two.

Lorev strode along the worn trail, Trav at his heel, tongue lolling. His mind was a whirl of emotions. He thought he'd shared something with Jath, something they might build on. Yes, he knew about her twin spirits, but she had been with him. But no, a spirit apprentice would never be enough, compared with the tall spirit messenger. He wondered if she would still have chosen Nuru if they'd travelled together.

He realised his pace had slowed, the immediate anger spent, simmering now as he wandered the path. Trav gave a yip, wondering why his friend was lagging.

"Go, if you want to," he said, signalling with his arm. The wolf bounded off to explore, while Lorev walked on.

He thought about his testing at Stanna. It would never be possible to learn all that they required of him. He would be an apprentice forever. His fingers strayed to the crusted scabs under his eye, itching now. This time, a girl of fourteen summers had rescued him. When would he ever take control of his own destiny?

The night was falling when he realised he would have to make camp. He pulled the hide from his pack, erecting a hasty shelter. The weather was still cold. Too cold for travelling, but there was no going back. Lorev was glad when Trav slept beside him. The warmth of his spirit animal made the night bearable.

* * *

The second day's journey was more challenging. He kept going over his thoughts again and again. Who was he supposed to be? The prophecy of the dying woman ran through his mind. 'Know what you want. Know what you need.' What did that mean? He had wanted Hessa, but she had left to be a chief's mate. He had wanted Jath. Now she'd found happiness with Nuru. Getting his messenger status was a dream he may never achieve.

And what did he need? Family? He'd argued with his parents, with Albyn. His birth mother had her own life. There was no room for him there.

His mood deteriorated, paces becoming smaller steps, then only a shuffle. Trav lost patience, leaving him for most of the day, returning at night to sleep.

On the third day, he wandered into a village. He had packed no food, and the smell of cooking meat drew him from his thoughts.

"Greetings," said a voice.

Lorev looked up to find a woman in her middle years, messenger tattoos under her left eye.

"Are you protected-of-spirit?" she asked.

His hand touched his scabbed cheek. "I am an apprentice," he said. "An outlaw captured me, he tried to mark me, but a friend rescued me."

"Rescued?" the woman said. "Perhaps you are the outlaw, and you escaped before they could mark you."

"I was at Stanna. Spirit Master Yalta treated the wound."

"Oh?" the messenger said. "Do you have an honour token? Something Yalta may have given you to verify your story?"

Lorev gaped at the woman. He never considered that someone may think him an outlaw marked for his crimes. "I am Lorev, Spirit Apprentice of the Hill Clan of the Tribe of the West. Plant Apprentice, Lore Apprentice, Fire

Keeper and Healer," he said, hands extended. He glanced down at Trav. "This is my spirit animal."

"I do not know of your tribe," she said.

"We are from far to the north, the Long Islands."

"Convenient," she said. "What about an honour token?"

"I left in a hurry. Yalta gave me nothing to carry," he said, realising that the woman would not believe him.

"I do not trust you, Lorev. If that is your name," the messenger said. "I think you and your wolf should move on."

* * *

Lorev sank deeper that day. Hungry now, he searched clearings and woodland edges for any dry berries still clinging to winter plants. There were few. Trav caught a hare, bringing it to his friend, and Lorev shared the meat, roasting the skinned carcass over a small fire.

He avoided villages now. If one person suspected him of being an outlaw, others could too. Perhaps they would chase him off, or even kill him. Trav hunted, some days catching something they could share. Other days, Lorev left the tiny voles and shrews for the wolf to eat.

Lorev wandered off the well-used trails, afraid of meeting strangers who might mistrust him. He grew thin on the lean winter game diet, tightening his waist-cord to keep the leggings from falling down.

Caring for himself became an afterthought. His thick, brown hair grew overlong, and he saw no point in combing or trimming the straggling beard he had always kept short and neat.

He stopped at a clear pool, dipping his water-skin to fill it, then scooping a cupful to drink. When the water settled, he stared at his reflection, the face gaunt, hair lank, beard matted. He inspected his apprentice tattoo. The scabs were long gone now, and it was hard to read his status from the scarred and faded marks.

Perhaps the ancestors, the spirits, had decided he was not fit to be an apprentice. Not fit to be protected-of-spirit.

Lorev pulled some cooked meat from his pack. Trav had tackled an elderly deer the previous day, and Lorev had been close enough to take a shot with his spear, killing the weakened animal. He'd stripped the meat, packing some to carry, cooking some. Trav had gorged on the entrails while Lorev cooked and ate the liver. He'd cracked open the skull and the long bones, looking for any trace of fat on the almost starved creature. If he couldn't find plant foods, fat was his best chance of survival.

He tossed strips of the chewy roast to Trav and wondered how far north he had come. The days had passed, and he'd kept no record. He tried to remember when he had last seen the moon. Black buds were forming on Ash trees. He remembered Ash from his story-walk when Ivarra taught him how to memorise the creation legend. He smiled at the memory of the yellow-haired girl. Without her, the outlaw tattoo would be complete, and he'd most likely be dead.

That night he watched the moon rise. It was fat, but past full. He wondered how he'd neglected to keep track of the phases, lost in his thoughts. How many moons had passed? It was just past new moon when he'd left Stanna, now it was past full. Had it been fifteen or sixteen days? Had he missed a complete cycle, and it was a moon and a half?

For the first time, he looked at the surrounding landscape. There was sparse woodland and a range of hills to his right. He wondered if he could chance a visit to a village. If they would suspect his scarred tattoo?

* * *

He kept Trav close to his side as he entered the settlement. The cluster of houses was small. If he was unwelcome, there would be fewer people to escape from.

"Greetings," came a voice. A man, not much older than himself, stood arms outstretched. "I am Gorg, Spirit Messenger of the Valley Clan of the Poan People. Plant Keeper, Lore Keeper, Fire Apprentice and Healer."

"Poan?" Lorev said. "Sorry. I am Lorev." He gave his status, watching the man's face. His eyes held nothing but a trusting smile. "You are Poan? My birth mother is of the Forest Clan. Is it nearby?"

Gorg beckoned, leading him into a small roundhouse. "You are near to home then, Lorev," he said. "A day, maybe two will take you there. Do you not recognise the landmarks?"

Lorev took the seat Gorg offered him at the hearth. "I was adopted at eight summers. I have only visited the Forest Clan, though I have sisters there. My status gives the clan I call home."

"I do not know of your Tribe of the West," Gorg said, pulling stones from the fire.

"The Long Islands, far to the north."

"Ah. Then your mother is Vinna? I have heard tell of you, Lorev. You fought off a wolf to save a man's life."

"A man I meant to kill," Lorev said, annoyed by his failure.

"As I understood it, the ancestors took him for you," Gorg said, dropping dried leaves into the steaming water. Lorev could see the plant in his mind's eye, though its name evaded him. He had never thought of his story like that, the ancestors on his side, not snatching away his free will.

"Perhaps," he said. "May I stay overnight?"

"Of course," the messenger said, handing him a steaming cup. "Drink this, and I'll tell our leader you are here. Your wolf is safe with the clan children, I take it?"

"Trav plays well with children," he said, sipping the hot tea.

"There is daylight enough to bathe in the stream if you wish," Gorg said when he returned. Lorev smiled at the messenger's subtle hint. He must stink. He couldn't remember bathing, unless it was in the crossing of some river, since leaving Stanna.

"Thank you," he said. "I'll take the chance to trim my beard and hair while I'm there."

Trav splashed and leapt around him as he scrubbed at his body with a handful of coarse grasses snatched from the stream bank. The wolf seemed happy to be back among people. Lorev was not sure if he was, yet.

* * *

He forced his pace the next day, following Gorg's directions. Dusk was falling as he saw the familiar houses of the Forest Clan's village. He went straight to the messenger's house, knocking on the split plank door. A familiar face peered around the frame as it opened.

"Lorev?" Mai, the eldest of his three sisters, paused a moment before leaping at him. He dropped his spear and grasped at the flying girl, holding her to him as she chattered. "We wondered if we'd ever see you again, Lorev. You've been away so long. Where have you been? I want to hear all your stories."

"Who is it?" Lorev recognised Govat's voice as Mai flung the door wide and dragged him inside.

"It's Lorev," she shouted as they buried him in a pile of bodies. His birth mother, Vinna, and his two smaller sisters were all trying to hug him and talk to him at once.

"Give him room," came Govat's voice again. "Let the man get his breath before you crush him."

The bodies retreated, except for Vinna, who stood, her hands on his shoulders, smiling.

"It is so good to see you again, Lorev," she said.

"And you, Vinna." He smiled at the woman who had given birth to him. He still couldn't think of her as his mother, but he was glad to see her again.

"I know you have just arrived," she said, "but do you have news of Verra?"

Lorev pulled her close, hugging her.

"Verra is free," he said. "Her spirit has crossed the river, and her bones lie in a tomb on the Isle of Pigs. I laid her there myself. She is at peace."

He could hear tears in Vinna's voice. "Thank you," she said.

"Have you eaten?" Govat asked. "You'll be looking for food and a bed, won't you, Lorev?"

Lorev smiled over Vinna's shoulder. "Yes, thank you, Govat. Food and a bed would be welcome."

Twenty-three.

There was a child in his arms when Lorev awoke. He'd eaten well with Govat and his daughter the previous evening, his sisters and Vinna staying for the meal. Comfortable in a warm bed for the first time in, perhaps, two moons, he'd slept until dawn.

"I missed you, Lorev," muttered Mai, the eldest sister. Another small body squirmed behind him. He turned to find Raya and Devra both in his bed, too.

"What are you lot doing here," he asked, smiling at Mai's sleepy face.

"Welcoming our brother home," she said, rubbing a fist at her eyes.

"You didn't go home last night?"

"This is our home," Mai said, sitting up. "Mother has bonded with Govat, we live here now, and Gianna is our sister."

Lorev felt a pull at his heart. Someone else who had found a mate and happiness. His sisters now with a father in their lives again, while he still searched for some kind of purpose.

"Let me up, girls," Lorev said, struggling to extricate himself from the pile of sisters. Devra reached for him, but he smiled, lifting her up as he climbed out of bed. He kissed the young girl on the forehead, setting her down.

"Good morning, Lorev," Govat said. "Raya, will you make tea for us all?" The child grinned and raked for stones in the ashes of the fire. "This is her new chore," Govat said, smiling. "She is our morning tea maker."

Raya dropped the stones into a pot of water, taking the bag of herbs Govat handed her.

"I must congratulate you, Govat. I hear you have a mate now," Lorev said. Vinna appeared, and Govat laid an arm around her shoulders.

"Thank you. Lorev. We make a wonderful family. The children were already friends, as were Vinna and I."

"It is a good pairing," Lorev said, smiling at them. He wondered when it would be his turn.

After they'd eaten, Lorev told the whole of his tale. The children all gasped at the story of his capture and rescue by Ivarra.

"I can repair your tattoo, Lorev," Govat said. "Shall I remake the marks for you?"

"I… I don't know, Govat," he said. "It seems I am not made to be a messenger. Perhaps they are best left."

Govat looked puzzled but nodded as Lorev explained his failure to learn plant names, legends and stories.

"So, I may never have the skills to progress to messenger," he said. "I am a healer, but no more."

"What will you do?" Gianna asked. "I have never heard of anyone leaving the protected-of-spirit."

"I don't know," he said. "Visit my family on the Long Islands, return the star charts to the Isle of Pigs. After that, I cannot tell you."

"I want you to stay here," Raya said, climbing into his lap.

"Me too," said Devra, clutching his hand.

"For a while, perhaps," Lorev said.

"Long enough to put some meat on your bones," said Vinna, putting the last of the cooked meat on a platter and handing it to him. "You're too thin."

* * *

"You are sad," said Gianna, sitting beside him. Lorev was cutting rawhide for a drum. A gift for Mai, who had set her heart on becoming a spirit apprentice at midsummer.

"I am fine," he said, smiling at the girl.

"No. Inside you are sad," she said. "You smile, but there is no joy in you any more. What is wrong, Lorev?"

Lorev looked at her. Gianna was mature for her years, and her eyes begged an answer. "There was a girl," he said. "I thought we were more than friends."

"And she?" Gianna asked.

"She was bonded to someone else when next I saw her."

"Your heart is sore. I had a sore heart when my mother died, but things are better now. Father has a new mate, I have new sisters." She patted Lorev's leg. "Perhaps a new brother."

The smile, this time, was genuine. "Yes, you have a new brother. Even so, I must leave again."

"I understand," she said. "This is not your home, is it?"

"No. I don't know if I have one any more," Lorev said.

* * *

Lorev hoisted his pack to his shoulder once again and called Trav to his side. He had said his goodbyes and didn't know when he would return. He waved at the women who were part of his family and walked out of the village.

There was food in his pack, and his confidence had returned a little, yet still, he avoided the villages he passed along the way. When he had exhausted his food, he foraged and hunted. Spring provided more for a traveller, and he and Trav lived well. He regretted leaving Vinna and the children behind. His life seemed to be one disappointment after another, and he wondered if the star masters on the Isle of Pigs would think him dead if he failed to return. No, that was unfair. They had trusted him with the star charts. He must go back.

After half a moon, he made for the west coast. If he wanted to return to the Long Islands, he would need to find a clan that made the crossing. The going was hard, and he realised he had come further north than he had expected. He travelled the coast for two days before he came upon a village, with boats on the beach of a sea-lake.

He made his way down the hill, past a tumbling waterfall, taking in the smells of wood-smoke and baking bread as he entered the village. A child ran off at the sight of him, emerging from a house moments later with a white-haired man.

"Greetings, traveller," the man said. "I am Tadd, leader of the Falls Clan of the Cheel people."

Lorev held out his hands, listing his achievements. Tadd bowed and led him into a house. "We have no messenger or master to greet you, Lorev. Our clan is small, and protected-of-spirit are few in the north."

"Do you need my skills?" Lorev asked, "I am qualified as a healer."

"It would be helpful if you would see my daughter. She is expecting her first child, and her time is near," Tadd said.

Lorev smiled. "I'm happy to help." He had only helped at two birthings, and both had gone well, but he knew the dangers and how to treat a new mother. Tadd sat him at the hearth, asking his mate to feed their visitor. They both looked alarmed at Trav's sudden appearance, but relaxed when the wolf settled at Lorev's feet.

"Will you stay a day or two?" Tadd asked once they had fed him and served tea.

"I will stay for your daughter's birthing if that would please you, Leader Tadd," he said. "I will treat any other ailments in your clan while I am here."

"There is a place here for you if you wished to stay," Tadd said.

"I need to get across to the Long Islands," Lorev explained, "Perhaps you make this crossing?"

Tadd smiled. "That will be our pleasure. If you see my grandchild born, I will see that we take you to the island."

* * *

Lorev was soon at ease with the Falls Clan. Tadd had the villagers clean an empty house, and Lorev moved in. They set two older children to keeping his fire and helping with foraging for herbs. Lorev taught them a little, asking them to name the plant while he told them its uses.

Dun, a boy of ten summers, and Bel, a girl of twelve, became his companions. He woke each day to breakfast, hot tea and a blazing fire, while his stock of treatments grew.

Cali, the leader's daughter, was huge. The girl was just seventeen and had only bonded with her mate at the winter solstice. Lorev could find no cause for concern and settled in to wait for her birth.

It was past midnight when Bel shook him awake. He found Cali and her mate beside his fire, Dun feeding logs into the growing blaze.

"I'm sure it has started," Cali said, hands hugging her bump. "I am getting pushing pains now, and the birth waters have come." He watched her tense as another tightening went through her.

"Do you have your birthing cloth?" he asked. She held up the decorated square, one that had been her mother's, that she had been born on. Families kept such cloths for generations if they had only held good birthings. If a baby or the mother died, though, they destroyed them.

"Lay it out, Bel," he instructed the girl.

Bel spread the cloth on the fresh straw of Lorev's floor, fussing over getting the edges straight. She looked up at Lorev, seeking approval.

"Perfect. Now help me with Cali." They guided the pregnant woman, helping her balance while she squatted down.

"When the next tightening comes, I want you to push," Lorev said, kneeling beside her. Her fingers dig into his shoulder as she grunted at the pain.

"Lorev. It hurts!" she cried.

"Birth is always like that, Cali. Just endure for your little one's sake."

The pains were coming more often now, though Cali was tiring. Lorev put an arm around her waist, getting Bel to do the same. He peered between her spread legs, spotting the crown of the baby's head.

"This time, Cali. Push with all your might."

The woman screamed as she bore down, and Lorev cradled the baby as it dropped to the cloth. He cleared the tiny mouth and sighed as the new life drew a breath and bawled. "You have a son," he said, pulling the small child clear and handing him to his mother. Cali was about to take him when she froze.

"I need to push again," she said.

"Yes, the afterbirth will come soon. Push when you are ready," he said.

He passed the child to Bel as Cali pushed again.

"Lorev, I feel something," she said.

He peered between her legs again, gasping as two tiny feet appeared. He knew the problem now. Twins were a danger. One or other came feet first and could drown if it were not birthed fast enough.

"Lay down on the blanket, Cali," he said, "you have another baby coming." He grabbed the corner of the decorated cloth, wrapping it around his hand so he could grip the wet feet. As Cali pushed, he tugged on the second child, drawing it from its mother as she screamed again.

Cali lay back, gasping as Lorev wiped at the tiny girl's mouth. There was no breath. He thought of his training, lifting the small child and locking his mouth over the blood-smeared face. He breathed into her, praying to the ancestors she would live. A weak cough followed a squeak, and her slight breath rattled in her throat as she cried.

"A son and a daughter," Lorev said, wiping sweat from his eyes. Cali unfastened her shirt as Lorev passed her the screeching girl. Bel set the boy to her other breast, then wiped her bloody hands on the stained cloth.

"Thank you, Bel," he said.

"I'm never, ever having children," the girl replied.

Lorev showed Bel how to wash the infants. Then he cut the cords to their mother and propped her up on pillows until her afterbirth came. Later they got Cali onto a spare bed, then settled her with the two babies.

Lorev walked out into the chilly dawn and drew in a deep breath. A hand clapped him on the shoulder, and he turned to find Tadd and his mate.

"Thank you, Lorev. Twins are a blessing, but so dangerous for our daughter," he said. "Come to our house when you have rested. We will have breakfast ready."

Cali was smiling as the twins suckled her when Lorev went back inside. "Thank you, Lorev. They're beautiful," she said.

He set his helpers to make food and tea for the new mother and then walked to Tadd's house.

* * *

The new babies thrived, and Lorev let Cali take them home the next day. Bel washed and dried the birthing cloth, returning it to Cali as she left.

"Thank you all," Cali said, "We will call our daughter Mila, for my mate's mother. Our son, we shall call Lorev."

Lorev blushed, smiling at the little family he had helped to complete. He bowed to Cali. "I am honoured."

Tadd watched the weather, while Lorev spent a few days treating the sick. He instructed Bel and Dun in a little more simple healing, showing them the use of honey for wounds and how to clean and bandage cuts to keep out bad spirits.

"The skies look clear, Lorev," Tadd said. "Will you make your crossing tomorrow?"

"If your sailors think it wise, then yes," he said. He packed his belongings again, more this time as he had gathered healing herbs and some extra clothes from the Cheel people. The boat was small, and just one man, a nephew of Tadd, sailed away with him the next morning, carrying him back to the Long Islands.

Twenty-four.

In the distance, the Stones of Classac crowded on their hilltop like crooked teeth. Lorev had taken the entire day to cross from the east coast, unsure what awaited him in his home village. He wondered why he was here, but he wanted to see his sister, Shilla, and find out what had happened to Hessa.

Lorev decided against going to the village that day, pitching camp by a stream in a valley. He'd just got the shelter up when Trav trotted to him, a fat grouse clutched in his mouth.

"Well, thank you, Trav," he said, taking the bird. He sat to pluck the feathers while Trav waited, watching the strange ritual, knowing he would get his pickings soon.

Lorev gutted the bird, adding the head, wings and feet to Trav's share. The wolf looked up at him, before bolting down the meal, slobbering at his dripping fangs as he finished.

"I'd better light a fire," he said, ruffling Trav's fur, "Seeing as how you've provided dinner."

The aroma of roasted meat made Lorev drool as he peeled the scorched dock leaves from the steaming bird. He pulled off a leg, biting into the moist flesh as he sat beside his fire. The light had almost gone, and the last red clouds streamed over the horizon, back-lighting the sacred stones on their hilltop. He wondered if anyone had seen the smoke from his fire. Perhaps they'd come looking the next day. Tomorrow he'd go to the village and find what awaited him.

He threw the bones of his meal to Trav and crawled into the shelter. Trav climbed in beside him, making his circular dance before settling. Lorev had been glad of the wolf's warmth in the winter, so he let him stay, closing his eyes as Trav gave a satisfied sigh.

* * *

The small boy came running into the roundhouse, his face red. "What's wrong, Glev?" Talla asked.

"Man. A wolf," he gasped, "Man. A wolf."

Col scooped him up, wrapping him in a hug. "Wolves don't come into the village, Glev," he said.

"Yes, man, wolf," the boy insisted. Col carried him to the door, peering out into the late morning sunshine. Someone was coming up the village path. The figure stopped to bow his head and touch the sacred bull's skull at the boundary post. As he turned back towards the village, a grey wolf bounded up to him.

"Talla. I think it's Lorev," Col said. Talla rushed past him, running down the path towards the figure.

"Lorev? Lorev!" she cried, flinging herself at him. He stood as the pale woman hugged him. "Oh, Lorev, I'm so glad you're alright."

"I'm well, Mother," he said, giving her a brief hug back.

"You're so thin and so tall," she said, taking his hand and dragging him towards the house. She helped him off with his pack, setting it on a bed platform, then set about boiling water.

"It's good to see you, Lorev," Col said, holding out his hands. Lorev copied the universal greeting, but his father took both his hands and squeezed them. "I am glad that you are safe and well."

"Thank you, Father. I am sorry to return to disappoint you once more, but I wished to see Shilla again."

"Your sister is at the shore… but what do you think has disappointed us, Lorev?"

Lorev turned. This was harder than he had imagined. His father and mother would have noticed at first glance that he did not carry spirit messenger marks. Yet they made this pretence of being glad that he had returned. "I must find my sister," he said, heading for the door, "Perhaps we can talk later."

Lorev spotted Shilla, down by the low tide mark, prising mussels from the rocks. She looked up at the crunch of his feet on the coarse sand.

"Lorev!" she squealed, dropping the basket of shellfish and rushing to him. He picked her up, strong hands around her waist, lifting her high before setting her back on the sand.

"I've missed you, Shilla," he said as she wrapped her small arms around him.

"Me too," she sobbed, "I thought I'd lost you."

Lorev looked around. "Where is Albyn?"

Tears filled her eyes as she looked up at him. "He died two moons ago. We interred his bones at the new moon."

Lorev gathered her to him again as her tiny body shook with her sobs. "I'm sorry. He was your friend; your teacher."

"I miss him so, Lorev. Every morning I start to make tea for him. Every time I come to the shore, I feel his hand in mine. When I tell a story, I hear his voice speaking the words."

"Then he has not gone," Lorev said. "He is still with you."

When her sobs subsided, she took Lorev's hand. "Come, let's go to the house."

"I'd rather sit here with you for a while," he said, picking up her basket. They walked to the top of the beach and sat. "Do you hear anything of Hessa?" he asked.

Shilla's hand came to her mouth as if to stop the words, but they came anyway. "She is bonded to Jorn, leader of the Bay Clan of the Tribe of the South. She is Messenger of her own village. They have a son."

Lorev heard the word 'bonded', then 'son' and his mind flew into a whirl. Why had he made his journey with Jath? Why did he not follow Hessa that day? All these tasks he'd undertaken, avenging Verra, returning the talismans, warning of the eclipse, and still he could not have her. Hessa was bonded, mate to a leader. All Lorev had achieved was growing a year older.

"Lorev?" Shilla said, clutching at his arm, "She waited for you, until that day she saw you with Jath."

"I know," he whispered. "Jath told me to go to Hessa that day, that she and I had been for fun. It was already too late when I realised Hessa had left."

"What has become of Jath," Shilla asked.

"She found her life's love. She too has a mate."

"I'm sorry," she said, taking his hand.

"I need to think," Lorev said, pulling his hand away. "Let me be alone for a while."

"Lorev…" Shilla began.

"Leave me be, Shilla. I have nothing left here. Nothing."

She watched her big brother storm off towards the north, his wolf trailing at his heel.

"You have me," she whispered as she watched him go.

* * *

Lorev marched along the cliff edge, making for the highest point. He stopped, panting, staring out to sea. Trav nuzzled his leg, and he sat, wrapping an arm around his spirit animal.

"Why did I come back here?" he asked the wolf. "What did I ever hope to achieve?"

He'd been twelve summers when he'd taken his apprentice vows, bearing the cuts of the tattoos with pride. He wanted to be like his parents, Col and Talla. To become a spirit master one day and make them both proud. He couldn't even master the skills to become a messenger.

That day he'd left his clan to avenge Verra, his sister, he'd dreamt of how he would emulate his father's courage and heroism. How he would confront Verra's killer and slay him. Instead, he'd almost saved him, watching him die from wounds inflicted by a wild animal.

The talismans Albyn had given him were nothing but a curse, dragging him far to the north. Images of his failures kept coming. The shame of being rescued by Jath. His parents intervening as the spirits of fire and air. Being taken by the outlaw at Stanna, then his reprieve at the hands of Ivarra. The moment he realised Jath was no longer his. That she had found someone better, a spirit messenger, to be with.

Then today, his parents pretending that they did not see that he had failed, yet again, to become a spirit messenger. The news that Hessa was bonded to someone far better than him, a clan leader. That they had a son.

This was not his home any more. At Classac, he would be a source of shame to his parents, and a figure of derision to the villagers. He had cut his ties at Stanna by storming off in anger. He could not return to his birth mother and his three sisters, he was not the hero they assumed he was. And the Isle of Pigs, where men of knowledge had trusted him. Would he return, still the apprentice that he was when he left?

Lorev climbed to his feet. He realised he was crying and scrubbed the hot tears from his cheeks. There was nothing left, nowhere to go. He would never be enough for himself or anyone else.

He stepped to the edge of the overhang, staring down at the slab of sea-blackened rock below. A few moments and it would all be over. The pain, the sadness, the not belonging, the being second best. Trav whined, unsure of why his human was standing on the cliff edge. Sensing something wrong.

"Go hunt," Lorev said, making the throwing movement he had taught the wolf. Trav turned, loping off, stopping as Lorev went back to the cliff edge.

"Spirits of the ancestors. I come to be with you now. Verra, come to greet me at the river."

Lorev toppled forwards, feet leaving the ground, then he was falling. The descent was slow as if he was floating. Above the wind in his ears, there was a child's voice screaming.

"No!"

A pitiful howl came next, before his back slammed down, driving the breath from him. Someone was talking, shouting, angry, then he was floating up into a bright light, clouds all around. The figure came towards him, its face a mask of hatred.

Twenty-five.

Hessa took the sleeping child from her breast. Pulling her tunic closed, she lifted him to her shoulder. She sat beside the hearth, throwing on some wood with her free hand. Jorn was gone again. He was an exceptional leader. In the last year, he'd built a herd of cattle by trading goods and favours. The houses of the Bay Clan were sturdy, and the people happy. The hillsides behind the village were green with barley, the first tinge of yellow tinting the seed heads. He'd overseen the building of two trading vessels, heading the exchange voyages himself, always returning with valuable goods.

Jorn would be back in a day or two, but there was no joy for her in his return. He loved his village, his people, but he didn't love her. Their relationship was professional, leader and spirit messenger. That they were mates, that they had a child, was incidental.

Her mind went back to her days, growing up with the Hill Clan at Classac. Her joy at being apprenticed, her time with Albyn and Geth, before Col and Talla's return. She'd learned so much from them, and revelled in the friendship of their son, Lorev.

Hessa hoped he was happy now. She wished she could be.

"Hessa? Are you here?" came a shout.

"In here, Dorlan," she called, wiping away a tear she didn't know she'd shed.

"Hello, little Saren," the apprentice said, taking the snoozing baby from Hessa's arms. She cuddled him, cooing as he fussed a little, then returned to sleep.

"Where were you yesterday?" Hessa asked.

Dorlan blushed. "I channelled the spirits," she said.

"Your gift? What did the spirits tell through you?"

"It doesn't always seem like a gift," Dorlan said. "I told Leader Sarn that he was old and that I should replace him. If I was not protected-of-spirit, I'm sure he would banish me."

"Is that all?" Hessa laughed.

"I told of a bloody battle, many tens of people died. It worried Rolva that it was a prophecy, but it was not here, not this island."

"Where then," Hessa asked, but Dorlan only shook her head.

"Come, I'll put Saren down to sleep, and you can help me make some wound cream," Hessa said, taking the baby.

* * *

Two days later, Jorn returned. The villagers welcomed him, and he stopped to chat with many of them. The widow, Goen, seemed happy to see him, too. At last, he came to their home, kissing Saren on the head, giving Hessa a distracted pat on the arm.

"I must meet with the older men tonight," he said as he finished the meal Hessa had cooked. "We have to discuss our next trading voyage."

"I'll clear the platters and bank the fire for you," Hessa said.

"Oh, not here. If Saren cries, it will distract us all. I'll go to one of their houses."

Hessa took out her sewing after he left, stitching the fine linen into a shirt to replace her old tattered one. Dorlan came in just before dark, sitting to talk.

"Can you watch Saren for a moment?" Hessa asked, "He's sound asleep and not long fed."

"I'd be glad to," the girl smiled, "Where are you going?"

"Oh, I forgot to tell Jorn something. I won't be very long."

Hessa pulled on her cloak against the evening's chill and went out. She walked down through the village, heading for the house of Jorn's trading partner. Stopping outside, she listened to the talk coming from within, but could only hear the voices of the family. Towards the edge of the settlement, was a smaller house, one just big enough for a widow and her child.

There was giggling, "Oh, Jorn, yes."

She heard Jorn's muffled voice, then Goen's gasp. Soon, the rhythmic creaking of a bed was the only sound. Hessa pulled her cloak tight and turned for home.

"Did you find him?" Dorlan said, pulling stones from the fire to heat water.

"I don't think he wanted me to disturb him," Hessa said, hanging up her cloak. She turned back to the fire to see Dorlan blushing. "You know, don't you?" she said.

Dorlan stared at the fire. "There are rumours, Hessa, that's all,"

"Rumours that appear to be true," she said.

"What will you do?"

Hessa shrugged her shoulders. "Leave?"

"And go where?"

"I don't know," Hessa said, running her palm over her face.

"This is your home," Dorlan said. "Don't let him drive you away."

* * *

"I have a proposal, Hessa," Jorn said, setting his spear beside the door. "We don't connect any more. I want to take a second mate."

Hessa stiffened and turned. "Do you have someone in mind?" she said.

"Perhaps the widow, Goen, would make a suitable sister-wife. She is lonely since the death of her mate."

"She didn't sound very lonely when I came looking for you last night," Hessa said, hacking at a joint of meat with a heavy flint blade.

"You came looking for me?"

"Yes. Goen sounded as if she had enough company to keep her busy."

Jorn stood gawping at her. "We talked. I asked for her promise of bonding."

Hessa walked over to him, waving the bloody blade in his face. "Promise? Do you know your tribe lore, Jorn? Do you know that for another mate to join a couple, both parties must agree?"

"We talked. She has already agreed."

Hessa stabbed a finger at her own chest. "Me! I am the other person in this bonding. You cannot ask for her promise without asking me."

Jorn frowned. "Very well," he said, "Will you agree to Goen joining our bonding?"

"Never."

"But…" Jorn began.

He felt the spittle on his face, Hessa's glaring eyes a hand's-breadth from his. "Sleep where you like. I will not give credence to your disloyalty. If you wish to take another mate, then cut me free first."

Jorn held her gaze, rage boiling. He could not cut the knot of a bonding less than a year old. He could not chance leaving his people without a spirit messenger. It would destroy his honour. He turned and strode out of the door.

* * *

"There are rumours you are not sleeping in your own bed at night," Sarn said. Jorn sighed. He seldom visited his parents, despite their living in the next village.

"Rumours have a life of their own, Father," Jorn said.

"Perhaps, but if I am hearing them here, what are the gossips saying in your own village?"

"Hessa has not complained," Jorn said. "She has her own interests, her plants, her ceremonies, her son."

"Saren is your son too, is he not?"

"Yes. I just meant…"

Sarn leant forward, poking at the fire with a stick. "Respect is hard won, Jorn, but lost all too soon. Your reputation is as a strong and fair leader. Do not gain one as a weak and disloyal mate."

Jorn stood, throwing the dregs of his tea into the fire. "I am the leader of the Bay Clan," he said, "I will do as I see fit." Sarn shook his head as his son threw down the cup and stormed out of the house.

"Is Jorn leaving already?" his mother asked.

"He has things to attend to," Sarn said, picking up the cup. "Or, at least, he should."

Twenty-six.

Shilla climbed the path from the beach, following her brother. She stopped, watching a vast wave crest off the shore. It rolled in, breaking on the blackened rocks. She saw him then, her big brother, silhouetted against the sky, perched on the very edge of the cliff. Shilla screamed as Lorev toppled forwards from the overhanging precipice. She turned to run to him but realised he was now on the rocks below. As she made for the steep path, she saw her uncle, Gren, on the beach, lowering his raised arms as the foam of the freak wave subsided.

She scrambled down the rocky path, feet slipping, hands grasping at grass to steady herself. As the wave ebbed, she spotted her brother lying on his back, motionless.

* * *

Lorev thought he heard someone talking, shouting, angry, then he was floating. Up into a bright light, clouds all around. Then the figure came towards him, its face a mask of hatred. The ice in the girl's eyes burned into him.

"Did you mourn me?" Verra shouted. "Did you grieve the loss of your sister?"

"Yes, but..."

"How many sisters do you desert now? Shilla loves you more than life. What of Isla, of Mai, Raya, and Devra? Don't you now consider Gianna a sister too?"

"Verra, I..."

"Shut up! You think you have failed? This is your greatest failure, to desert six girls who look up to you, for your own self-pity."

Lorev was sobbing now. "I cannot be what people want me to be. Everything I love is taken from me."

"What of those that love you?" Verra's spirit said, pacing. "You have taken everything from them."

"I'm sorry."

"How old are you, Lorev?"

"Sixteen," he replied.

"What might your lifespan have been? Sixty years or more? One-fourth of your life, and you think you have failed? What about the promise of those other years? What could you have done? And without you, what will not be done?"

Lorev tried to sit up. "I don't know. I couldn't go on, not like it was."

Verra strode over, glaring down at him. "I refuse to speak for you with your ancestors. You may not cross to the land of the dead."

"What do you mean?" Lorev asked.

Verra's foot kicked out, sinking into his ribs. He winced at the sharp pain. "You may not die," she said. "Breathe!"

* * *

Shilla ran to the prone figure on the wet rock. She watched his chest, but there was no rise and fall of breath. She kicked out at his body in a rage.

"You can't die," she screamed. "Breathe." The kick connected with Lorev's ribs, and he coughed and retched, vomiting seawater. Shilla threw herself at him, sprawling on top of him, her arms wrapped around his chest. "Breathe," she shouted, burying her face in his neck. "I hate you. I hate you."

When her sobs subsided, she stood, looking down at him. "Why?" she asked.

"I am a failure, Shilla. I am not the brother you deserve."

"Can you walk?" she asked.

"I think so."

Shilla held out her hand. "Come on. We'll climb back up and try again, but this time I'm jumping with you."

"What? No. Shilla, you have your life ahead of you. You are a talented storyteller. One day you will be a Lore Master."

Shilla scrubbed at her eyes. "You were always there, Lorev. My big brother, my protector, my teacher, my friend. Then you left. I cried for days, but Albyn tried to explain that you had something to do, that you would be back. You returned, with Jath. I hated her because she took you away once more. Now you come back again. This time to let me watch you die."

"Shilla, I didn't mean for you to see this," Lorev said. "I'm so sorry."

She took his hand. "But I did see it." she said, "Come on, if you live, I'll live. But I'm not letting you out of my sight."

* * *

They had no sooner reached the top of the cliff when a wall of grey fur knocked Lorev to the ground. The excited wolf licked at his face and neck as he struggled to sit up.

"Someone else who's glad to see you," Shilla said, pulling him to his feet again.

"What happened," Talla asked as she saw his wet clothes. She fussed over him as Shilla retrieved his pack, searching for clothing. Lorev stripped off the wet things, shivering by the fire.

"Your chest," said Zoola, spotting the darkening bruise on his ribs. "Shilla, what happened?"

The girl looked at Lorev. He nodded, hanging his head. "Lorev tried to jump off the cliff," she said, "He thinks he's a failure, that he doesn't belong."

In a moment, everyone was talking. Col and Talla, Zoola and Gren, all clustered around him, asking questions.

"Stop it," Shilla shouted. There was silence for a moment. "Lorev needs to sleep. You can talk to him later," she said. She went to her bed, pulling back the thick furs. She pushed her brother onto the bed, tucking him in, then took Gren aside.

"You saved him," she whispered.

"It was all I could do," her uncle said.

"He has been rescued too many times," she said. "Never speak of it."

"You are wise, Shilla."

Shilla pulled him down to her level, kissing his cheek. "Thank you," she said.

Lorev stared as she pulled off her moccasins and climbed onto the bed beside him. "Are you tired too?" he asked.

"No, but I'm never leaving your side again."

* * *

Lorev felt uneasy. Shilla was still asleep beside him when he woke, but there was no one in the house. He stooped to the hearth, reviving the fire.

"Good morning," Shilla said, sitting on a bench nearby.

"Where is everyone?" he asked.

Shilla shrugged, squinting at the open door. "It's late, maybe they just let us sleep."

"You're awake," Talla said, carrying in some fresh bread. "What do you want to eat?"

"Cheese and bread," said Shilla, running to help her mother.

"What's going on, Mother?" Lorev said. "Where is everyone?"

"They've left us alone to talk, once you've eaten," Talla said.

Shilla broke a chunk from a cheese and tore a loaf in half, placing the food in front of her brother. She served herself and sat beside him, packing her mouth. "Eat," she mumbled.

Lorev picked at the food, watching his mother heat water and make tea. "I'm sorry," he said.

Talla smiled. "When you've eaten, we'll talk. Unless you'd rather talk to your father, or Gren and Zoola?"

"No," he said, "I'll speak to you."

* * *

Talla cleared the platters and sat opposite Lorev, smiling over the fire. "Perhaps you should leave us to talk, Shilla," she said.

Shilla jumped onto the bench beside her brother, wrapping herself around his arm. "I'm not leaving him."

"Very well," she said, "Lorev, why did you want to leave us all? What had we done?"

He looked down at his hands, fidgeting in his lap. "I must be a disappointment to you and father," he said. "I have been an apprentice for four years, and may never be a messenger."

"Some take longer," Talla said. "Is that why you tried to kill yourself?"

"In part."

He told his story from the time he left Classac, right until he arrived back on the Long Islands. Shilla gasped at the parts where his life had been in danger, her small fingers digging into his arm. His mother nodded, saying almost nothing until he had finished.

"You say that you have disappointed your father and me. Why?" she asked.

"You asked me to become a spirit messenger. I have tried, but I cannot pass all the tests."

"We wanted you to try, to give yourself a chance. If you cannot pass, we are not ashamed of you, Lorev. Your father and I love you, whatever you achieve."

"But I have failed at everything," he said.

"You made sure that Verra's killer did not rest," she said. "It was you who aided the Princess Jath in exile, who returned the talismans and laid Verra to rest. You warned the land of the coming eclipse, found a new family of sisters, and delivered twin babies. How is that failure?"

Lorev opened his mouth, then closed it. He had never thought of it like that. All he saw were the things that had gone wrong.

"Stay here with us, Lorev," his mother said. "Be part of our family again."

"Yes, Lorev. Stay," Shilla said.

"For a while," he said.

Talla smiled. "Let me spoil my son again. Put a little meat on your bones."

Lorev managed a smile for his mother. He had missed his family. He nodded.

* * *

Lorev sat in the sand, watching Shilla chasing Trav around the beach, squealing and giggling. He heard someone behind him.

"She is so much happier since you returned," his father said, sitting beside him.

"I am glad," Lorev said, smiling at the excited girl as she ran over to Col.

"What is my spirit animal, Father?" she asked, crawling into his lap.

"I don't know, you are not an apprentice," Col smiled.

"I want to be," she said. "Can I apprentice?"

"You are young," Col said, "I will speak to your mother." He turned to Lorev. "Do you feel up to a short journey and some healing work?" he asked.

"Perhaps. Why?"

"The Spirit Messenger of the River Clan is sick. He needs care, and the village needs a healer. I can send an apprentice, but I thought you might be ready."

Lorev looked at Shilla. "Yes, we will go," his sister said.

Col chuckled. "I'm sure Lorev can manage this on his own."

"No," Shilla said, standing. "I meant what I said. I will not leave Lorev's side."

* * *

It was late when they spotted the River Clan village. Lorev carried his pack, filled with medicines, herbs, and a few clothes. Shilla carried a small bag, her cloth doll poking from the top. Lorev had smiled when she packed it. It had a splint tied to one leg, a sewn wound on its arm, and a bandage around its head.

"Greetings, Apprentice. Thank the spirits you are here. I am Yorra. I will take you to Spirit Messenger Borv," the woman said, leading them into a house. The fire blazed, and an elderly man lay motionless on a bed.

"Borv has no apprentice?" Lorev asked.

"None since Rolva, eight summers ago," Yorra said.

Lorev tipped his pack out onto a spare bed. "I know Rolva. She is at the Boat Clan in the south. Shilla, heat water, please."

"Your helper?" Yorra asked.

"My sister," he said, examining Borv. "Shilla. The small tree with white flowers… soft wood."

"Elder. You'll want willow too?" she asked, twisting a green stick into tongs and raking in the fire for stones.

"Yes. The tall herb, feathery leaves, and white flowers too."

"Yarrow," Shilla said, dropping the hot stones into the pot, "Shall I add honey?"

"Yes. Now, I must get some of his clothes off. He is burning with fever."

Yorra helped to undress the old messenger, while Lorev checked his body.

"What are you looking for," Yorra asked.

"A wound, perhaps. He is plagued by bad spirits, they got into him somehow."

"He has no wounds," she said.

"Food then, or dirty water," Lorev said. He took the cup Shilla gave him, sipping the hot infusion. "Perfect," he said, smiling at her. He lifted Borv's head, tipping the drink into his mouth a little at a time. The messenger stirred, coughing, then swallowing the healing tea.

His eyes opened, lucid for a moment. "Thank you," he whispered.

Shilla brought cold water and a cloth, bathing his face and neck, as Lorev made up the fire.

"The spirits will make him hot one moment, cold another," he explained. "We must keep the fire going tonight."

Once they had made Borv comfortable, Yorra brought them food. They sat, learning of the River Clan as they ate, then after rechecking their patient, they climbed into bed.

"We make an excellent team," Lorev said.

Shilla grinned at him in the firelight. "Good, because you're not getting rid of me."

Twenty-seven.

"Lila, help me up," came Borv's croaking voice. Lorev jumped up, rushing to his side.

"Borv? Can you hear me?" he asked, feeling the old messenger's forehead.

"Lila, please," he said.

"Fetch Yorra," Lorev said, turning to Shilla.

"I'm here," Yorra said, carrying in firewood and setting it at the hearth. "What is wrong?"

"Borv. He is asking for Lila."

"His mate," Yorra said, brushing dirt from her hands. "But she crossed the river six years ago."

"This is bad," Lorev said. "If he is speaking to her, he must be at the death river. I should go to him. Oh, why did I not bring a drum?"

"He's a spirit messenger," Shilla said. "He must have one here somewhere." She searched around the house for a few moments, then clambered into the roof timbers.

"Lorev, catch," she called from above him. She tossed down a dusty drum, then another.

"Two drums?" he said.

"I'll help."

"You're not apprenticed, it may not be safe."

Shilla grinned. "My big brother will be with me. I will be safe."

Lorev took the beater from the rawhide bindings and set a slow heartbeat rhythm. Shilla sat beside him, matching his beat.

The grey world below was becoming familiar to Lorev. His training was barely enough for him to take such journeys, yet he had done it for Verra, and for Jath's brother already. He turned to see Shilla standing behind him, gazing about in wonder.

"Is this the land of the dead?" she asked.

"Beyond the river there," Lorev said, pointing. They both spotted the prone figure on the near bank and ran over to him. Borv was staring across the water at a wraith-like figure opposite.

"Come for me, Lila," he pleaded.

"It is not your time," she called back. "The clan needs you still. I cannot come for you. You must come to me when your time is done."

"I miss you," he said.

"I miss you too, but you have promises to fulfil. Time will pass, we will be together again, Borv."

"Soon," Borv said. "Soon."

Lorev reached down, helping the old man to his feet. He wrapped an arm around his waist, holding him up.

He turned, about to call for their return, when he froze. Shilla stood, staring at the spirit of Verra.

"I am his sister," Verra said.

Shilla stepped between Verra and Lorev. "You can't have him," she said.

Verra smiled. "I don't want to take him from you. I care for him from here. You care for him in the living world. We are sisters now."

Shilla's tense shoulders relaxed, and she held out her hands in a formal welcome. "Greetings, Verra," she said.

"Greetings, Shilla." She turned to Lorev. "You have resolved to live?" she asked.

Lorev nodded.

"Do not try that again," Verra said, "I will leave you to roam as a ghost, as I did. It is not pleasant."

"Thank you, Verra," he said. "I will not anger you again."

"I'm sure you will," the small spirit said, laughing, "But I will be your guardian nonetheless. Farewell for now."

Lorev smiled. "Back," he called.

As soon as he opened his eyes, Lorev jumped to his feet and went to Borv. The spirit messenger's brow was cool, his breathing steady. "I think he's over the worst now," he said to Shilla.

"I'll make more of the healing tea for when he wakes," she said, reaching for a pot of water.

"You remember the ingredients?"

"Elderflower, willow, yarrow, and honey," she said, not looking up. Lorev grinned.

"Spirit Apprentice," came a voice from the doorway. Lorev turned to find an older warrior coming in, followed by Yorra.

"This is our leader, Caman," she said.

"Greetings, Caman," Lorev said, hands held out.

"Greetings, Spirit Apprentice. You and your sister honour us by coming to tend our messenger. How is he?"

"Improved," Lorev said. "The fever has passed, I think. He needs rest now and nutritious food."

"I will see that he, and you, are well-fed, Lorev," Yorra said.

"Please, eat with us tonight," Caman said. "My mate would like to cook for you both."

Lorev smiled and was about to answer when a man rushed in, clutching a bloody forearm.

"I must deal with this," he said, bowing his head to Caman.

"We hope to see you later," the leader said.

Lorev inspected the wound, a long slash inflicted when butchering an ox. Shilla appeared with his tool pouch and boiling water before he had time to ask, then cleaned the cut ready for sewing. Lorev pierced holes for the stitches, then watched as his sister threaded and tied the sinew.

"Have you done this before, with mother or father?" he asked.

Shilla smiled. "No, but I have watched it many times. Is it correct?"

"It is perfect," he said, washing blood from his hands and reaching for the pot of honey.

* * *

Lorev passed his empty platter to Caman's mate, thanking her. The gathering had been larger than he had expected with the leader's three children, the mates of the two who were bonded, and several grandchildren.

"May we impose on you for a story?" Caman asked.

"Ah, I'm not the best at stories," Lorev said.

"Can I?" Shilla said, getting to her feet.

"One so young?" Caman said. "Please do."

Shilla flattened the fire a little, and the house became darker. Lorev watched as she placed dry timber close to the embers, though not where it would burn. She selected a long stick from the pile of firewood and stepped to the hearth.

"This is the tale of Tarren, the first warrior," she said, launching into the creation story. Lorev watched her, spellbound. He knew Shilla was well versed in the tribe lore, but her acting was something he'd never seen. She paced, arms moving. The stick, as her prop, was a staff for the hero. Lorev noticed she knocked the timber into the fire, just as she got to the part where Tarren set light to the sun. Her stick rested in the embers so that when the glorious hero took his spear to throw it into the sky, the end was aflame.

"Tarren cast his spear up into the sky, trying to see more of his world," she said, imitating the throw. "It reached the sun and illuminated the skies as it burst into flame."

Right on cue, the fire flared to life, the fresh logs igniting. There were gasps from the audience and squeals from the children as Shilla told the last part of the tale, still moving, still gesturing, pacing. "And that is how the first warrior created the world we know," she finished.

The usual polite clapping that followed the telling of a well-known story became a loud round of applause, with whoops from many men.

"You are a true entertainer," Caman said, as he stopped clapping. "Thank you, Shilla."

Shilla gave an exaggerated bow and moved back to sit with her brother.

"Well done," Lorev whispered. Shilla blushed.

* * *

It was the eighth day after their arrival that Borv got up from his bed. Lorev walked him around the house in the morning and, by the afternoon, he was accompanying him around the village. The old messenger watched as Shilla changed the dressing on the wound she'd sewn. Borv patted her on the head and muttered his approval. They stayed another two days and were glad to find that Yorra, a widow, had moved in to keep house for him.

"We owe you a debt," Caman said as they prepared to leave.

"Nonsense," Lorev said. "The protected-of-spirit serve where they are needed."

"We would like you to accept these gifts," Caman said.

Lorev knew that to decline would be a great insult, so he smiled. Caman's son brought forward a beautiful bow with a quiver of arrows. Lorev took it, holding it to his heart before making a show of examining the gift. It was a valuable weapon, traded, not made on the Long Islands. The workmanship was stunning.

"Thank you, Caman. I am honoured by the generosity of the River Clan," he said. Caman smiled at the thanks, then turned to Borv. The spirit messenger took his best drum and walked up to Shilla.

"Young woman," Borv said. "You had a significant part in my healing and recovery. The spirits tell me you will apprentice to this path, so please take this drum as a token of my gratitude."

Shilla was old enough to know the protocol of gifts and held it to her chest before inspecting it. "You have painted a wildcat on it," she said, fingers tracing the simple brush-strokes.

"I spoke to the ancestors," he said. "When you apprentice, this will be your spirit animal."

Shilla rushed to him, hugging him. "Thank you," she whispered, tears in her eyes. "But how does it represent me?"

"Patient, tenacious, loyal..." he smiled, "vicious if angered. Is that you?"

Lorev chuckled. "Yes, that's Shilla," he said.

* * *

It was late when they got back to the Classac. Glev, their small brother ran to them, asking Lorev to lift him. Baby Isla was crawling on the floor, and Shilla picked her up, cuddling the youngest sibling.

"Tell us of your visit," Zoola said when they were all gathered. "Is Borv well? Has he recovered?"

Lorev told the story, turning to let Shilla fill in details from time to time. Talla smiled at the way her children interacted.

"Borv gave me this drum," Shilla said, taking the instrument from the cloth wrapping. "He spoke to the ancestors. I am to apprentice to the protected-of-spirit, and the wildcat is my animal."

"You are decided?" Col said, sitting beside his daughter.

"Yes, Father. I want my tattoos."

Col glanced at Talla, then nodded. "You shall have spirit apprentice and healing apprentice tattoos," he said, "But I cannot let you have plant and lore apprentice marks."

Shilla looked up, surprised. "Why not?"

Col ruffled her hair. "Because you are already a plant and lore keeper," he said. "You shall have them at the full moon."

Col showed the beautiful bow and arrows he had received, vowing to practise now that he had such a well-made weapon.

* * *

The drum journey was complete. Col stood and addressed the tribes as the bright moon's disc climbed into the sky. The prophecies were positive, which pleased the clan.

"There is another matter tonight," Col said, taking Shilla's hand and leading her into the stone circle. "Our eldest daughter wishes to apprentice to our path."

There were cheers from the villagers, Shilla was a popular child. Col lifted her onto a rock, facing the circle's centre. Her mother came to her first.

"I cleanse you with the element of air," she said, wafting the smoke of burning herbs over Shilla.

Zoola came next, marking Shilla's cheeks with ochre. "I ground you with the element of earth," she said.

Gren walked up to the young girl, blue ribbons flying in the breeze. He gave her a drink from a cup of water. "I quench you with the element of water," he said.

Her father, Col, came last, placing his palm on her forehead. "I give you the passion of the element of fire," he said. He turned, nodding to Lorev who approached his sister, setting his tool pouch on the stone. He took the finest flint blade and held it close to her upturned face.

"Make them look good," Shilla said.

Lorev smiled. "I'll try."

Shilla grabbed his wrist. "Then stop shaking," she grinned. She closed her left eye. "I'm ready. Do it."

Lorev took a deep breath and whispered a prayer to the ancestors. He had never made tattoos, but Shilla would hear of no one else doing it. The blade made shallow cuts in her skin, the spirit eye first. He rubbed in the lamp-black, engrossed in his task now. The plant and lore marks were next, then healing and fire. Shilla was shaking, her fists clenched at her side, though she never moved. Lorev rubbed in the last of the black dye and wiped the blood from his sister's face.

"All done," he said, as Shilla opened her eyes. "Greetings, Spirit Apprentice Shilla."

Shilla wrapped her arms around him as the villagers cheered. "Thank you," she said.

Col gave the signal, and they served the feast.

Twenty-eight.

The family had finished their meal one evening, and Shilla was collecting the platters when Lorev stood up and walked to the hearth.

"I need to return to the Isle of Pigs," he said, trying to gauge his parents' reaction. "There are charts that belong to Star Master Brode. I was learning from him, something that I understood, numbers and the movements of the moon and sun; the meanings of the stars."

"How long will you be away?" Talla asked.

"I don't know. There is much to learn. Perhaps I may become a Star Keeper in time."

Shilla came and took his hand, looking up at her big brother. "You must do what makes you happy, Lorev," she said.

"You're taking it well, Shilla. I thought my leaving would upset you," Lorev said.

Shilla smiled. "Why? I'm coming with you."

There was a chorus of voices. Col, Talla and Lorev all talking at once. Col held up his hands. "Quiet. Shilla, you are too young for that journey, and we don't know how long Lorev will be away."

"How old were Uncle Gren and Aunt Zoola's children when they travelled here?" she asked.

"They were with their parents, Shilla," Talla said.

"And I will be with my big brother. I am an apprentice now. Are we not taught that the protected-of-spirit value honesty and keep their word?"

"Of course," Col said.

"Well, I promised to never leave Lorev's side. Will you have me break that promise?" she asked.

Col shook his head. "We will discuss this later," he said.

* * *

"I will try to talk her out of this," Talla said. "I know you don't want to take her on your journey."

The younger ones had gone to bed, and Lorev was just banking the fire. "It's not that I don't want her, Mother," Lorev said. "Shilla and I are the best of friends. We work well together. I assumed that you and father would not allow it."

"I am concerned either way. If we let her go, I will worry about her. If she stays, she will pine for you. Last time you left she didn't speak, except to Albyn, for two moons."

"I want Shilla to be happy, but I want to find my own path too," Lorev said.

"She will never be happy without you, Lorev. Let me speak to your father."

* * *

It was six days later that the trading ship sailed into the bay. They had flint, a rare commodity on the Long Islands, and Col took most of their cargo for a litter of young pigs and two bull calves. Lorev spoke to the Boat Master, asking where they were bound.

"North, to the Isle of Pigs. These calves will bring us good trade there," he said.

"Would you take passengers with you?" Lorev asked.

The master looked at the penned livestock, working out the room needed. "One or two," he said, "Can you pay me?"

Lorev noticed the row of teeth strung around the man's neck. An animal spirit, or tribe mascot, he guessed. "I have an entire wolf skin, including the head," he said, watching the man's eyes widen.

"How many passengers?"

"Me, my sister, and my spirit animal, Trav," he said, giving a whistle. The wolf bounded down the beach, jumping to place his paws on Lorev's shoulders. He licked at his face, powerful jaws mouthing his throat.

"I'll take you," the boat master said, his eyes never leaving Trav. "I am Folon. My people are the Boat Clan of the Wolf Tribe from Manu's Isle. The wolf is our symbol. A whole hide would have great value."

"Will you wait until tomorrow to sail?" Lorev asked. "We have farewells to say. We will feed and house you."

Folon smiled. "Will you show me the wolf skin?"

"Come on," Lorev said, "Let's go to the village."

Lorev laid the thick pelt on the bed, and Folon ran his hands through the soft fur. "It is well cured," he said.

"Oak bark tanned by the Poan Tribe."

"They are famous for their skins and leather," Folon said. "This will more than pay for your passage to the Isle of Pigs."

Lorev thought for a moment. "Then perhaps we can make the debt even," he said. "You know the village between the worlds? The Drogga people?" Folon nodded. "When you travel that route, come to me, or my sister, for a message and deliver it here, to our mother."

Folon held out his hands without hesitation. "A deal," he said, as Lorev clasped them.

* * *

Shilla hugged each of her extended family as they all stood on the shore. It was mid-morning, and Folon was keen to be away. Lorev said goodbye to his small siblings, to Gren, Zoola and their children. He stood in front of his parents.

"Thank you," he said. "I was so lucky that you adopted me. I will take great care of Shilla, and Folon will bring messages whenever he sails this way."

Talla smiled at Folon, fidgeting a few paces away. "There will be a meal and a bed for you," she said. She hugged Lorev, her face buried in his neck.

"I love you, Lorev. Find who you are."

Col took her place, clasping Lorev to him. "Find what you love, and embrace it," he said, tears running down his cheeks. "You will never disappoint us, Lorev. Never."

Lorev nodded, unable to form words, then pulled away, throwing his pack into the boat. He carried Trav into the vessel and watched as Shilla hugged their parents. She ran to Lorev, arms up, waiting for him to lift her. Lorev swung her into the boat, then helped the crew shove off from the beach. The two crew hoisted the square sail, while Folon steered a course along the sea-lake and towards the open ocean.

* * *

South-westerly winds drove them north, then east. Folon traded the piglets for grain on the Great Island coast, then made for the Isle of Pigs. Lorev drank mint tea to battle the sea-sickness, and they put ashore to sleep each night. The ear piercings helped when the sea's motion became too much, and Lorev would sit, eyes on the horizon, as he twisted the bone ornaments. There was a crowd gathered on the shore as the boat crunched into the shingle.

"We saw your sail," shouted a warrior, "Are you traders?" Lorev noticed that each of the warriors carried either a bow or spear. Had they been expecting trouble?

"I am Folon, trading from Manu's Isle," the boat master called.

"Come ashore," the warrior said.

Folon leapt into the shallow surf, passing ropes to two men as they came to help.

"Lorev?" came a voice as he jumped ashore. He turned to see Kimmi, Star Keeper Urdan's daughter, running to the boat. She looked tired and dirty.

"Kimmi. It's good to see you," Lorev said, hugging the young woman. "How are your father and Star Master Brode?"

The smile left her face. "Both are dead," she said. "Come, you must speak to Norlyn."

"Wait, I am not alone." He reached over the side of the boat, lifting Shilla clear and depositing her on the beach. He whistled for Trav, who leapt out to stand beside her. The wolf spotted Kimmi and went to the familiar woman, sitting to have his ears scratched.

"This is my sister," Lorev said.

"I am Shilla, Spirit Apprentice of the Hill Clan of the Tribe of the West," she said, hands extended. "Plant Keeper, Lore Keeper, Fire Apprentice and Healing Apprentice."

"I am Kimmi, Spirit Apprentice of the Bridge Clan of the Drogga people," Kimmi replied. "Plant, Lore and Fire Apprentice, and healer."

Lorev noted the raised, fresh scars of the healing tattoo. "A healer already?" he said.

"There has been much healing to do. I wish there had not been," she said. "Come, but prepare for a shock."

They followed Kimmi back to the walled settlement, seeing the destruction as they approached. Several of the houses were blackened ruins, the heavy slate roofs missing. People were milling about, unsure of what to do.

"When did this happen?" Lorev asked. The fires that had burned the houses were long gone, yet they had done little to repair or rebuild.

"Over two moons ago," Kimmi said, leading them to Chief Norlyn's house. "Chief Norlyn, Lorev has returned," she said, as the crippled leader struggled to his feet. The withered right arm hung uselessly at his side, the faint marks of the lightning strike still apparent on his skin.

"Greetings, Lorev," he said, extending the good arm. "You are still an apprentice?"

"Yes, Chief Norlyn." He realised that this was the first time he'd said that without a feeling of shame. "This is my sister, Shilla," he said, pulling her forward. Shilla reeled off her status, and Norlyn gave her a weak smile. "Welcome, Apprentice."

"What is being done with the burned-out houses?" Lorev asked. "Are you not repairing?"

"For what?" Norlyn said, slumping onto a bench. "The next attack will destroy us. We have only half a dozen warriors left, fit to fight. We have sacrificed a whole generation of young men to this war, and now we will all die."

"Are the Eagle Tribe still that strong?" Lorev asked. "They must have had casualties too?"

"Oshyn, their king, is dead. Beyond that, we do not know."

"What of Brode and Urdan?"

Norlyn pushed back his mane of hair. "All gone. Dreena and Kimmi survived. Gelyn lives, but sending over twenty of our loved ones across the river has been hard on him. Like me, he can see no hope for us." His face contorted as he pressed a hand over his eyes, sobs escaping as he spoke. "They slaughtered my mate and my children."

Shilla ran to him, embracing him. "They are no longer in pain, Chief Norlyn," she said, her small hand rubbing his shoulder.

"Thank you, Shilla," he said, wiping away tears. Lorev was pacing now, his mind working fast.

"We must do something," he said.

"There is nothing I can do," the leader sighed.

"Perhaps there is something I can do," Lorev said. "What if we sent a peace party to talk?"

"They would kill us."

"Oshyn is dead," Lorev said. "Jath was planning to return to the Isle of Eagles when I last saw her. It is a gamble, but if Kimmi and I go, two people she knows, perhaps we can agree."

"The Eagle Tribe have never had a queen," Norlyn said, "What makes you think they will have accepted Jath?"

Lorev smiled. "Because Jath gets what she wants."

"I cannot spare any warriors."

"No, it is better if we go unarmed," Lorev said.

* * *

"Keep down," Lorev said.

"Why?" Shilla said, making no attempt to hide. "They look like a bunch of women. Maybe one or two warriors."

"I didn't want you to come. I told mother that I'd look after you."

"And I promised to never leave your side," she grinned.

"How did I get talked into this?" Folon said, turning the boat towards the shore. "Hail them, Lorev. I'm not putting ashore until they promise our safety."

"I am Lorev, Spirit Apprentice from the Long Islands," he called. "We are unarmed and mean you no harm."

"Come ashore," called a woman's voice. "I will vouch for your safety. We were expecting you."

Twenty-nine.

Hands grabbed at the ropes as the boat slid onto the soft sand. Lorev climbed out, lifting Shilla and helping Kimmi onto the beach.

"I am Brinn of the Eagle Tribe," said a skinny woman, holding out her hands. Lorev gave his status, but Brinn held up her hand. "I'll take you to the village," she said, "You can give your achievements to Jath."

"Jath is here?" Lorev said.

Brinn nodded and strode off, avoiding further questions.

The village looked much like the Drogga settlement, many houses burned or damaged. Here, though, rebuilding work had started. The main house was larger, and a sea-eagle perched on a post beside the door. Lorev watched as two women came out. Nuru's skin gleamed in the sunlight. Jath walked out, head high, tight leather leggings and tunic clinging to her body. Held tight to her shoulder was a baby.

"Hello Lorev," she said, smiling at him. "Kimmi, it's good to see you again, welcome." She turned to the Shilla. "You have your apprentice marks! Congratulations, Spirit Apprentice Shilla. Nuru is my mate and joint leader," she said. "Introduce yourself, my love."

"I am Nuru, Spirit Messenger of the Eagle Tribe. Plant Keeper, Lore Keeper, Fire Keeper and Healer," she said.

Lorev gave his achievements more for the gathering crowd than for Jath and Nuru. Kimmi followed, then Shilla.

"You have a child," Lorev said, looking from Jath to Nuru.

"Yes, his name is Loryn," Jath said, smiling down at the infant. "Would you like to hold your son?"

Lorev was reaching for the child Jath offered, as the words sank in. "My son?"

Jath placed the baby on Lorev's arm, so he supported his head. "Yes, he is yours. There has been no one else, and much as I love Nuru, fathering a child is beyond her."

Lorev looked down at the tiny bundle, just as his eyes opened. The chubby baby stared at his father, and a slight smile crossed his face.

"I thought, perhaps, you had heard about him. Is that why you're here?" Jath said.

"No," Lorev said, his eyes never leaving the baby. "I didn't even know for certain you had returned."

Shilla walked over to inspect the child, smiling as he grasped the finger she gave him. "This is not good, Lorev," she said.

Lorev looked at the child, then at Shilla. "What's wrong?"

"I am only seven summers, and you have made me an aunt," she said.

As the laughter faded, Shilla walked over to Nuru, taking her hand and leading her towards the door. "Tell me you have nettle and rose-hip," she said, "I need a cup of tea." Kimmi followed them.

"He's beautiful," Lorev said.

"What we had was beautiful," Jath said. "It wasn't meant to be forever, but it was good. He was your gift to me, and now he is my gift to you."

"We cannot be together," Lorev said.

"No. I am happy with Nuru. We complete each other, but Loryn will know his father. We must visit each other often as he grows."

"I would like that," Lorev said. Jath reached in and planted a soft kiss on his lips.

There was a cough from the doorway. "We are making tea," Nuru said.

"We'll be there in a moment," Jath said.

"Is Nuru alright with this... with Loryn?" Lorev asked.

"There was some jealousy at first. She thought I'd leave her and come to you. Now she understands Loryn is a child with a father, and two mothers. We will make it work." She pecked him on the lips again. "Come inside," she said.

Shilla had made herself at home and was pouring her favourite tea into wooden cups. She passed one to Lorev, one to Jath, as they sat at the hearth.

"So, why did you come?" Jath asked, as Nuru sat beside her and took her hand.

"We came to negotiate peace," he said. "The Drogga are broken people. Norlyn will not even rebuild for fear of another attack."

"My father is dead," Jath said. "You know there was no love lost between us. I bear the Drogga no ill will. Anyway, do you think I would attack the home of my child's father?"

Lorev smiled. "No more than I would attack the home of my son's mother."

"Then we agree," Jath said. "Perhaps we can trade again, too."

"I'd like that," Lorev said.

***

They stayed the night, Lorev, Kimmi and Shilla visiting with Jath and Nuru, while Folon and his crew found lodgings with a widow. The next morning, Lorev was up early. He went to the village centre, walking around, looking at the repairs being made.

"There is still much to do," said Nuru, from behind him.

"It is something I must start when I get back to the Isle of Pigs," he said. "Norlyn is so saddened by all the killing, I'm not sure he'll ever recover."

"Thank you for accepting Loryn," she said. "I wasn't sure how you'd take the news that you had a son. Jath was convinced that you'd be happy."

"It shocked me," he said, "But, yes, I am happy." He looked at Nuru, considering. "You have nothing to fear from me, Nuru. Jath is yours, anyone can see it. I wanted more from her once. I was angry when I found you two were bonded, but I have had time to think. Love her well, Nuru."

Nuru wiped a tear from her cheek. "Come on," she said, "Help me make breakfast."

* * *

Lorev walked into the walled compound of the Drogga village, making for Chief Norlyn's house. The journey back from the Isle of Eagles had taken all morning. He knocked and entered.

"You have survived, then?" Norlyn said, rising from his seat by the fire.

"We are at peace with the Eagle Tribe," Lorev said.

"For how long?"

Lorev smiled. "As long as Jath and I live," he said. "Jath has become the leader of the Eagle Tribe, and she has a son now."

"You think that will stop her from attacking us?" Norlyn asked.

"Yes, because I am the child's father."

"So, you'll be moving to the Isle of Eagles."

"No. We have to rebuild here. I will help with that," Lorev said.

Kimmi and Shilla arrived, bringing Gelyn, the clan's elderly spirit master. They all found seats near the hearth.

"How shall we go about rebuilding?" Lorev asked.

Norlyn shook his head, staring at the floor. "I am tired, Lorev. My family is dead. It is too much."

"There are those that live, Norlyn. Can we not rebuild for them?"

"Why not let the boy organise it?" Gelyn said. "The people know him, and he has skills in measurement and numbers."

"Will you do it?" Norlyn asked.

"Yes, but I also need to learn as much as I can from the star charts. There is no one to carry on the mastery of the skies."

"Perhaps there are other star masters," Gelyn said.

"We found one on our journey," Lorev replied, "But he was ancient. Master Gelyn, will you be able to take on Shilla as well as Kimmi as an apprentice?"

Gelyn nodded. "There is much to do, I would be glad of the help," he said.

"Then I will split my time between the charts, and the building work," Lorev said. "They did not damage the temple?"

"No," Kimmi said. "They did not dare. It was where mother and I hid during the attack."

"Then I'll see which houses we can salvage and work out where to start," Lorev said.

* * *

Lorev and Shilla moved in with Kimmi and her mother, Dreena. Lorev got the few fit warriors to start work on the houses needing the least repair, and within half a moon there were just four damaged houses left to deal with.

Shilla enjoyed the company of Kimmi and took to Gelyn straight away. She helped with the wounded who were still recovering, dressing wounds and cooking for the patients.

One of the first repairs was a house belonging to a young widow, Joreen, who had a two-year-old son and a baby daughter. Her mate had been killed in the attack on the Eagle Tribe village. Lorev soon found himself invited to eat with her.

"I'll be at Joreen's house tonight," he said, one evening. "Don't keep food for me."

"She's feeding you now?" Kimmi asked. Shilla giggled.

"I think she's lonely," Lorev said.

"Yes, I'm sure she'll be glad of your company," Kimmi said.

"Take your cloak," Shilla called after him.

"It's mild tonight," he said.

"Yes, but it will be cold in the morning," she said, as she and Kimmi dissolved into laughter.

Lorev blushed and left.

* * *

The sun was just clearing the horizon when Lorev opened the door of Joreen's house and stepped out. The naked woman wrapped her arms around him and gave him a last kiss, waving as he crossed the square. He slipped into the house, stripping and climbing into his own bed.

"Did Joreen give you breakfast?" Shilla mumbled from her bed.

"Shut up," Lorev said, pulling the furs over himself.

It seemed only moments later that Shilla was prodding him awake. "Come on, sleepy-head, the men are waiting to start work."

Lorev struggled out of bed, and Kimmi placed a hot cup of Rose-hip tea in his hands. "Get them started, then I'll make you breakfast," she said.

The warriors, their numbers swelled a little as the injured recovered, greeted him with knowing smiles. There were few secrets in the small settlement, and when Joreen fetched water a little later, there were some good-natured howls from the men. Joreen took it well, tossing her hair and winking at Lorev.

The clan worked hard, the men rebuilding, the women tending the children, the cattle and the crops. Lorev discovered it was the same in every village. Old folks, women and children, but few men. He worked the mornings on the reconstruction of the houses and the afternoons poring over the star charts. He learned of the skies' movements, the figures that could be traced among the stars, and the wandering stars that often appeared close to the horizon. Many nights he lay, staring up into the sky, matching what he saw with Brode's old charts.

* * *

Lorev was watching the movements of the red star when he felt someone sit beside him. A hand stroked his cheek, and Joreen's face appeared. She bent for a kiss, then stretched out beside him.

"Are the children asleep?" he asked.

"Yes, I'll hear them if they wake." Her fingers trailed down his chest. "I have something to tell you," she whispered. "I'm going to have a baby."

Lorev gulped and turned to her. "I – um..." he began.

"I don't expect to be your mate," Joreen said. "There are so many young widows now. Every warrior has taken a second partner; nevertheless, there are ten women without a mate." She snuggled up to Lorev, her head on his chest. "My friend Loria gets lonely at night too," she said, giggling.

"Loria? You expect me to..."

"She's beautiful, and only a few years older than me," Joreen said. She straddled Lorev's body, hands on his chest. He saw her, silhouetted against the starry sky, hair like a halo. "We may never find partners now, Lorev, but we can still bear the children our mates would have given us."

"You want me to father children for you both?" he asked.

"How else will the clan grow?" she asked, standing and pulling him to his feet. She led him back towards her house. "And there are so many lonely widows."

Thirty.

Summer was past now, and autumn chilled the morning air. They had completed the building work, and Shilla and Lorev had moved into an empty house. The population was so reduced that they had stripped the last two buildings, but not rebuilt.

Shilla raked at the ashes of yesterday's fire, breathing life into the embers. She pulled hot stones from the hearth to heat water. There was a muffled yawn from Lorev's bed, and she wandered over, pulling back the furs. Sona's face smiled back at her. Lorev's latest woman friend.

"Tea?" she asked.

"Mm, please," Sona said, climbing from the bed and putting on some clothes. Both Joreen and Loria had distended bellies now, though they still spent the night sometimes. It had annoyed Shilla, at first, that all these widowed women thought it was acceptable to use her brother so, but he appeared not to mind, so she kept her peace.

"I'll get breakfast for you both," Sona said, as Lorev surfaced. One benefit of Lorev's many lovers was that Shilla seldom had to cook, clean, or carry firewood. It was all done for them.

"How many now?" Shilla asked as Lorev sat up in bed.

"What?" he mumbled.

"Babies," she said. "How many?"

"Four of them are pregnant, that I know of," he said. "Sona told me last night that she has conceived."

"Are you happy about it?" Shilla asked. "None of them seems to want to bond with you, yet they seem to like you well enough."

Lorev smiled. "They are doing their duty to the tribe, to replace those lost to the war."

Shilla sat on the bed beside him. "Do you love any of them?"

Lorev saw the concern in his little sister's face. "I have some feelings for each of them," he said, watching Shilla. "I am happy to help the tribe."

"Do you think you will bond with one of them, perhaps Joreen, one day?"

"No," Lorev said, "I think it unlikely." Shilla shook her head.

* * *

"What do you remember of the star master's ceremonies?" Lorev asked.

Gelyn sighed. "They celebrated each full moon and new moon, separate from my marking of the day. Offerings of meat, bread and fruit were made to the moon spirit. There were acknowledgements of the wandering stars too, marking their rise and set. Each of the constellations represented one moon. The bull, the sow, the snake, all of them. Each has a time."

"I am nearing the end of my studies from Brode's charts," Lorev said, "Yet I still cannot see the entire purpose of some parts."

"You need to find a star master to learn from before it is too late," Gelyn said. "Many were trained when I was young, but they will be old men and women now. When the spring comes, you must search for a new teacher."

"I spoke to boat master Keld, when he last visited," Lorev said. "He may have found out if any still survive."

* * *

Lorev sat at Norlyn's hearth, sipping a cup of nettle tea. Norlyn had turned down the offer of a housekeeper. One older widow had suggested something more, but the chief was still deep in mourning.

"Our clan appreciates all you have done, Lorev," he said. "The houses you have rebuilt are strong, they will last lifetimes."

"The credit is for the warriors who did the work," he said, "I only directed."

"And measured, and calculated, and sourced the correct timber. Do not belittle your skills," Norlyn said.

Lorev blushed. "Thank you, Chief Norlyn."

"Just Norlyn will suffice. You are at least a star keeper now, though I do not know how we can progress you further."

Lorev was explaining about his enquiries through the trading network when there was a clatter at the open door. Trav jumped to his feet, alarmed, as a red-faced boy barged in. Lorev grabbed the wolf's thick fur, holding him back.

"A boat... an eagle tribe boat," he wheezed, hands on his knees. "Coming up the sea-lake."

Norlyn glanced at his spear, gathering dust by the doorpost since his arm was crippled. Lorev stood, placing a hand on his shoulder. "They are no longer a threat," he said. "It will be Jath coming to visit with our son, I expect."

Norlyn relaxed as Lorev smiled and thanked the boy. "I'll go to meet them," he said.

The outrigger vessel was just reaching the shore as he got there. He ran to the water's edge, catching a rope and hauling the bow onto the sand as Brinn leapt ashore. She took the baby as Jath climbed onto the beach.

"Hello, Lorev," she said, walking to him and embracing him. Lorev hugged her back. Jath's touch was familiar, and his mind slipped back to when she was his. He let the thought go. They must allow things to work out as the ancestors intended.

"You look well," he said, holding her at arm's length.

Jath squeezed his upper arm, smiling. "You have grown again." She turned to take the baby back from Brinn, who stepped forward, extending her hands in welcome. Lorev ignored them and pulled her into a hug. A gasp escaped her as she relented and wrapped her arms around him.

"It's good to see you again too, Brinn."

"Thank you, Spirit Apprentice," she said, bowing her head.

"Call me Lorev," he said, reaching for the baby. Jath handed Loryn to him, noting how he held the boy, head supported. "Come, let's go to the village."

Jath turned. "This is Gwyn," she said, as an older man climbed out of the boat. "He is hoping to set up trading agreements here and begin a trade route."

Lorev extended his free hand, reciting his status.

"We thought he would be an agreeable man to introduce to your tribe," Jath said. "Bringing a warrior would raise too many awful memories."

Lorev smiled at Jath's wisdom. They hauled the boat above the high-tide mark, securing it to a large rock, then made for the village.

* * *

Norlyn stood as Lorev led the small party into his house. He held out his good arm in welcome, and Jath clasped his hand in hers. "Greetings, Chief Norlyn," she said.

"Greetings, Queen Jath," he replied.

"Chief will suffice," she said, smiling. "They voted me as the leader, we plan to dispense with hereditary titles."

"And this is the child who has brought us peace?" Norlyn asked, nodding to the baby in Lorev's arms.

"No doubt we would have come to an arrangement anyway," Jath said. "He has guaranteed it."

Lorev introduced Brinn and Gwyn, then left them in Norlyn's care to discuss trade. He took Jath to his house so she could put Loryn down to sleep.

"He's grown so much already!" Shilla said when she saw her nephew. "Can I hold him?"

"When he wakes," Jath said, laying him on a bed. She looked around. "This house is rebuilt?" she asked. Some wood shavings still littered the floor amongst the straw, but much of the stonework was blackened.

"Yes, the tribe did not need it, so we took it," Shilla said. "Will you stay with us tonight?"

"That would be nice," Jath said.

"None of your girlfriends tonight, Lorev," Shilla giggled. Jath looked confused as Lorev blushed and stared at the floor. "He has made it his mission to repopulate the village," Shilla said. "How many now?"

"Four," Lorev muttered.

"The clumsy lad I took to my bed?" Jath said, smiling. "You were a quick learner."

Lorev wished he could disappear. He was not used to such teasing, except from his sister. Things got worse, though, when Joreen wandered in with an armful of firewood, her belly bulging through her linen dress.

"Oh, you have a visitor," she said, dropping the logs beside the hearth and bowing.

"You remember Jath, don't you?" Shilla said.

"Yes. You are a leader now, aren't you?" Joreen asked.

Jath nodded. "And you are one of Lorev's conquests."

Joreen looked up, anger in her eyes. "There are no menfolk left for us, Chief Jath," she said. "Lorev is allowing our tribe, our clan, to continue. So, no, I am not a conquest, I am a clan woman who can still bear children."

Jath rushed over to the distraught widow, hugging her rigid body. "I meant no disrespect, Joreen, forgive me. We were only ribbing Lorev. Our own tribe is the same, each warrior has taken another mate. You are right, it is your duty."

Joreen smiled at last. "Thank you. Rebuilding the clan will be harder work than just rebuilding the houses," she said, "But Lorev is helping with both."

* * *

Jath pulled aside the leather curtain and entered the temple. She had stayed two nights, giving Lorev time to get to know his son a little, but it was time to return. She saw him, hunched over the stone slab of an altar, drawing marks with charcoal on the flat surface. His fingers traced across a painted hide, then he threw the charcoal aside.

"Spirits! It makes no sense," he shouted. He turned from his work and spotted Jath. "Sorry," he said. Loryn was sleeping in her arms. "I just can't make sense of this part."

"Can you go back to the star master on the Great Forested Isle?" she asked.

"Dorbna? If he still lives," Lorev said. "I have sent out word along the trade routes. It is a journey I must make soon if I can find a teacher."

Jath's fingers traced the ruined apprentice tattoo under his eye. "Shouldn't you have a star keeper's tattoo by now?" she asked.

"Perhaps. Norlyn and Gelyn seem to think I am ready."

"Then get them before you leave," she said.

"Gelyn's sight is too poor for the work now, and Kimmi has no experience," he said.

"I'll do it," came a voice from the back of the temple. Shilla wandered over, though neither had been aware she was there. "I was practising my counting," she said, holding up a charcoal stick in blackened fingers.

"Have you done them before?" Lorev asked.

"No," she said, "Had you done them before your first time?"

* * *

Lorev lay on the bed, Shilla perched beside him. She clutched the blade from her healing kit in her fingers. A pot of lamp-black was balanced on his chest. The eight-pointed design was drawn on a piece of birch bark beside his head.

"Ready?" she asked.

"As I'll ever be," Lorev smiled. He knew his sister would do her best, but it was her first attempt. He winced as the blade cut into his forehead, passing through his existing plant and lore marks. Shilla cut the second parallel mark, then rubbed in the black dye. The lines on his cheek passed through the scarred remains of his apprentice marks. Shilla moved on, double lines again for the horizontals, then single for the diagonals.

"There, done!" she said, sitting back and admiring her work. Lorev glanced at Kimmi, but her smile told him that Shilla had not messed up his new status tattoos.

"Thank you," he said, sitting up and taking the damp cloth she handed him. He dabbed at the wounds, seeing the straight patterns of blood on the fabric, knowing the tattoos were a success.

* * *

Half a moon had passed since Jath's visit, and Lorev was poring over the star charts yet again. He had just rolled the hides up and returned them to their store when a shout came from outside.

"Traders coming," called a voice. Lorev wandered outside to see who had returned. The trading party carried jars of grain and leather hides as they came in through the village gate. At their head was Keld.

"Keld," Lorev called, "It's good to see you."

The sailor put down his roll of hides and pulled Lorev into a hug. "Greetings," he said. He inspected Lorev's tattoos and smiled. "Star Keeper," he added.

"What news?" Lorev asked.

"I was at Classac. Your parents and family are all well. Talla sends her love to you and your sister."

"And star masters?" Lorev said.

"I have word of one," he said. "As soon as I've conducted my business, we shall talk."

Thirty-one.

Shilla settled Keld at their fire and gave him tea and a platter of bread and cheese.

"You are most generous, Spirit Apprentice," he said, accepting the meal. Lorev's young sister impressed him. Lorev was becoming an important man in his village, and the Drogga were superb trade partners now the war was over.

"So, you have news? Is Dorbna still alive?" Lorev asked, taking a cup of tea from Shilla.

Keld shook his head. "No, he has crossed the river, but there is word of a reclusive star master in the east of the Great Island. She is supposed to be of the Poan people, but she lives on the southern edge of their lands."

"I have family in the Poan Tribe," Lorev said, "But they are in the north of the territory and far inland. Do you travel down that coast?"

Keld shook his head. "No, I keep to the west. Do you know Folon from Manu's Isle?"

"Yes, he carries messages for us, like yourself."

"He is your man," Keld said, tearing a piece of bread and biting into it.

"When did we last see Folon, Shilla?" Lorev asked.

"A moon and a half ago, he brought flint."

"That's why he trades the east coast," Keld said. "There are many flint mines there."

"Then I must await his return," Lorev said.

* * *

The first of the winter storms came in days later and confined Lorev and Shilla to the house for all but the essential things. Lorev worked on making arrows. He was getting better with his bow, but targets had a habit of snapping the shafts. Shilla had become fascinated with weaving the linen thread they produced into fabric for clothing. Lorev had built her a loom frame, and she'd carved a bone needle for weaving the threads. Shilla was sitting, humming a melody as she worked, and Lorev asked her what she was singing.

"Nothing. It's just a little tune." She continued on, weaving her linen cloth, mumbling along to her tune.

"Are there words?" Lorev asked.

She smiled and started putting the words of the creation story to her melody. Lorev stopped shaving the arrow shaft, and listened to her clear voice, rhyming the words at the ends of alternating lines.

"That's beautiful, Shilla," he said, "Will you sing it at the solstice?"

"I don't know if I'm good enough," Shilla said.

"Well, I don't mind if you practise here. I love your voice."

* * *

The day of the winter solstice dawned bright, a few patches of snow glistening in the first rays of sunlight. Lorev put offerings in a linen bag, tied it to his belt, and set off for the circle of death. He played a steady rhythm on his drum as he walked, chanting a call to the ancestors to honour the sun on this shortest day. In the distance, he could hear Gelyn, at the circle of life, conducting his ceremony. He walked around the circle of stones, sun-wise until he came to the north stone. North, the place of earth, of winter, of darkness. He placed his palm on the icy slab. The image of his aunt, Zoola, flashed in his mind. The spirit of earth. This was her place. He closed his eyes.

"Spirit of Earth, I call to you on this solstice day." He could see Zoola's smile. "I ask for your blessing and offer you the bounty of our village." He took out a fresh loaf, a small joint of beef and a basket of dried berries, setting them on the ground outside the circle of stones.

"We know that the sun was created by Tarren, the first warrior. The sun rests low in the sky now, but we ask for its renewal to bring the spring."

Lorev whispered a prayer and stepped into the ring of stones. A shiver coursed through him, even now after standing in this circle so many times. He drummed, walking sun-wise again within the stones.

"Winter, time of darkness and hibernation, bring forth Spring." He stepped on, reaching the east.

"Spring, time of growth and new birth, element of air, bring forth summer."

"Summer, time of fat cattle and tall crops, element of fire, bring forth autumn," he chanted as he passed the south.

"Autumn, time of harvest and fruitfulness, element of water, bring forth winter."

Lorev stopped again as he reached the north stone, bowing his head and waiting a moment. His parents' voices thanked him, then he heard Gren and Zoola whisper his name. They all knew he was there, each acknowledging his new role. He made prayers for the recently deceased, summoning the ancestors to witness their first solstice from the land across the death river.

"You are ancestors now," he called, "Join the generations past and bring prophecy and protection for those living." He had timed it well. The sun's red orb cleared the horizon to the south-east and began its low arc across the southern sky. Lorev kept his eyes to the front as he walked back to the village. The spirits may be feasting on his offerings, and it was bad luck to see them in the human world.

Gelyn joined him as he entered the village gate.

"Did it go well?" he asked.

"I think so."

"Did the spirits come? Did you summon the ancestors?"

Lorev smiled. "Yes, Zoola, Gren, and my parents were all there. I felt the ancestors too. It worried me that I did not know the form of the ceremony, only an outline."

"It is your intent that matters, Lorev," Gelyn said. "The spirits, the ancestors, would not have come if your intent was not pure. There is no right or wrong. Just success, or failure."

"Thank you, Gelyn. I will know, next time," Lorev said.

Shilla rushed to meet him. "Did you see mother and father?" she asked, "Did Albyn come?"

"Our parents and our uncle and aunt were there," he said, pushing open the door of the house, "But the ancestors were not recognisable. I'm sure Albyn's spirit was there, though."

"He comes to me still, in dreams," Shilla said.

"He haunts you?" Lorev asked.

"No. He has crossed over, but he comes to look at me. Sometimes he gives a little advice."

"Like Verra does for me?" he asked. Shilla nodded. "I am not aware of others who have this."

"Do you know of walking spirits," Shilla whispered.

Lorev spun to look at her, searching her eyes. "It seems that you do," he said. "This is a spirit master teaching, we should not have this knowledge."

"Sometimes, when they thought I was asleep, I wasn't," she said.

Lorev grinned. "Same here," he said. "Do you think that's what Verra and Albyn are to us?"

She shrugged. "What else?"

* * *

As the sun sank below the horizon, the villagers gathered at the circle of life. The fire crackled in the hearth, and Gelyn stood, arms wide.

"We honour our ancestors tonight, on this shortest day," he said. "We will journey to the world below to seek the wisdom of our forebears." Gelyn sat close to the fire in the evening chill, Kimmi and Shilla just behind him, drums in hand. "Lorev," he called, "Join us."

"I am just an apprentice," Lorev said, "Perhaps I should drum."

Gelyn patted the ground beside him. "You are a star keeper, sit." The girls began a heartbeat on the drums, the pace rising until Lorev felt the pull of the lower world again.

They were close to the death river. Gelyn and Lorev stood side by side, Shilla and Kimmi behind them. Gelyn beckoned the girls forward, then raised his arms.

"Ancestors that love us, come. We seek your wisdom for the moons ahead."

Across the water, shapes formed. A woman stood opposite Gelyn, and he conversed with her. Albyn appeared for Shilla, and the girl smiled at her mentor. Kimmi had tears in her eyes when her father, Urdan, came to her. Lorev smiled as his sister, Verra, appeared at the water's edge.

"Greetings, brother," she said, arms outstretched.

"Verra, it's good to see you again. What message do you have for me?"

The child paced back and forth. "You are going on a journey," she said. "Be careful of those you meet, be sure of who, and what they are."

"The star master?" he asked.

"Yes, and others. Be sure to keep Shilla out of harm's way. She is precious to you, and to the ancestors alike."

"Shilla will be safe on the Isle of Pigs," he said.

Verra looked at him and smiled. "How did you intend to prevent her from going with you?" she asked.

"I... I must take her?"

"She will follow if not. Guard her well," Verra said. "I will be close."

"Are you a walking spirit now?" he said.

"I serve in that role, for you. Now go, the master is waiting."

Lorev turned to see Gelyn, Shilla, and Kimmi watching him. Lorev smiled.

"Back," said Gelyn.

* * *

The feasting had begun, and Chief Norlyn stepped forward to fill his platter. There were tears in his eyes as he remembered why he was alone. That his mate and children were now gone. Gelyn stepped up to get food for Kimmi and himself, then nodded to Lorev. This was a first, an acknowledgement as the third family. He took a platter and filled it with food for himself and Shilla, moving almost half to his sister, then sitting beside her to eat.

"You talked of walking spirits at the river," Gelyn said.

Lorev swallowed his food. "Shilla and I are children of masters. We learned by mistake."

"The old man is a walking spirit for Shilla?" he asked.

"Yes," she said, "That is Albyn."

Gelyn frowned "He and I were acquainted when we were much younger."

He rubbed at his chin. "If you know, I suppose there is no harm in telling you. They are guardians and helpers for you. Everyone has a spirit that loves them, but only spirit masters can communicate with them. You may converse with your spirits when they come to you. In time, you may call them, perhaps even visit them in the upper world."

"May we always trust them?" Shilla asked.

Gelyn nodded. "They will not lie to you, but you must listen to their words. They are given to talking in riddles."

* * *

Spring came early. It was just two-and-a-half moons after the solstice, when the weather became warm, if still wet. Norlyn mapped out the land for tilling, while Gelyn distributed the grain for sowing. Seven days later, the rain stopped, and a dry spell had the villagers busy in the fields.

"Traders already," said Shilla, as a line of men bearing bundles and jars walked up from the south. Lorev went with Norlyn to meet them and was happy to see Folon from Manu's Isle at the head of the line.

"Greetings, Folon," Norlyn said, holding out his arm. "You are early this season."

"The winds and the seas are kind, Norlyn," he said, setting down his load. "We are hoping you have use for some of our goods."

"What do you have?"

"Fine pots," said Folon, "Baskets and bowls, soft hides for clothing, and a little bloodstone."

"Bloodstone we have," Norlyn said, "But the rest is of interest. We have surplus salt meat, linens, and some fine stone orbs."

"We can work a deal with that," the trader smiled. "We are going south for flint from here."

Lorev glanced at Norlyn, who nodded.

"Will you have room for passengers?" Lorev said.

"You and the wolf? Yes, I'm sure of it," the sailor smiled.

"And Shilla too?"

He nodded. "Will she make me some of her rose-hip and nettle tea?" Folon said.

Lorev smiled, "Of course, come on, the trading will wait."

They were soon at the hearth of Lorev and Shilla's house. Folon relayed messages from their parents and told of his journey north. Shilla displayed her linens, offering some to Folon as payment for their trip.

"No, I will take you south. You do not owe me. The ship will be half empty this early in the year. Where are you going?"

"The very south of the Poan lands. There is an old star master I must learn from."

"I know the coast you mean, but not of a star master there," he said. "They mine flint there. I will go ashore nearby."

"When do we leave?" Shilla asked.

Folon smiled at the girl's eager grin. "Two days," he said. "Be ready."

Thirty-two.

The journey down the east coast was quick, Folon stopping at only a few selected tribes. He knew his route well, trading the salt beef for grain in the fertile flatlands. They swapped the linens for heavy hides and the precious stone orbs for other valuable ornaments.

"What of the bloodstone?" Lorev asked him as they set sail once more.

"The flint miners of the Poan cherish it," he said, "and I know they'll need the grain. This should be a good trip." He smiled at Lorev, Trav and Shilla. "I think you three bring good luck."

Lorev was becoming used to sea travel, and the ear piercings and mint tea helped. He sat in the front of the vessel, eyes on the horizon as Folon steered in towards the shore. They were greeted well, for Folon was a respected trader here, and his goods were popular.

"How far are we from the Forest Clan?" he asked the spirit messenger that greeted them.

"Oh, a day's walk," he glanced at Shilla, "perhaps two. Do you have family there?"

"My mother is Vinna."

"Then please pass on my greetings, Vinna and Govat are my friends," he said.

"Do you know of a reclusive star master, south of here?" Lorev asked.

"Bron," he said, his smile gone now. "You seek her out?"

"I need to complete my training, there are few star masters left," Lorev said. "She may be the only one in the Great Island."

"Needs must," the messenger said. "Leave your sister with your family. Bron is… eccentric."

Lorev felt uneasy about the exchange but decided he had to find a teacher.

Next morning they said their farewells to Folon and his crew and set off towards the north-west.

* * *

Shilla and Lorev followed broad pathways through the thick woodland, Trav often running ahead to investigate smells, or hunt small animals. They camped overnight, pitching their shelter in the lee of a huge rock. The second day was colder, and it had begun to rain when Trav gave an excited yip and ran off.

"Do you think we're close?" Lorev said.

Shilla stopped, sniffing the air. "Woodsmoke. Do you smell it?"

They walked a little further, hearing the bustle of a village now as they emerged into a large clearing that Lorev recognised. The two girls sitting de-fleshing an ox hide looked up from their work. Shilla smiled at them, then they spotted Lorev. With a squeal, they threw aside the task and ran to him.

"Lorev, you came back," the older child said.

He crouched down, hugging the girls. "Hello Raya, hello Devra."

"Who's this?" Devra said, looking at Shilla.

"This is our sister, Shilla. Shilla these are Raya and Devra, daughters of Vinna of the Poan Tribe."

"You're an apprentice," said Raya. "Come meet our other two sisters. They are also apprenticed."

Devra grabbed Shilla's hand. "Come and meet mother," she said, tugging the surprised girl across the clearing.

"Mother, Mother, this is our sister, Shilla," Devra said, running into the house. Vinna looked up from the food she was preparing to find her youngest girl holding hands with a stranger. Then the excitable wolf bounded in behind them.

"Is Lorev here?" she asked, as he came in the door with Raya. "Oh, Lorev, it's good to see you," she said, rushing to hug him. He heard running feet, then more arms held him. Looking down, he found Gianna and Mai clinging to him. Govat's voice rose above the excited chatter.

"Why am I never greeted like this?" he said with a laugh. "Welcome, Lorev. Come in, if the women will let you."

Lorev pulled a bewildered Shilla forward. "Perhaps my sister should give her status," he said, smiling at her.

"I am Shilla, Spirit Apprentice of the Bridge Clan of the Drogga people, Plant Keeper, Lore Keeper, Fire Apprentice and Healing Apprentice," she said, arms extended.

Govat, Gianna and Mai all bowed, each giving their own achievements.

"And I am Vinna, Lorev's…" she paused.

"Vinna is my birth mother," he said, causing the woman's face to light up.

"Thank you, Lorev," she said, clasping Shilla's hand. "I am glad to meet one of Lorev's adopted family."

"He's always been my brother," Shilla said.

"And he still is," Vinna said. "But he has an extra family here too."

"Your tattoos are well healed, Shilla," said Mai. "When did you apprentice?"

"At the summer solstice," she said, "How about you?"

"The same! Lorev made me a drum. Do you want to see it?" Mai said, leading Shilla to the back of the house.

* * *

"Will you stay long?" Govat asked when the excitement was over.

"No, I must go south to find a star master. I believe her name is Bron."

"Bron the mad?" he gasped. "Why would you seek her out?"

Lorev's fingers traced his star keeper tattoo. "I must complete my training somehow."

"Leave Shilla here," he said. "Bron's cave is no place for a child."

"So I am told," Lorev said. He turned as Shilla came into the house with Mai. "Shilla, I leave for the south in the morning."

"Don't worry, I'll be ready," she said.

"No, I must go alone."

Shilla frowned. "I said I would not leave your side, and I meant it."

"I know, and I appreciate it," he said, "but this is too dangerous. The woman I must learn from is eccentric, maybe mad."

"I'm coming with you."

Lorev knelt beside her. "I love you, Shilla, and I'll miss you, but I need to learn the ways of the stars, and you need to continue your apprentice training. You can learn from Govat, and I will go to Bron and ask her to teach me."

"How long?" she asked.

"A year, no more."

"A year! Not a day more," Shilla said, taking Mai's hand and heading outside.

"What has made Shilla cry?" Gianna asked, coming in the door.

"Me, I'm afraid. I must leave again in the morning," said Lorev.

* * *

Shilla stood holding onto her new sister, Mai. Lorev knew he was being punished for leaving her when she refused him a hug. The journey would be several days, and the star master was well known as a recluse. His sister would be safer here with a teacher and other children to play and learn with. He lifted his pack, slipped his bow over his shoulder, and waved goodbye. Shilla gave him a defiant stare and turned, dragging Mai into the house.

Lorev headed south, Trav trotting at his side as he made a fast pace along well-worn trails. He stopped at a village the first night, receiving the hospitality of a young spirit messenger. She shook her head at his destination.

"I have never met this Bron," she said, "But I have yet to hear anyone say anything good about her. Is there no one else?"

"Not that I can get word of," Lorev said.

She showed him to a spare bed. "I wish you well then, Lorev. Goodnight."

In the morning, he was on his way again, heading for the next community.

* * *

The seventh day took him to the Gorge Clan of the Poan people. Their community lived and traded along a river that ran west to east across the land. They were a prosperous people, and Lorev was taken to meet their chief.

"Greetings, traveller," the warrior said, hands outstretched. "I am Rogan, leader of the Gorge Clan of the Poan people."

"I am Lorev," he said, smiling at the chief. "A star keeper of the Bridge Clan of the Drogga people, from the Isle of Pigs."

A tall, elegant woman joined the chief, taking his arm. She peered at Lorev's tattoos. "You have apprentice marks also," she said.

"This is my mate. Our spirit master, Zaron," Rogan said, introducing the woman. Lorev bowed.

"I was apprenticed at twelve summers," he said, "but I have discovered a talent for numbers and cycles. I come in search of a star master called Bron."

A murmur ran through the small crowd gathering around the chief, and Zaron put up her hands in the warding sign.

"No one seeks Bron," she said. "Are you mad?"

"It seems she is poorly thought of by those that know her," Lorev said. "She may be the last surviving star master. I have no choice but to persuade her to teach me."

Rogan glanced at the curious people around him. "Go about your business," he said, "Leave us to speak with our visitor in peace."

Zaron took his arm. "Come inside," she said.

The house was one of the largest Lorev had ever seen. The roof timbers disappeared into the darkness above him, and a forest of poles supported the framework. At the centre, a fire blazed. Zaron led him to a bench and sat him down.

"Make tea for us, Sheen," the spirit master called. A lad of about twelve ran to the hearth and heated water, as Rogan sat opposite Lorev.

"This woman you seek, Bron. She was of this clan in her younger days, gifted at numbers and the movements of the moon and stars. She travelled far to learn, then returned to our tribe. Bron is reputed to have been an outstanding beauty. Hair of chestnut, eyes so dark they seemed black. She took a mate here."

Zaron continued. "She became pregnant, but the babe she birthed was dead. It crushed her, and she tried to drown herself in the river. Her mate rescued her, and over time, she became herself again. When a second pregnancy ended the same way, she argued with her mate. She disappeared that night, they found her mate with his throat slit."

"Why was she not punished?" Lorev asked.

"She is a star master," Rogan said. "No one has the rank to bring her to account. She banished herself to a cave downstream. The clan could do nothing."

"But how does she survive?" Lorev said.

"We feed her," Rogan said, looking at the fire. "My predecessor thought it a waste and stopped the practice. She came to the village and cursed him. He died of the curse, and a third of the villagers along with him."

"Are you thinking again about your desire to have her teach you?" Zaron asked.

Lorev sighed. "A war has raged in the Northern Isles for thirty years. In the last attack, they killed both the star master and the star keeper. I have learned all I can from the charts, but there is knowledge I do not have, that I cannot learn alone. I must try to save the wisdom of the skies."

Zaron nodded. "Stay tonight. Tomorrow I will take you to her."

* * *

The path along the gorge was overgrown and ill-defined, but Zaron pressed on. Around noon they arrived at an overhanging stone on the bank of the river. Zaron set down the baskets she was carrying. She searched the bushes nearby, finding four empty baskets.

"This is as far as I go," she said.

"You do not meet with Bron?" Lorev asked.

"Once. She met me to foretell the eclipse of the sun last year. She is a hideous, filthy hag. I still have terrible dreams about our encounter."

"Where do I go?" Lorev asked.

"Follow the path," she said. She lowered her voice as if someone could overhear them. "Do you have a family? Someone who would like to know where you went?"

"Yes, a sister with the Forest Clan. Why? I will return when I have learned all I can."

"There have been visitors over the years," Zaron said. "None has returned." She gave a sad smile, and touched Lorev's shoulder, then turned and retraced her steps.

Thirty-three.

Lorev lugged the heavy baskets of food down the overgrown path. He wondered how the old woman managed. Up ahead he spotted movement and Trav froze, a low growl coming from his throat.

"Who are you? What do you want?" came a thin voice.

"I am Lorev, Star Keeper of the Bridge Clan of the Drogga Tribe. I seek knowledge," he called, still unable to make out anyone ahead.

There was a hoarse chuckle. "So, after all these years, the Drogga seek knowledge from Bron? Where are the grand star masters now, Eh?"

"Dead," Lorev said, walking closer. "They were killed in a raid last midsummer. I am the only one left with the skills to learn of the stars and moon." Beyond an ivy-clad rock face, Lorev could make out the black mouth of a cave. Cords hung across the doorway, each with an item tied to its end. Leg bones, a skull, carved wooden masks. A whole fox hung by the neck, a cloud of flies covering its rotting corpse.

"Step closer so I can see you," Bron said. He walked towards the cave, stopping when he saw movement in the shadows. "Turn your face to me."

Lorev watched as a hunched figure shuffled out of the darkness. The creased brown skin of her face peered out from a mass of tangled locks. Around her left eye were the fading remains of a star master's mark.

"Seek to know the secrets of the stars, do you?" she said, walking up to him. She was more than a head shorter than him, and he watched in fascinated fear as a long finger reached up to his face. The filthy nail dragged across his tattoos, and the reek of fetid breath sickened him. "Bring the food inside," she ordered.

The cave was small, and rats crawled amongst the decaying debris on the floor. Bron gestured to a rough shelf. "Put the food there," she said, dropping onto a low bed, "Then come and sit."

The rickety bed creaked as Lorev lowered himself as far from Bron as possible. She studied him for a while, and Lorev opened his mouth to break the silence.

"How many days since the full moon?" she snapped.

"Twenty-four."

"And how many moons until the midsummer solstice?"

Lorev closed his eyes, seeing the counting marks in his mind. "Four moons and… three days."

"How many days make one year?"

"Three hundreds, sixty and five."

"Hmm," Bron said, "You can count."

She questioned him on the stars and the meanings of the night sky patterns, then asked about the wandering stars. Lorev told what he knew of the morning star and the red star, drawing with his finger in an imaginary sky.

"Enough. You may be teachable," she said. "Build a bed over there for yourself, then light the fire. Sleep after noon, we will be awake much of the night."

Lorev noticed the old woman laying down and pulling tattered furs over herself as he cleared a space to the side of the cave. He kicked at the rats, vowing to tidy the place once he had settled in. He cut bracken to cover the hard floor and spread his fur blanket and cloak over it. Taking his fire bow, he crouched at the hearth and got a small blaze going. Firewood seemed to be scarce, so he went along the river path, collecting dead-fall. A clean pot stood by the cave wall, so he filled it from the river and heated water. He'd just added nettle and rose-hip when Bron stirred.

"You can make tea?" she asked. "Can you cook too?"

"I can feed myself," Lorev said. "Stew, roast meats, bread."

Bron nodded towards his bow, laid beside his bed. "Can you hit anything with that?"

"Small game, deer, if I'm lucky."

Her first smile revealed long, yellowed teeth. "Perhaps you'll be of use," she said.

* * *

Bron poked him awake as the sun set. Lorev climbed from his bed as bats flitted in and out of the cave mouth. He pulled on his cloak against the chill as the old woman made for the doorway.

"Come on, come on, we will catch the evening star yet if you don't dawdle," she said. Lorev rushed after her as she hobbled along the path, making for a clearing on the hill. Bron spread a hide on the ground and sat, waiting for Lorev to join her. She waved her arm across the darkening sky.

"Tell me what you see," she said.

Lorev pointed out the evening star, glimmering above the horizon, then the red star. He repeated the names of the star-patterns, drawing them with his finger against the emerging night. It still amazed Lorev that he could remember all the names and attributes of the stars. The bull, the goat, the serpent, he knew them all.

"This one," Bron said, pointing.

"I don't know a star-pattern in that part of the sky," he said, trying to make sense of the shining lights.

"There," she said, drawing lines with her finger. "A fish, do you see it?"

Lorev stared. "Yes, the head to the left. Is that it?"

Bron nodded. She told him about the significance of the pattern. What energy it held. They lay back for a moment, eyes on the dense swirl above them.

"There!" Bron said, "A flying star."

Lorev watched the bright light streak across the sky, disappearing in the west.

"A sign," she said. "The spirits say you are ready to fly with the stars now. Tomorrow we will make preparations."

"Fly? How?" he asked.

"Tomorrow," she said. "Now, tell me what you know of the bull."

* * *

It was close to dawn when the lesson ended, and Lorev crawled into his bed, soon falling asleep.

When he woke, it was past noon. He lit a fire and took meat from the bag hung high in the roof, cutting rough chunks and beginning a stew. Barley thickened it, and he set the pot in the embers at the fire's edge. Lorev added water to some meal and left the bowl out to gather the bread spirits. In a day or so the batter would froth, and bread made from it would be lighter than the hard biscuits he could make without. Bron woke as he made tea, sitting up and peering at him as if she'd forgotten about his presence.

"Is there tea?" she asked. Lorev nodded and poured some into a cup, passing it to her. She rummaged in the supplies, finding a stale loaf and attacking it with vigour. She paused after a few mouthfuls, tore the bread in half, and passed some to Lorev.

"May I tidy the cave after we have eaten, Star Master?" he said.

"As you please," she said. "It does not bother me. The rats are company, though I have you now, I suppose."

He carried refuse from the cave all afternoon. A fallen tree provided timber for a bed frame, and he covered the platform with bracken. They ate the stew in silence, and Lorev collected the bowls to wash in the river.

When he returned, Bron was crumbling something dry and brown into a pot of steaming water. She steeped it for a while, straining it through a cloth.

"This is the flying potion," she said. "We will take it tonight, and I will introduce you to the stars."

* * *

Back on the hilltop, at dusk, Bron poured two cups of the earthy drink and passed one to Lorev. "Drink it down, the taste is foul," she said.

Lorev gulped the lukewarm tea, almost choking as the bitterness registered. He coughed, and Bron slapped him on the back as he regained his breath.

"Lay back and take my hand," she said. "Do not close your eyes, or I cannot control what you see."

He stared up at the stars, Bron's bony hand in his, as the sky swam and flowed. He gripped Bron's hand tighter as he lifted from the ground, floating. A voice, slow and deep, called his name. Then they were flying. He gasped as they soared high into the air, the stars becoming brighter, closer. Bron kept up a commentary as they flew, showing him the star groups. Lorev could see the lines now, joining the twinkling lights to form the bull, the goat. They travelled on, Lorev reaching out with his free hand to touch the canopy of the sky.

At some point they returned to the hilltop, collapsing as they touched the ground. Lorev was aware of being guided to his feet and led back to the cave.

When he opened his eyes next, it was past noon. His head ached, and his mouth was dry. Bron was sitting by a small fire, making tea.

"You want some?" she asked, leering at him. "Sore head?" Lorev nodded. "Drink this then and tell me what you remember."

He relayed his memories to Bron, and she nodded as he pieced together their trip around the night sky.

"What else do you remember?" she asked.

Lorev shook his head. "I think you led me back here," he said. "That's all I can recall."

"Good," she said, "We travel to the stars again tonight."

* * *

The days passed, but it was the nights that Lorev came to live for. He craved the flying potion and suffered when, after half a moon, Bron stopped their nightly flights.

"You need a rest for a few days," she said.

"I'm alright," he said, "I can carry on."

"No, two or three days. You will make bread and hunt. I will collect the tribute the villagers leave. We will fly again soon."

The first day was torture. Lorev's hands shook, and his mind was heavy. By the second day, he felt well enough to bake bread and gather firewood. He stalked a deer on the third, bringing it down with a single arrow to the heart. He gutted the animal and half dragged, half carried the carcass back to the cave. He cooked stew and even ate a little, but his appetite was for a return to the stars.

Bron was tucking into a bowl of stew, sopping up the juices with bread. Lorev nibbled on a half loaf. "Will we fly tonight?" he asked.

"Yes. Sleep after lunch, and we'll go at sunset," Bron said.

* * *

Lorev gulped the flying potion, not noticing the rank taste now. He lay back and took Bron's hand as the sky flexed and twisted before him. They flew higher and further than before, touching the smallest of stars as his teacher kept up a commentary all the while. The night was too short and, before he was ready to return, he found himself in his bed. He knew he must have slept, as the shadow on the cave wall said it was past noon again. Something came back to him, then. Someone being with him. His head ached. A dark-eyed beauty had shared his bed. He remembered the weight of her body on him — the feel of her soft hair, smooth skin. Lorev crawled from his bed, poured water for himself, and then took a cup to Bron's bedside.

"Thank you," she said, sitting up and taking the cup.

"Was someone else here last night?" Lorev asked.

"Who?"

"A woman," Lorev said. "Young, brown hair and black eyes. She was with me, I'm sure."

"The image of me as a youthful woman," Bron said.

"Is she your daughter? Someone from the village?" he asked.

"She is of my blood, yes. Did you enjoy her?"

"You do not mind that I bedded your daughter?" Lorev asked.

"Her will is her own. She does as she pleases," Bron said.

"Where is she now?"

"She comes in the night," Bron said. "Perhaps she will return."

"She is not a ghost, is she?" Lorev asked.

"No, she is real. Now light the fire, we must eat."

* * *

The climb to the hill was becoming harder. Lorev struggled to the top and sat, gasping. He ran his hand over his belly.

The muscles he used to feel had gone. He looked down at his aching legs. Thin, scrawny thighs led to huge knees, then skinny calves. He noticed his arms for the first time in many moons, they too were thin and wasted. Bron arrived with the flying potion, and he forgot the physical again.

The girl came again that night. He woke with the memory of her, but she was always gone when the sun roused him.

Lorev knew he was growing weaker, but he needed just a moon more, maybe two, and he would have all the knowledge he craved. Bron had told him so. Winter came, and the nights on the hill were longer and colder. He slept most of the day now. The breaks from the nightly flying had stopped, and Lorev was glad. He needed the flying potion to learn… to live.

Thirty-four.

Shilla and Mai sat working the soft leather between them. They pulled the hide back and forth over a smooth log, softening the fibres. Shilla had learned each step of the process to make the tribe's fine clothing leather now. She and Mai were inseparable, both working hard towards becoming messengers one day. Mai learned the stories from Shilla and taught her friend to make leather in return.

They took the finished hides back to the house, rolling them and storing them in the roof space.

"How many do you have now?" Vinna asked as they climbed down.

"Twenty," said Shilla. "Perhaps we can go on the trade trip this summer."

"Perhaps," Vinna smiled.

"It is past time for Lorev to return," Shilla said. "If he does not come back soon, I will go to find him."

"That is too long a journey to make alone, Shilla."

"I would not go alone," she said. "Gianna has offered to go too."

"She is only twelve," Vinna said.

"Danat would jump at the chance to go with us," Shilla giggled. Danat was two years older than Gianna but was sweet on her.

"Ask Govat," Vinna sighed. "He is the spirit master."

* * *

It took Shilla half a moon to convince Govat that she needed to retrieve Lorev. She got Gianna and Danat to agree to accompany her, and Govat mapped out a route that would have them staying at a village each night. He knew the neighbouring clans well and sent gifts for each of the hosts they would meet.

Shilla packed her bag and hugged all her newfound family. She gave special attention to Mai, who had become her best friend. The trio waved as they left the village, heading south. Danat carried his spear, gifted by his father. Gianna took a bow and arrows. Vinna had ensured they had food for two days, in case they needed it.

They made the first village well before nightfall, and Shilla introduced them all, giving Govat's gift to the spirit messenger.

"You are young for such a trip," the messenger said.

"I am fourteen," said Danat, standing as tall as possible. The messenger smiled.

The days passed, and Shilla grew excited at the thought of seeing her big brother again. They came at last to the Gorge Clan, and Shilla sought Zaron. She gave the tall spirit master the final gift, an exquisitely polished bloodstone axe-head, and told her of the reason for their journey.

"Yes, Lorev was here a year ago, but we have had no word of him since," Zaron said.

"Can you take us to this Bron tomorrow?" Shilla asked.

Zaron looked at the axe-head. Its value was great, and they would give the lodgings the young travellers had requested for free. She didn't know Govat well, but she realised that the gift was for more than shelter, it was to ensure the safe return of the child and her friends.

"I will take you in the morning," she said. "But now, eat and tell us of your travels."

Danat was quite the storyteller, describing an uneventful journey as if it were a grand adventure. Shilla could see that Chief Rogan and his mate were humouring the lad, smiling and nodding in all the right places, never interrupting.

"You tell it well, Danat. You will be an excellent warrior before long," Rogan said. "But now it is time for bed." They led the trio to beds at the back of the large house, and they were soon asleep.

* * *

Zaron led them west from the village as soon as breakfast was over, and they followed the faint river path upstream. It was close to noon when they approached the cave, and Zaron stopped well back from the entrance.

"Bron. It is Zaron, Spirit Master of the Gorge Clan of our people. Are you there?"

There was silence.

"Bron. Are you there?" she shouted again.

"What do you want?" came the voice from the cave.

"I bring visitors for Lorev."

There was muttering and cursing, then the ragged star master appeared in the cave mouth. "Who do you bring?"

"Lorev's sister, Shilla. She asks him to return."

"Lorev," Bron called. "Your sister wants you to return with her."

Shilla waited. A shambling, emaciated man shuffled out of the cave, and she wondered who it was. Then she saw his eyes.

"Lorev? Oh, Lorev. What has she done to you?" Shilla ran forward, standing in front of the shadow of her brother. His ragged clothing was dirty, his hair and beard matted. He stank of carrion, and worse. "Do you never let him eat?" she squealed at Bron. "Do you not allow him to wash?"

"Lorev does as he pleases," Bron said, glaring at the girl.

"I want to speak to him," Shilla said. "Alone."

Bron dismissed her with a wave of her hand and turned back into the cave. "Light the fire when you've finished talking," she called to Lorev.

"What has happened?" Shilla said, taking her brother's hand. The fingernails were long and broken.

"I am learning from Bron, as I said I would," he said.

"You are wasting away. Are you sick? Why are you so thin?"

"The teachings take the use of a special potion. It allows me to fly through the stars and learn from them. I am not sick."

"Flying mushrooms?" Shilla said. "How long have you been taking them? Not for the entire year?"

"Has it been a year?" Lorev asked. Shilla noticed how slow his speech was now.

"Come back with me," she said. "Vinna will feed you. We will make you strong, and we can go back to the Isle of Pigs."

"I need longer, Shilla. A moon, maybe two. That is all."

"No," she said. "You promised me a year, no more."

Lorev stared at the ground. "I need to light the fire for Bron," he said. "I'm sorry, Shilla."

"Lorev. Come back with me now. You promised!"

He never turned. Just shook his head and disappeared into the cave.

"Make him come with us," Shilla said, turning to Zaron. "He promised me, a year."

Zaron took the girl's hand and led her away. "He is free to do as he wishes, Shilla. I'm sorry if he has broken his promise, but I cannot force him to come."

"Danat. You could make her let him go. I want my brother back."

"She has the highest rank I know, Shilla. You cannot threaten a star master. She did not force him to stay, did she?"

"No… but," Shilla burst into tears. Lorev had always been her hero, even when he'd tried to take his own life, she still loved him. How could he desert her like this? She turned from the cave, scrubbing tears from her cheek, and followed Zaron.

"Shilla, look out, a wolf!" shouted Danat, raising his spear.

Shilla turned, spotting the grey shape slinking out of the bushes behind them. "Leave him, It's Trav," she said. The wolf walked up to her, ears and tail low. She ran her fingers through his thick fur. "Why are you not with Lorev?" she asked.

"Shilla, you saw how he has been caring for himself," Zaron said. "It's likely that he has neglected his spirit animal too."

"Come," Shilla said, using Lorev's hand motion for the wolf. "I will care for you."

* * *

Shilla paced up and down in Zaron's house, trying to think how to get Lorev back. "Ask the spirits," Gianna said, stepping in front of her.

"What? How?" Shilla asked.

"Zaron, may we conduct a drum journey to ask for help for Lorev?" Gianna asked.

"If you wish, though, I would like to travel with you," she said. "Are you comfortable with drum journeys, Shilla?"

"Yes, Spirit Master, very," she said.

Zaron retrieved drums from a shelf, passing one to Gianna, then sat close to the hearth. The two girls joined her as she set up the steady rhythm.

Shilla found the lower world familiar now and headed straight for the river. Glancing back, she saw Zaron and Gianna following. She raised her arms and called out across the water. "Ancestors that love us come. Spirits of mine, spirits of my brother, Lorev, come to me."

She watched as two indistinct forms solidified on the far bank. The old man she had loved all her life and Lorev's small sister. She beckoned, and both spectres stepped into the water, Albyn helping Verra as they waded the river.

"No. This cannot happen," Zaron shouted, her voice breaking. "The dead cannot return."

"They come at my bidding," Shilla said, "They will do no harm." She turned to Verra. "Do you see Lorev? Do you see what he has done to himself?" Shilla asked.

"I cannot reach him when he takes the flying potion, Shilla," Verra said. "His mind is closed to me."

Shilla turned to her old mentor. "Messenger Albyn. Can you do nothing to help him?"

"I may not intervene unless directed by a spirit master," Albyn said.

Shilla turned to Zaron. "Can he help Lorev?" she asked.

"What are you?" Zaron asked Albyn.

"I am the child's walking spirit."

"She is but an apprentice," Zaron said.

Albyn nodded. "Nevertheless, it is true. May I intervene?"

Zaron looked at Shilla's pleading face. "Very well," she said.

"What methods may I use?" he asked.

"Any method," Shilla shouted.

Albyn turned to Zaron, and she nodded. "It will take time," Albyn said. "Do not wait for him. We will work together to bring him back to you if we can. When the time is right, he will find you."

"*Lorev is my brother, he freed me,*" Verra said. "*I will do all I can.*"

The two figures turned and stepped back into the river, wading to the far shore before fading from sight.

"*Back,*" called Zaron.

As soon as the drumming stopped, Zaron turned to Shilla. "What just happened?" she asked. "A spirit apprentice should not know of walking spirits, far less have one of their own."

"I learned of them from my parents. They are both spirit masters. Their names are Col and Talla."

Zaron's eyes opened wide. "You are the daughter of the Fire Spirit and the Air Spirit?" Shilla nodded. "That explains much," she said.

* * *

Govat was coming out of the house as Vinna entered. She nodded towards Shilla, sitting on a log at the forest edge.

"She's been home four days now," Vinna said, "And all she does is sit on that log and stare at the south path. Even Mai can't get her moving."

"Gianna said that the spirits told her not to wait," Govat said. "What can we do?"

"She asked about the trade journey north. Do you think the traders would take Shilla and Mai? They have fine hides to trade."

Govat sighed. "I will ask. We have to get her mind off Lorev."

"You believe he will return, one day, don't you?" Vinna asked.

"If the spirits foresee it, he will come back," Govat said, hugging his mate.

When Shilla came in for dinner that evening, Govat took her aside.

"Would you still like to trade your leathers?" he asked. "The trading party leaves tomorrow for the Atay lands."

"What about Lorev?" Shilla asked.

"Where will he go, when he gets back his senses?" Govat said.

"North."

"And you will go north. You will not miss him."

"Is Mai going?"

Govat smiled. "She will go if you do."

Shilla nodded. "I will be ready tomorrow."

* * *

The trek north was long and the loads heavy. The two girls carried ten hides apiece, plus their belongings, and the traders were used to a fast pace and long days. Mai dropped to the ground, throwing her pack aside, as the head trader called a halt for the day. Shilla sat beside her, Trav still at her side.

"Not much longer," she said. "One of the women said we should reach the Atay port tomorrow. Perhaps there will be people I know. The Long Island tribes trade with the Atay too."

The following day was bright and calm as the party made its way into the Shore Clan village. They called greetings and made introductions. The Clan leaders were a couple, Gan and Solla, and it soon turned out that they knew Shilla's parents. As both girls were spirit apprentices, they were taken to the spirit master, a woman called Genna.

"So, you are Col and Talla's daughter," she said, smiling at Shilla. She spotted Trav sitting by the door. "Is this your spirit animal?"

"My brother's. He is… sick," Shilla said.

"And who is this?" Genna asked.

Mai reeled off her status for the spirit master, but Genna looked puzzled.

"She is Lorev's sister, and Lorev is my adopted brother," Shilla explained.

"Then she is your sister, according to our lore," Genna smiled.

"Boats!" came a cry from outside. Genna ran to the door, Mai and Shilla close behind. Four sailing vessels were making for the shore, each carrying six or more men.

"Traders?" asked Shilla.

"No, there are too many," Genna said. "Both of you, in the house and hide!"

Thirty-five.

Hessa raked at the cold ashes in the hearth. The fire was out, there was no firewood, and Saren was screaming. She sighed and unfastened her tunic. She'd think better once she got her son settled. Silence returned as she lifted the sobbing boy to her breast.

The house was her prison now. She left each day to fetch water or fuel, but the villagers did not speak to her anymore. Her mate, Jorn, had taken to sleeping with his mistress, Goen. Hessa had refused to move out of the main house. The house Jorn had built for himself, Hessa and their son. There had been a fight, and Jorn had moved out, leaving Hessa and Saren behind.

She heard the whispers in the village. Jorn was an honourable man, they said. Hessa dishonoured him by refusing to give him the house. She should leave, they said. Hessa wondered how they would cope with their illnesses and injuries, births and deaths if she went. She wouldn't go, though. He had taken her as a mate, and if he wanted to be rid of her, he'd have to cut the knot himself, not her.

Saren slipped into sleep, and she laid him on the bed, pulling a fur over him. She knelt at the hearth and began the daily ritual of lighting the fire.

She'd just got a flame kindled when the door creaked open behind her. Dorlan's smiling face peeked in.

"Need some firewood?" the apprentice asked.

"Please," Hessa said.

When Dorlan returned, Hessa stacked wood on the fire and pushed in stones to heat. "What news from the Boat Clan," she asked.

Dorlan shifted from foot to foot. "Jorn was visiting yesterday. I was channelling the spirits. He told Rolva they should banish me from the Clan because I was mad."

Hessa rushed to the girl and hugged her tight. "It is not his village. He has no right to ask anything of Rolva." She held Dorlan for a little longer. "You are not mad, you are gifted. You can speak to the ancestors."

"He frightens me, Hessa," Dorlan said.

Hessa glanced at the door. "Why are you here if you fear him?"

"He is away trading again. Did you not know?"

"He doesn't live here, and no one speaks to me. How would I know?"

"I'm sorry," Dorlan said, hugging Hessa back. "You could leave. No one would think any worse of you."

"They couldn't think any worse of me than they do, but I will not give him the pleasure," Hessa said.

* * *

"You insult me," Jorn shouted. The traders of the Atay Tribe hated doing business with him. He overvalued his goods and lost his temper at the slightest thing.

"Your salt beef is excellent, Jorn," said the trader, "But we have plenty of stores, and it is almost summer. If you need flint, we can spare that." He pointed to a basket of rough nodules at his side.

"That is not enough. There is almost a whole cattle beast here," Jorn ranted.

"Perhaps, but that is all the flint we have to trade. We can give you barley if you wish."

"I have no need of barley," Jorn said. "We grow plenty for our needs." He turned to the sailors. "Load this meat back in the boat. I refuse to deal with these thieves."

The trader shook his head and picked up the basket of flints.

"You've not heard the last of this," Jorn shouted from the shore.

* * *

Hessa heard the yelling coming from the beach. Jorn was back, and she was glad that Dorlan was not there if her mate was in a foul mood again. The shouting drew closer, then Jorn kicked the door open, and appeared, red of face and scowling.

"I want you out," he said, levelling his shaking finger at Hessa.

"And go where? This is the house you built for us, and our son, to live in."

Hessa had no time to dodge the back-handed blow, and her head snapped around as she lost her balance and fell to the floor. She wiped at her face, finding blood at the corner of her eye. Her gaze never left his as she climbed to her feet.

"I will not leave," she said, her voice quiet now. "Cut the knot with me, or go back to your fancy woman." She turned to pick up Saren but felt Jorn's hands grip her neck from behind. Her elbow shot back, knocking the wind from him. As he doubled forward, Hessa turned and brought her foot up between his legs. He gave a sharp cry and fell to his knees.

"Get out," she said.

Jorn looked up at her and struggled to his feet. There was rage in his eyes as he left.

* * *

Hessa heard whispers as she returned from the river with her water skin. Her blackened eye was closed, and she had left the dried blood on her face. After the failed trade journey, perhaps this would make them think again about their paragon of a leader.

Rolva, the spirit messenger from the Boat Clan came running over. "Hessa, what has he done to you?"

"He hit me, then tried to choke me," she said, loud enough for a passing busybody to overhear.

"Come into the house," Rolva said. "I came to see if the rumours were true. Is he still trying to get you to move out?"

Hessa nodded and sat to feed Saren as Rolva heated water to clean her eye.

* * *

Jorn strode into his father's village, making for the chief's house. His mother was standing talking to Dorlan. The girl flinched when she saw Jorn approaching.

"Is this mad girl still here?" he shouted. "I told Rolva to banish her."

"Do you assume you can eject the apprentice of my spirit messenger from my village, Jorn," his father's voice said from behind him.

"The girl is crazy. She brings bad spirits and poor luck," Jorn said.

"On the contrary. She is a gifted seer and a great asset to the Boat Clan," Sarn said. "It is time you left, Jorn."

"You would throw me out of the village? Your own son."

"I think you should go," Sarn said. Jorn stepped forward, pushing his father in the chest. The older man stepped back a pace, then came at him. Jorn's anger resurfaced, and he drove his fist up into his father's jaw.

The old man's eyes rolled back as he fell, his head striking a rock as it met the ground.

Dorlan rushed forward, her hand going to the chief's head. It came away covered in blood.

"I need to treat this," she said, looking at Jorn.

"Get away from him, you madwoman," he said, kicking out at the girl. "I'll take him to Hessa."

Jorn pulled his father up by his tunic, lifting him to his shoulder.

"You shouldn't move him," Dorlan said, but Jorn was already walking away.

* * *

Rolva was rubbing wound cream into Hessa's eye when the door burst open. Jorn stooped to get his heavy load in through the low frame, dropping the unconscious man onto a bed.

"He fell and hit his head," Jorn said, "Treat him."

The two women rushed to Sarn. Rolva checked his head while Hessa inspected the abrasion on his swollen jaw.

"Who hit him?" Hessa asked.

"Just treat him," Jorn snapped, turning for the door.

Hessa looked at the split in his scalp, pressing over the cut. "The skull is broken, I can feel the dent in his head," she said.

"What can we do?" Rolva asked.

"I have seen this done, once," Hessa said. "If the brain is bruised, I think it is good to let the bad spirit that made him unconscious leave. I must cut a hole."

Hessa ran to get her tools, then turned Sarn onto his side. She cut back the skin around the wound, exposing the skull, took a heavy blade, and scored along a line. It didn't take long to pierce the thin bone of his head. Then she cut a second groove, a third and a fourth. The piece of bone came away, and she peered inside. Blackened blood lay pooled against his brain. Hessa wiped her bloody hands on a cloth and reached for her drum. She set a steady beat and closed her eyes as she dropped to the world below.

"Sarn," she called as she spotted him crossing the river to the land of the dead.
"I am to leave the land of the living now, Hessa," he said.
"No, I have cut a pathway for the bad spirit to leave. Come back."
"I am past halfway," he said. "I cannot return."
Hessa watched as he waded the last few paces to the bank. Two ancestors took his hands and led him away.
"Back," she said, already processing the implications of the loss of Sarn.

"He is dead," Rolva said, as Hessa opened her eyes.
"I know I saw him cross the river."
Jorn came in the door, looking from Hessa to the lifeless body. "You have killed him!" he said, "You killed my father."
Hessa rolled Sarn's body onto its back and laid hands on his head and heart, whispering a prayer. She turned to Jorn. "I think the person who punched him in the jaw killed him," she said.
"I must get back to the Boat Clan," Rolva said, "I need to arrange a vote for a new chief."
Jorn stepped in front of her. "You will not," he said. "There will be no vote."
"But our lore says…" Rolva began.
"I will be chief over both villages. Tell your people that," Jorn said.

Rolva scurried out, heading for the Boat Clan settlement. Hessa knew she was worried about the safety of her family with Jorn in charge.

* * *

Sarn's mate, Calda, was at the house and Rolva gave her the news. She broke down for a moment, but soon composed herself and wiped at her tears.

"Jorn hit him," she said, "His own son."

"He has forbidden me to seek a new leader," Rolva said. "Jorn says he will be chief to both villages."

"Then I must leave," she said. "It will be dangerous here for me."

"Perhaps I will bring Dorlan and my family and come with you," Rolva said. "Where is Dorlan?"

"She is missing. I don't know where she has gone," Calda said.

* * *

It was past midnight when the group of people left the Boat Clan village. Rolva and her mate carried the two smallest children, while Calda took the older two's hands. They had searched for Dorlan, but her things had gone from the house. Rolva hoped she had the sense to head north, as they were doing. The party climbed the hill in the light of the gibbous moon, making for Classac.

* * *

The baby was fast asleep in Hessa's arms. If she kept him fed and cleaned, he was a contented child. Hessa's thoughts went back to the prophecy that she had from the spirit of Geth, the day she left Classac.

"You will be bonded, but this is not the time or the place. You will bear a son first, then a daughter. Your home will be elsewhere, not at Classac. In time, you will know happiness."

Hessa had been bonded to Jorn. She had borne a son, but there was no chance she would bear a daughter to a man that slept in another woman's bed. If that was the case, would she never be happy now? A knock on the door pulled her from her thoughts, and Hessa opened it.

"Can I speak with you, Messenger Hessa," the woman said. Paal, the gossip of the village.

"Why would you want to do that?" Hessa said, not trying to hide her distaste.

The woman came to the hearth and sat beside Hessa. "They say that Jorn killed his father. Is it true?" she asked.

"Ask him that. All I know is that he brought Sarn to me with a head wound. I could not save him."

Paal nodded her head. "He did that too, didn't he?" she said, pointing to Hessa's blackened eye.

"Jorn wanted me to leave this house. I refused. There was an argument, and he hit me." Hessa waited, but Paal was silent. "Where is he now?"

"He has taken four boats and all the warriors," Paal said. "They say he will raid the Atay lands for the way they insulted him on his last visit."

Thirty-six.

Lorev stumbled from his bed and took a long drink straight from the waterskin. He wiped his mouth with the back of his hand and hung up the empty skin. The sun through the cave mouth told him it was past noon. Bron's bed was empty. It was early for her to be up. There was coughing from the entrance, and the old woman shuffled in.

"Good morning, Bron," he said. The star master lowered herself to the bed and caught her breath. "Are you sick?" Lorev asked.

"I am fine," she wheezed. "Prepare yourself. Today you will receive your star master's tattoo."

"I have completed the master's training?" he asked.

"A master's training is never complete," Bron said, "But you have enough knowledge to learn for yourself now."

A smile was on his lips, perhaps the first in many moons, as he lit the fire.

* * *

"Hold still," Bron said as she took the fine blade in her shaking fingers. Each tiny cut stung as she filled the space between the vertical tattoo marks with intricate spirals and scrolls. The lamp-black burned as she rubbed it into the fresh wounds. Bron stopped, racked with another bout of coughing. She wiped at her mouth with a blood-flecked rag, then continued with her task.

"There, finished," she said, gathering her tools and shuffling back to her bed.

"Thank you," Lorev said. "Shall I get some food for us?"

"Feed yourself," she said, steadying her breathing, "I will eat later."

The Gorge Clan had brought fresh supplies the previous day, and Lorev took bread and cheese, walking outside to eat by the river. His muddled memories told him that Shilla had been there. Was it yesterday? The day before? She wanted him to go with her, but he needed to study the stars, needed his nightly journey. He craved the flying potion. He tried again to think how many days since his sister had been at the cave. The supplies had come yesterday, left upstream as always. The previous day it had rained. He shook his head. The flying potion made it so hard to remember anything but his lessons.

* * *

Lorev followed Bron to the hilltop, stopping several times for her to catch her breath. They laid out the blanket, and she passed him a cup of the potion.

"Is this all there is?" he asked.

"Yes, drink it, and I will observe tonight," she said.

"You must show me how to make it."

"Tomorrow," Bron said, laying back on the ground.

Lorev swallowed the foul liquid, then lay down, eyes on the skies as the magic seeped into him. Soon he was soaring amongst the stars. He was drawn to the pattern of the wildcat. Tracing the outline of the pouncing animal as he flew.

Wildcat. Shilla's spirit animal.

* * *

The dream woman sat astride his naked body, smiling down at him. She had whispered her name to him one night as they shared his bed. Brona. Lorev was sure she was Bron's offspring, come to check on her mother, then distracted by her new companion. It puzzled him that she never came by daylight.

His body spasmed as he reached his climax and Brona slipped off him, tucking herself tight to his back.

* * *

The spectre of the old man stood watching the sleeping couple. Lorev, he knew well. The woman he knew of. Albyn reached out his hand and drew in a deep breath. As he sucked in air, it left the lungs of the sleeping woman. He sucked again. Her eyes flew open as the last breath left her body, and she tried to scream at the sight of the ghost. No sound came as her heart gave its final beat.

* * *

The shadow on the cave wall told him it was still before noon. Lorev stirred, smiling as he remembered his nocturnal visitor. He went to climb from his bed but sensed a weight behind him. She was still there. Brona, his night-time companion.

Lorev rolled over, hoping to see her smile. He froze, bile rising in his throat. The face was familiar, yellowed teeth bared in a silent scream. Cold, terrified eyes bored into him — dead eyes.

He scrambled from the bed, kneeling as he retched. When his stomach calmed, he turned again, sitting on the cave's filthy floor. How had Bron got into his bed? Had she crawled in when Brona left, then died there? Another horrible thought came into his addled brain, and his empty belly heaved again.

"No," he whispered, staring at the corpse. "No."

* * *

Dragging the star master's body to the hilltop took him half the afternoon. There was no strength, now, in his starved body. He could not build a sky-burial platform, nor could he get the body into a tree for the carrion birds to clean.

Laying her on the top of the hill, he placed his hands on her head and her heart. He chanted the prayer to the ancestors for her passing, then took one last look at her and turned for the cave.

The drum was dusty from disuse. Lorev warmed the slack skin at the fire until it was playable, rubbing at the grime coated instrument. The faint picture of a swan appeared. Had that been Bron's spirit animal? Despite spending a year in her company, he had discovered little about her. He set up a steady rhythm and closed his eyes.

The black waters of the death river were high, splashing and foaming over submerged rocks. Lorev stood on the bank, staring across at the vague shape across the water.

"Bron?" he called. The figure turned. The familiar features looked younger.

"I have crossed. It was my time," she said.

"What of Brona? What has happened to her?" Lorev asked.

The features of the spectre continued to look younger, years dropping away as he watched. "You know what has happened to her."

The face became Brona's face. The body became full and youthful.

"No."

Bron, or Brona, chuckled. "You got what you wanted, Lorev. I got what I wanted. Go back to your life, if you can." She turned and walked away from the river, her body melting into the air.

"Back," Lorev whispered.

* * *

Lorev stood panting. He had torn the cave apart, looking for the flying potion. The empty leather bag hung from his fist, barely a crumb remaining for him to take that night.

He tried to think if Bron had mentioned the ingredients, but nothing came. He'd assumed the red, white-spotted mushrooms were a part of it, but the pouch contained traces of leaf and a few tiny black seeds too. How would he fly to the stars without it? How would he cope?

Lorev lit the fire, then set about cooking a stew with the supplies left by the villagers. After eating a tiny portion, distracted by his thoughts, he stored the rest in a covered pot. The bed beckoned, and Lorev climbed over the disarray that he'd created to stretch out on his furs. He couldn't go to the hilltop, that was where he'd laid Bron's body. There was no flying potion, and, as the light faded, he began to sweat. He needed to fly. Needed to feel the potion's ingredients rushing through his body, lifting him up to the skies. He shivered, the night air cooling his sweating skin. Pulling the furs tight around him, he slept at last.

* * *

"So, you are back," the voice said. Lorev sat up in his bed, peering into the darkness. Verra stood a few paces from him, a frown darkening her face.

"I never left," Lorev said.

"Your flying potion cut you off from everything. You could only see Bron and the stars. You even ignored our sister when she came to get you back."

"When did she come?" Lorev asked. "I lose track of time."

"Seven days ago. She travels north on a trade journey now, with our sister Mai. Your flying potion makes you lose track of more than time, though. Look at your body."

Lorev looked down, seeing his physical state for the first time without dulled eyes. His ribs protruded through loose skin, his arms and legs were wasted. His body was filthy, he couldn't remember when he had washed or bathed.

"How has this happened?" he asked. "I cooked. I ate."

"Yes," Verra said, "But how often?"

"Each day."

Verra shook her head. "You woke, made a fire, cooked perhaps every third or fourth day. It's why you lose track of time. Some days you slept through, others you just woke and crawled back to your hilltop for the potion."

"Do you know it's ingredients?" Lorev asked. "Tell me, please, I need it. I cannot fly to the stars without it."

"Have you tried?" Verra asked.

"No, but…"

"Lay down and close your eyes," she said. "Now, see the star pattern you know best in your head."

"I see it. The wildcat."

"Good," Verra said, "Now fly there."

Lorev was floating out of his body, soaring up to the skies above. He navigated the stars, weaving around the pattern of the wildcat. He was flying again. Something tugged at him, and he was in his bed once more.

"I don't need the potion?" he asked as he opened his eyes.

Verra frowned. "You never did. Oh, perhaps once or twice, but you have been using it for over a year."

"But why? Was it for the sake of Brona? So she would never meet me?" Lorev asked.

"There were only ever two people in this cave, Lorev," she said, "Bron and you."

Nausea took him. He had lain with the haggard old woman, night after night, convinced she was a youthful beauty. Bron had tricked him. Verra picked up on his thoughts.

"She used you, Lorev, just as you used her."

"Used her?" he said.

"You wanted the star master teachings, at any cost?" Lorev nodded. "That was the cost. Now, get back your strength, your sisters need you."

* * *

The following day dawned bright and dry. Lorev's head was clearer as if someone had lifted a veil. He ate some cold stew, then took all of Bron's possessions outside. He built a fire, throwing on her bed frame and bedding, her spare clothing and belongings; a knife, a comb, her cup and bowl. He rested for a while, exhausted, but set to again as soon as he could. He made a broom of birch twigs and swept the floor, piling his own few things on his bed.

The array of suspended decorations hanging across the cave mouth was next. In his dulled state, he'd never examined them. Two wooden masks, one suggesting a swan, the other a cat, he kept. The bones and skulls were human, and he set them aside. He would have to determine if Bron had given them proper rites to cross the river. The last two items were grotesque leather dolls. He cut one down, inspecting the work involved in making it. He gasped and dropped it to the floor as he realised what he had been holding. The 'dolls' were the dried out remains of two tiny children.

Lorev thought back to his journey to the cave, a year or more ago. Had the Gorge Clan not mentioned that Bron had lost two babies? He picked up the shrunken child's body, then cut free the other. Lorev laid them on his bed and retrieved his drum. After placing his hands on each child's head and heart, he sat to begin the drum journey.

As Lorev opened his eyes in the lower world, he heard the screams of babies. On the ground at his feet, the two infants wriggled and cried. He went to pick one up.

"No, Lorev," came Verra's voice. "I will take them."
The girl knelt, picking up the babies, hugging them to her.

"What will become of them?" Lorev asked.

"I will return them to Bron," she said, stepping into the water of the death river. She waded across and, as she stepped onto the far shore, Lorev saw Bron, or Brona as she appeared now, standing with her head bowed. Verra handed the children to their mother, then turned to cross back to Lorev.

"How will she calm them?" he asked.

Verra shrugged. "That is for her to discover," she said. "She left them to roam the earth plane for over thirty years. They will now be her punishment. Death is a great balancer or things."

"The other bones..." Lorev began.

"They have had rites, lay them to rest," Verra said. "Each was like you, in her thrall. Neither survived. Be glad that you did."

The girl's body became transparent, and Lorev reached for her. "Will I see you again?" he asked.

"I will watch you. I'll be here when you need me," Verra said, as she faded from sight.

"Back," Lorev said.

Thirty-seven.

Over the next half a moon, Lorev ate well from the supplies left for Bron. He found the strength to draw his bow, enough to kill small game, and walked a little to discover his surroundings. He ventured almost as far as the Gorge Clan, but stopped short, watching from a distance, not ready to face other people yet.

Lorev searched for Trav, giving the call he used for the wolf, but he never came. He assumed he must have returned to the wild, perhaps found a pack.

Lorev laid the bones and the tiny baby bodies at the back of the cave. It was time to go. He'd caught sight of his reflection in a still pool that day. His cheeks were no longer sunken, and he'd filled out a little.

He climbed to the hilltop, bringing the star master's bones back to the cave for the last time. He stacked them beside her children and her victims, then went to the river to bathe. Taking a flint blade and a bone comb, he trimmed his hair and beard as best he could. He packed Star Master Bron's charts, picked up his belongings and made for the Gorge Clan village.

* * *

"Greetings, stranger," Rogan said. "You are welcome."

"Hello, Rogan."

The chief looked at the tired, thin man before him. He spotted the tattoos as their eyes met. "Lorev? Is it you?"

"Yes, Rogan, I have survived." He handed the chief a sack. "The remains of the provisions for Bron," he said, "She will not need them."

"She is dead?" he asked.

"Yes. A bad spirit took her breath, little by little. She crossed the river half a moon ago."

Zaron, the clan's spirit master, joined her mate. "You are sure?" she asked.

"I drummed for her. She has crossed."

"Your tattoos," Zaron said, "You have star master's status."

"Bron gave them to me the day before she crossed over," Lorev said. "Perhaps she knew. I have left everything in order at the cave."

"You are thin," Zaron said, squeezing his arm. "Will you stay awhile, let us feed you a little?"

"I should like that," he said.

That evening, Rogan gathered his two most trusted warriors, while Zaron brought her messenger and two apprentices. They ate together, then sat while Lorev gave his account of the last year spent with Bron. As usual, his story was disjointed, though he tried to use some tricks Ivarra had taught him for telling tales. The chief and his warriors seemed relieved that the old woman was no longer a threat, but Zaron was more interested in the star teachings.

"Will you teach this once you return to your home?" she asked.

"To preserve the knowledge, I must," he said.

She turned to a girl with apprentice marks. "Alb has skill with numbers, and can track the moon's cycles well," she said. "In a year or two, may I send her to you?"

Lorev smiled at the girl. "How old are you?" he asked.

"Nine summers, Star Master Lorev."

He smiled at the first use of his new title. "I have a sister just a year younger than you. I look forward to teaching you, Alb."

"Thank you," she whispered, blushing.

"Have you seen a lone wolf nearby?" Lorev asked Rogan.

"Your spirit animal?" Rogan smiled. "Your sister, Shilla, has him. The wolf seems to love her as much as you."

"Perhaps more," Lorev said. "I was worried he would be in danger."

They talked long into the night. Rogan told the story of Bron's past life again, and Lorev tried to memorise it for the histories.

* * *

Lorev was flying again. Not to the stars this time, but over land. He saw vast tracts of forest, the occasional village in a clearing here and there. He came to the coast, following it with his flight. Then he was skimming down to a settlement. He hovered, taking in the scene. He knew this place — the Shore Clan of the Atay Tribe. Four boats skimmed across the waves, filled with armed warriors. The village people were curious at first, then panic set in as they realised they were being raided.

Lorev recognised Genna, the clan's spirit master, standing at her house's door, fear on her face. He swooped inside, finding two girls huddled behind a bed, clinging to each other. Shilla and Mai.

Soon there were the sounds of fighting, and two men rushed into the house. They threw aside Genna, ransacking the spirit master's house, taking anything they thought to be of value. They spotted the girls — the larger man grabbing them by the hair and dragging them from their hiding place.

"Protected-of-spirit," he shouted to his companion, "Fetch Jorn."

Lorev screamed and flew at the man, determined to free his sisters, but he passed straight through him. He was being granted this vision, but he was not there. He saw Shilla look up and her lips formed his name.

Jorn appeared, blood running from a cut to his brow. He pointed to Shilla. "I know this one. She's one of Col's brood. Take them prisoner," he said.

"No," Mai shouted, as a back-handed slap knocked her to the ground, and she lay still as stone.

* * *

"I'll kill you, you evil pig!" Lorev shouted as he sat up in his bed. Moments later, Zaron was at his side.

"What is it, Lorev? A nightmare?"

"They have taken my sisters prisoner," he said, reaching for his clothing.

"Who? Where?" Rogan said, rushing to his bedside.

Lorev pulled on his leggings. "They are at the Shore Clan of the Atay tribe. A chief from the Long Islands has attacked. I must go to them."

Zaron placed a hand on his arm. "It is midnight, Lorev. There is no moon, you can do nothing until morning."

* * *

Lorev had packed and repacked. He talked with Rogan, finding the fastest way north. Zaron called in as many favours as she could, to get him any form of travelling food. There were some fat cakes with seeds and dried meat in them, cooked and raw meats and bread. Lorev tried to memorise his route, anything to get him to Shilla and Mai as soon as possible.

As the first grey of dawn showed, he picked up his bow and said his goodbyes. He kept a steady pace, stopping only long enough to take a drink along the way. He ate as he walked. His strength was returning, and the meat and fat-rich food helped. As the light faded on the first day, he pulled out a thick hide and rolled himself in it. He lay awake, watching the stars for a while, wondering when this had happened. Yesterday? Longer ago? Might it be a premonition? He drifted off to sleep with nothing but questions in his head.

The sun woke him as it cleared the trees, and Lorev took a long drink. He ate bread and meat as he set off once again. He avoided villages as much as possible. He had no time for polite greetings. He walked into the night until he could no longer see, then rolled in his hide once more.

* * *

It was the tenth day, and Lorev was becoming more and more worried about his little sisters. He didn't know where they were or how Jorn was treating them. He assumed he would have to cross to the Long Islands to find them.

"Hello!" he called, as he wandered into the Shore Clan village. He spotted several burned-out houses, and there was no one about. "Hello!"

"Who are you? What do you want?" came a voice.

"Genna? Are you alright?" he asked, running to her. Her face was bruised and swollen, her left arm hung limp at her side.

"Lorev? It's good to see you. They raided us…"

"Jorn. I know. Where has he taken my sisters?" he said, leading the woman back to her house.

"How did you know?" she asked.

"I had a dream, I was flying. I saw it all and came as fast as I could. Now, where are Shilla and Mai?"

"He took them," she said. "He came with twenty warriors, shouting that we were thieves and cheats. Seven men are dead. Jorn's men took what food they could, then burned our grain. Yella, my young messenger, is missing, and Gan, our chief, has a severe wound."

"Your arm," Lorev said.

"It's broken, I cannot set it myself," Genna said, crying now. "What can we do, Lorev? We will die of starvation."

"Take me to Chief Gan," he said, "Then I will set your arm. Bring any others who have wounds, too."

* * *

Lorev cleaned the open wound in Gan's side. It was days old and past stitching, but he had no choice. He brought the edges together, piercing the flesh and threading the sinew through, tying it tightly. He asked Genna's advice on herbal treatments, then smeared the wound in honey and bandaged it. Gan was already sweating and speaking to the ancestors. Lorev hoped they could get him past his fever.

He had two warriors hold Genna down while he pulled her arm straight. Her screams were deafening, and he was glad when she passed out from the pain. He worked fast, splinting the arm and binding it. He held her and whispered as she woke, apologising for the pain he'd caused.

"You had to do it, Lorev. I'll need some willow bark tea though," she said.

Lorev moved to the fire, but a woman stopped him. "Help the others," she said, "I can make tea."

He cleaned some smaller cuts and bandaged them, then checked on Gan. "I need to get across to the Long Island," he said to Genna. "Can you cope with him now?"

"Yes. The pain is bearable now," she said. "I'll send for Ket. He was at sea when the raiders came. His boat is undamaged."

"I will cross tomorrow, if your boat master agrees," Lorev said.

"How will you take on Jorn's tribe?" Genna asked. "We have no warriors to spare, we are weak and vulnerable."

"I will find a way," Lorev said. He stepped outside, looking across the broken village as the light faded. There was whining from the bushes behind the house.

"Trav? Trav is that you?"

The grey shape limped from its hiding place, head down, tail low. A broken arrow trailed from his hind leg. Lorev dropped to his knees, running his fingers through the thick coat. "I'm sorry I abandoned you, my friend," he whispered. "What have they done to you?" The warm nose grazed his cheek, and Lorev stood, leading him into the house.

"Clear a space," he said, taking Trav to the fire. He laid the wolf down and talked to him as he grasped the arrow shaft. "I'm sorry," he whispered, yanking the arrow from the yelping wolf's leg. Trav curled round, licking the wound as Lorev stroked his head.

"Tomorrow we find Shilla," he said.

* * *

The east wind was ideal for their crossing, but Lorev and Ket left it until late afternoon to sail. They were making good time, and the coast south of the Bay Clan village was drawing closer as the light faded.

"I will slip ashore," Lorev said, "I want you to sail further south and wait."

"I will come with you, Star Master," Ket said.

"No. If I fail, you must get a message to my father at Classac. If I succeed, I will light a beacon on the hill above the Bay Clan village. When you see that, come for me."

Ket nodded as the small craft drifted to the beach.

"If there is no beacon by tomorrow night, get a message to my father," he repeated.

"You will not fail, Star Master," Ket said, as Lorev jumped into the shallow water and lifted Trav out of the boat.

Thirty-eight.

Darkness cloaked the Bay Clan village as Lorev crept closer. The night was black, one or two shafts of light leaking from the eaves of a central house. He placed each foot with care. One moment of carelessness and he would be captured. The bigger house would be the chief's house, Hessa's house if she was still here.

He glimpsed movement from the corner of his eye, and dropped to the ground, his arm reaching out to grab Trav. The man walked through the door of the house. Lorev was about to run after him when a hand clutched his shoulder. He froze, turning to his left.

"It's only me," the voice whispered. He leant back, allowing the light from the house to illuminate the face. Dorlan.

"What are you doing out here?" he whispered.

"Jorn wanted me banished," she said. "I have been hiding for half a moon. I saw your boat land and followed you."

"Do you know who is in there?" he said, nodding toward the house.

"That was Jorn, going inside," she said. "There's Hessa and three girls. I know one is Shilla, I don't know the others."

"One is Mai, our sister. The other will be Yella. They took her from the Shore Clan. I need to rescue them. Do you know if there are guards?"

"No. Jorn has them tied up," Dorlan said, "Even Hessa. I sneaked a look inside at dusk, but he came back before I could help them."

"Follow me in, we'll help them now," Lorev said. "Go to the right once we're in the house, I'll go to the left, he won't be able to watch both of us at once." Dorlan nodded and followed Lorev to the open door.

Hessa, Yella, Shilla, and Mai were sitting on the floor, hands, and feet bound. There was a baby on the bed, screaming his hunger to the world.

"Shut him up!" shouted Jorn, his spear a hand's-breadth from Hessa's face.

"Then let me go. I need to feed and clean him," she said.

Jorn moved his spear to the baby. "Make him shut up, or I will."

Lorev saw Dorlan fly across the house, getting between Jorn and his son. "Don't you dare hurt him," Dorlan shouted.

"Oh, the mad one returns," Jorn said.

"And she's not alone," Lorev said from the door.

"Another of Col's brood," Jorn said, glancing over his shoulder, "I'll kill you in a moment."

Lorev saw him thrust his short spear forward. Dorlan's eyes bulged, and her mouth formed a silent scream. She gave a cough, and a gout of blood oozed over her chin. As Jorn turned to him, he saw the spear protruding from under Dorlan's ribs. The girl crumpled, still impaled, to the floor as Jorn drew a flint axe.

"Now for you," he said, advancing on Lorev. He raised his arm for a blow, but Lorev sidestepped, drawing his own blade. Lorev crouched, but as Jorn raised the axe again, Trav flew through the door, jaws crunching on his wrist.

"Get it off!" Jorn screamed as Trav worried at the arm. Lorev picked up a stool from the hearth and smashed it into the side of Jorn's head. Trav followed him down, still snarling as the leader's body crumpled.

"Enough, Trav," Lorev called. Jorn's hand was a mess of torn flesh as the wolf dropped it and walked to his master. Lorev rushed to Dorlan, but the pool of blood told its own story. She was dead, the spear shaft still wedged in her body. Lorev closed her eyes and then went to the captive women, cutting Hessa free to care for baby Saren. She smiled as she rushed to her son, pulling open her shirt to feed the wailing child.

He cut Shilla's bonds, then freed Mai and Yella. The girls all had wounds, and he was checking them when Trav growled.

"Enough, Trav," Lorev said, standing to greet the recent arrival. "What are you doing here, Father?"

Col stepped inside. "I came to rescue my daughter," he said. He looked at the body on the floor.

"It's Dorlan," Lorev said, "She died protecting Hessa's child from Jorn."

Col went to the fallen girl, drawing the spear from her body and laying her flat. He placed a hand on her head and one on her heart, calling to her ancestors.

"Lorev?" He turned to find his mother, Talla, coming in the door. "Are you alright?"

"Yes, Mother, but the girls are hurt. Help me with them," Lorev said, turning to Mai, while Talla fussed over Shilla. Gren and Zoola arrived, rushing to help the others.

"How did you know Shilla was here?" Lorev asked, rubbing salve into a welt on Mai's cheek.

"Jorn sent a message," Col said. "He wanted twenty head of cattle for Shilla's safety."

"And you brought them?" Lorev asked.

There was a muffled scream from outside. "No, I brought twenty warriors instead."

Trav growled again as Jorn stirred on the floor. He lifted his ruined hand and moaned. Lorev stood over him. "So, Chief Jorn," he said. "This is how you treat the protected-of-spirit – kidnapping and imprisonment, threats, and beatings. You killed a spirit apprentice. What do you think your punishment will be?"

"Kill him," said Col, not even looking up from working on Mai's leg.

"Get it over with," growled Jorn, meeting Lorev's icy gaze.

Lorev kicked at the bleeding mass that had been Jorn's hand. "Too easy," he said when the chief's screaming had stopped. "Father, hold him down," he said. "Shilla, fetch my tool pouch."

Shilla ran to his pack by the door and found the leather pouch with the wolf's-head engraving. She passed it to Lorev. "No," he said, "You do it." He drew two fingers under his right eye, and Shilla nodded.

Lorev grabbed Jorn by the hair, keeping his head still, while Col held his body. Shilla glared into his eyes as she took the tiny blade to his face.

"What are you doing?" Jorn said. "Just kill me. Col said to kill me."

Shilla's trembling hand cut line after line under his right eye. Lorev's fingers tightened in his hair as he tried to struggle.

"My sister is giving you a tattoo," Lorev said. "Now you are an outlaw, an outcast. You have no tribe now, no clan. You're alone in the world."

"My supporters will take me in and feed me," Jorn said through clenched teeth.

"Oh, I will not leave you here. Not on the Long Islands. I'm taking you to the Atay lands. You can live like the rat you are. But if they see you, if they catch you, what do you think they will do to you?" Jorn shuddered. "And when you die, no one will speak for you. Your spirit will roam this plane forever, never granted rest."

"No. Kill me!" Jorn shouted. "Lay me to rest with my family."

"Your family?" Hessa asked, walking over, Saren asleep in her arms. "The father you murdered? Do you think he will welcome you to the land of the dead?"

Jorn was sobbing as Shilla rubbed the lamp-black into his scars and stood from her task. She peered at the blade in her bloodied fingers and glanced at her brother.

"Throw it in the fire," he said. "His blood has soiled it, and I have others. Be sure to wash his blood from your hands too."

"What about his hand?" Shilla asked.

"Honey, and bind it," Lorev said.

Shilla lifted it, inspecting the wounds and shaking her head. "We should amputate it," she said.

Lorev frowned. "I'm not wasting time on him. If he dies, I don't care, as long as it is slow and painful."

Col put a hand on Lorev's shoulder. "Perhaps we should treat him," he said.

"Do you think I'm being harsh, Father?" he asked. "He killed an apprentice and imprisoned four protected-of-spirit, two of them my sisters. Across the water, the Shore Clan is destitute. He killed seven men and injured their chief, Gan, and their spirit master, Genna. He has taken their food and burned their houses and their grain. Now, do you think I'm being harsh?"

Col nodded. "No, Son, you are right."

"Can we get a beacon lit on the hillside?" Lorev asked. "My boatman is waiting for a signal."

Col walked to the door, calling to one of his men. They exchanged words, then he returned. "One of them will light a beacon. I have set a guard around the village. No one leaves here tonight. Tomorrow we will find a way for the Bay Clan to make amends. Now, can we get the fire going and have some tea?"

They settled around the fire, each with a drink, Lorev going to the women and girls to check on them.

"Are you hurt, Hessa," he asked.

"No," she said, pointing to her fading black eye. "These are old wounds. We fought before he left for the raid. He hit me." She reached up and traced Lorev's fresh tattoos. "What are these?"

"Star master marks," he said.

Hessa nodded. "It seems like you have found yourself, Lorev."

* * *

Lorev had lain awake all night. Thoughts of how the Bay Clan could hope to make restitution to the Shore Clan running around his head. He smiled at the two girls who had insisted on sharing the bed with him. Shilla was tucked into his left side, Mai to his right. Both slept well, despite their ordeal. As dawn broke, he climbed out of bed. He pushed the two mumbling girls together and watched as they clung to each other and drifted back to sleep.

"Good morning, Lorev," Zoola said, standing from the kindled fire. She reached for him, hugging him. "You have changed," she said.

Lorev accepted the warm hug. Zoola was like an aunt. Almost a second mother. "How so?" he asked.

"Last night," she said, "You took control. You are your own man now, aren't you?"

"I suppose so," he said. "I rushed to get here, to save Shilla and Mai. When I saw the destruction at the Shore Clan, it took me back to the war on the Isle of Pigs. So much senseless loss."

"You have seen too many unpleasant things, Lorev."

"As did you, on your travels," he said.

"What do you think will happen today?" Zoola asked.

"I have a plan. Do you think my father will allow me to take control again today?"

"I'll have a word with him," Zoola smiled, kissing his cheek. "Now. Rose-hip and nettle tea?"

"Of course," Lorev grinned, "With honey, if there's any left."

* * *

Lorev paced up and down in front of the packed village square. He had assembled every person from the Bay Clan. Jorn stood against a pole, his hands tied behind his back. Though Lorev had tied his ruined wrist loosely, he winced at every movement. Lorev stopped mid-stride and turned to the people of the Bay Clan.

"This is Jorn, your Chief," he said. "A man who murdered his own father. A man who struck his mate. This is the leader who raided a village of innocent people, killing seven men and injuring others. Jorn imprisoned four protected-of-spirit, threatened his own baby son, then killed Spirit Apprentice Dorlan."

The villagers gasped at the last piece of information. They'd all noticed the covered body by the roundhouse door, but none knew who it was. Lorev stepped up to Jorn, pointing to his face. "This is an outlaw tattoo. He is no longer Jorn of the Bay Clan, he is no one. He has no people, no tribe, and when he dies, he will have no rites. I will take him to the Great Island and release him in the

Atay lands. If he can keep out of sight and catch his own food, he may survive."

The gasp this time was loud.

"Quiet," Lorev shouted. "Those of you who followed Jorn on the raid, step forward now." No one moved.

A man with a wound to the side of his head stepped out. "He ordered us to go. Gave us no choice," he said.

"And you are?"

"Lart," he said. Lorev nodded.

"Did no one stand against Jorn?" Lorev asked.

To one side, an older man shifted from foot to foot. "I did."

Lorev noticed a black eye and split lip. One of the man's front teeth was missing. "And that was your punishment?" Lorev asked.

The man nodded.

"Gather your family. You are free," Lorev said.

Lart spoke up again. "What do you mean, free? Aren't we all free?"

"I haven't decided yet. Now, those on the raid, step forward. Come on, there are witnesses. Do I have to cross to the Great Island to get them?"

They drifted to the front, eighteen in all. Lorev walked along the line. "Which of you killed a man?" he said. Five hands rose. "Stand to the side," Lorev said. "Now, you and you," he pointed out two more men.

"You pushed aside the spirit master and broke her arm," he said to the first. He turned to the second. "You dragged my sisters by the hair, then stuck Mai, an eight-year-old apprentice."

"How can you know that? You weren't there," the man said.

Lorev's finger stroked the lines of his tattoo. "I am a star master," he said, "I was there. I saw. Join the others."

His confidence wavered for a moment. He glanced up, and Col gave him a tight smile and nodded.

"Each of you eighteen will have a single line tattooed under your right eye. The seven picked out here, will go to the Shore Clan as slaves to the village."

"Slaves?" shouted Lart.

"You have another choice," Lorev said, "Take an outlaw tattoo and join your former leader." Lart bowed his head.

"You will be slaves," Lorev said. "You will rebuild, work with the crops and animals, whatever the chief asks of you, you will do. When the village is back to its former strength, when you have paid your debt, you may return to your homes here."

"Why the tattoos?" asked a woman from the crowd.

"So they cannot escape their debts," Lorev said. "People will know that mark in every tribe and clan within two moons. There will be no running away."

He turned back to the crowd. "The tattooed ones left here will do the work of those paying the clan's debt. You will be responsible for this clan's survival. Step up now to receive your tattoos," he said.

Col and Talla, Gren and Zoola, all stepped forward, tool pouches in hand. One by one, the men came to be marked. Lorev watched as Mai came and stood before the man who had hit her.

"Kneel," she said. The man glanced at Lorev, then knelt. Mai took a blade and reached for his face. He twisted away, glaring at her.

"Which tattoo do you want?" she said.

"Line," he said, closing his eyes. Lorev smiled.

Hessa came to stand beside him, Saren in her arms.

"What's wrong, Hessa?"

"You will release Jorn on the Great Island, to die?" she asked.

"That is what I intend to do. Don't beg for him, Hessa, I'm not sure I could refuse you."

"Beg for him? I am glad to be rid of him," Hessa said. "No, he and I are still bonded."

"Do you want the knot cutting?" Lorev said. He saw hope in Hessa's eyes. "I cannot do it. I have… I had an interest in you. It would not be right."

"Who then? I won't be the mate of an outlaw."

Lorev thought. "I'll ask mother. Be ready later, we must leave here in the morning."

Thirty-nine.

The furs were warm around him as Lorev closed his eyes. It had been a hard day. Dealing with the Bay Clan raiders, giving the tattoos, watching Talla cut the bond between Hessa and the outlawed chief. He felt a presence by the bed and opened his eyes.

"Can we talk?" Hessa whispered.

Lorev threw back the furs so she could slip in beside him, as they did when they were children. "What's wrong, Hessa," he asked.

Her eyes flicked to his, then away again. "You said earlier that you had an interest in me. Do you still?"

"Hessa, a lot has happened…" Her finger went to his lips, silencing him.

"Do you?"

"Yes."

"Good," she said, throwing back the furs and sitting on the edge of the bed. "I have an interest in you too."

"That's all you wanted?" Lorev asked, surprised at her abrupt departure.

She grinned back at him. "No, I'm just getting undressed."

* * *

Hessa's body was still draped over him when Shilla carried a grumbling baby to their bed just after dawn. Lorev's sister smiled at him and pushed the baby at Hessa.

"Thank you for looking after him," Hessa said.

Shilla shrugged. "He slept all night." She looked at Lorev. "Tea?" she asked.

They were sitting at the hearth, Hessa feeding Saren, when Col and Talla joined them. "You are still going to the Great Island today?" Col asked.

"Yes," Lorev said, "I will set Jorn free, to live or die, set the slaves to work for the Shore Clan, then return Mai to her mother."

"She doesn't want to go back," Shilla said. "We want to stay together."

"So you want to live at the Forest Clan?" he said. Shilla's glare cut into him. "Um, Mai wants to come to the Isle of Pigs?" he asked.

"I want that so much, Lorev. Will you allow it?" Mai said.

"We must still return," he said. "You need your mother's permission, but yes, I would welcome you."

Both girls squealed and ran to hug him.

"You are gathering quite a little community in your new home," Talla said.

"We need it. The Drogga Tribe will take years to recover from the war, and I must salvage the star teachings," he said.

* * *

They loaded the last of the slaves into the boat, and Lorev pushed it away from the shore. He checked the supplies in the second vessel, then helped Shilla, Yella, and Mai aboard. Trav leapt in at his command.

"I'll see you soon," he said to his mother and father, hugging each of them. He turned to Hessa. "I'll be back as soon as…" Her fingers on his lips silenced him again. This was becoming a habit. He smiled.

"Don't make promises to me, Lorev," Hessa said, "Just come back." She kissed him and watched as he shoved the boat off and clambered in.

* * *

The journey was quick and smooth, and Lorev had no time to think about his sea-sickness before they were landing at the Shore Clan. Genna and the remaining warriors met them as they came ashore.

"Yella! Are you hurt?" Genna said, hugging her young apprentice.

"Nothing serious, Spirit Master," The girl replied.

"Who are these men? Why the tattoos?" Genna asked.

"They are here as slaves," Lorev said. "They will rebuild, work in the fields, whatever you need. When they've paid their debt to the Shore Clan, you may send them home."

Genna nodded. "Is this your doing?" she asked.

"Yes. Is that acceptable?"

Genna looked at the men, though none made eye contact. "We accept. What of him?" she said, pointing to Jorn.

"I will set him free. He is an outlaw now. If anyone sees him again, kill him on sight."

Genna took her water skin, handing it to Jorn. "Take this," she said. "You have until sunset. After that, if we see you, we will kill you."

Jorn turned and trudged away from the boats, heading for the forest. One warrior nocked an arrow and raised his bow.

"No!" shouted Genna. "We have more honour than that." The man nodded and lowered his weapon.

"How is Gan?" Lorev asked, worried that the Clan may also need a new leader.

"He is past the worst. The bad spirits left him last night. He is in pain, but he will recover, spirits permitting," Genna said.

* * *

The next day, Lorev's party left the Shore Clan and headed south. The journey was less rushed, and there were two eight-year-olds to hold him back. He didn't mind, though, as he enjoyed teaching them both a little about the moon and stars as they travelled. It was half a moon later that they walked into the Forest Clan village. Gianna, Raya, and Devra clung to him and Mai for a long while before he could sit and tell of his journey. Mai and Shilla told their tale to the horror of Mai's mother.

"Vinna," Lorev said. "Shilla and I must return to the Isle of Pigs soon." Vinna nodded. "Mai wishes to come with us."

Her face blanched. "You want to take my daughter from me?" she asked.

Mai ran to her mother. "No, Mother. Shilla and I have become such wonderful friends, we don't want to be parted. Lorev's tribe will welcome me, and I'll continue my spirit training. Please!"

"We would get word to you, by travellers, whenever we could," Lorev said. "Any of you are welcome on the Isle of Pigs anytime."

Shilla walked to Mai's side, taking her hand as if to add her support. Vinna turned to her mate. "She is not your blood, but you are her father now," she said. "What do you think, Govat?"

"If you can bear it, let her go," he said. "It will help with her training, and it's good for her to have such a close friend. Lorev has already proved that he takes care of his sisters."

Vinna considered for a moment and nodded her head. "You may go, Mai," she said, as the girls screamed and hugged her.

* * *

Lorev was amazed at the improvements to the Shore Clan in the moon they'd been away. They had rebuilt two of the burnt-out houses, and the barley crop was green and weed-free. Gan limped out to greet them.

"Greetings, Star Master Lorev," he said, hands extended. "Our clan owes you a debt of thanks."

"Pay me by thriving," Lorev said, clasping the chief's hands. "How is your wound?"

Gan pulled up his shirt. The scar was ragged and red. It would always be ugly, but it had healed and was dry.

"I only wish I'd got to you sooner," Lorev said.

"You saved my life, be content with that," Gan said. "Come, join us for a meal."

Genna joined them to eat, and they discussed the slaves and their contribution to the Shore Clan.

"They work well," Gan said. "I think they are sorry for their actions. If we get a good crop this year, I think I will send them home before the winter."

"That's your decision, Gan," Lorev said. "Be sure you get enough work from them first, though. You cannot call them back."

* * *

They crossed to the Long Islands as soon as the weather was in their favour. Lorev was glad to see that Rolva and her family had returned to the Boat Clan, and they spent the night in her home. The following day, they interred the bones of Dorlan in the Clan's tomb. Lorev and his sisters were quiet as they watched Rolva deal with the ancestors and set the apprentice's spirit free.

"Will you cope with the two clans' needs?" Lorev asked her when they returned to the house.

"Yes. And your father has promised me an apprentice from Classac before the full moon."

"I am sorry that I could do nothing to save Dorlan," he said.

"I spoke with Shilla and Mai," she said, taking his hand. "You did what you could."

Lorev nodded. "We will travel to Classac tomorrow. It will be nice to spend time with my family again."

"Going home," Rolva said.

"No. Home, now, is the Drogga Tribe, on the Isle of Pigs. The girls and I will return there soon."

"And Hessa?" Rolva asked.

"We — have not discussed the future," Lorev said.

* * *

The three travellers walked up the village track. They stopped to pay respects to the ancient bull's skull on the boundary post, then entered the settlement.

Col stood outside his house, arms extended, a grin on his face. "Star Master, Spirit Apprentices, you honour us with a visit. Welcome."

Lorev smiled back. "Thank you, Spirit Master, you honour us with your hospitality." The two men fell into a fierce hug, while Talla fussed over the girls. When Lorev turned to enter the house, Hessa was standing in the doorway.

"Hello, Lorev," she said. Her face betrayed no feeling.

"Hello, Hessa."

"Oh, for Spirit's sake," Talla said, pushing them together. "Kiss her."

Lorev's arms found her waist as she clung to his neck and their lips met. Mai and Shilla giggled behind them.

"Come, I'll show you to our house," Hessa said, taking his hand.

* * *

"So, we have a plan," Shilla said, sitting beside him. Lorev had been enjoying the evening sun on a bench outside the house.

"Hessa will try for her spirit master status at midsummer," said Mai, sitting on his other side.

"And you have a job to do at the stone circle," Shilla finished.

Lorev laughed. "My sisters are planning my life for me," he said.

"Of course," Mai giggled.

"Once Hessa is a spirit master, and you have finished your work, we will all go back to the Isle of Pigs," Shilla said.

Lorev froze. "I have asked nothing of Hessa," he said.

"Do you still love her?" Mai asked.

"Still? I…"

"You've loved her ever since I can remember," Shilla said. "Do you still?"

"Yes," Lorev admitted.

"Good," Shilla said, taking Mai's hand. She looked back at her stunned brother. "Oh, father and Gren want to talk to you in the morning."

Forty.

Massive wooden clubs pounded the wedges into the crack in the rock. It had been generations since they'd used the quarry, but legend said that each of the Classac stones had come from here. Fitting, Lorev thought, that the fresh additions should too.

"It's lifting," someone shouted. Lorev ran forward as the slab groaned at being disturbed from its slumber.

"Stop," he said. He knelt on the glistening rock, palms flat on the rough surface. "Rock Brother," he said, "We need your help. We ask you to come with us and join your siblings at our circle. We need your power." He felt a warm sensation in his belly as the stone agreed.

* * *

"Will they be ready for summer solstice?" Gren asked.

Lorev sat at the fire. "Yes, once we quarry them, the biggest task is to drag them to the circle. We will build a sledge tomorrow and bring down the first one."

"You have checked the alignment?" Col asked. "Albyn maintained those wooden posts until he lost his sight, but we need to be sure."

"I consulted the charts from two star masters. Both agree. If we place them where the stumps of Albyn's posts are, they will show the moon-rise at the low-of-the-moon."

"Have you thought of staying here?" Gren said. "We could use your knowledge and abilities."

Lorev shook his head. "I must return to the Bridge Clan. The Drogga people need me, Shilla and Mai too. Perhaps I should have told you sooner, but I have a child on the islands. A son called Loryn.

"I am a grandfather?" asked Col. "When? Who?"

"Jath is his mother," Lorev said. "He will be two summers at the solstice, I have not seen him in over a year."

"If you and Jath are together, Lorev, you must not lead Hessa on," Col said.

"Jath is chief of the Eagle Tribe now, and bonded to a woman I think you know, called Nuru."

Col looked at Gren and sighed. "How the world moves on around us," he said, "It almost makes you feel old. Nuru bonded. She was little more than a child when we made our journey."

Gren chuckled. "Well, you have a grandson, and you'll have twenty-five summers this year. Perhaps you are getting old."

Col grinned and punched his arm. "Shut up!" he said.

"What has got you three so happy," said Talla. Zoola and Hessa followed her in.

"You are a grandmother," said Col. "Lorev informs me he has a son with Jath."

Lorev saw Hessa's face pale. He patted his father's knee and nodded towards the door. "Back in a moment," he said.

He caught up with Hessa just outside and grasped her arm. "No," he said. "No more running away."

Hessa spun around. "Are you going back to her?"

"No. I will return to the Bridge Clan. Jath is chief of the Eagle Tribe and is bonded to her own mate, Nuru. She visits from time to time, so our son will know his father as he grows up. Is that so wrong?"

"You are not together?"

"We never were," Lorev said, taking Hessa by the shoulders. "I was her toy for a while. Yes, I took it hard when she left, but we are friends now. There is no one else."

"Tell her," said a voice behind him. Lorev turned to find Shilla and Mai. "Tell her about the others," Shilla said.

Lorev glared at his sister. "Others?" said Hessa.

"Sit down," said Lorev, walking to the bench. "Shilla. Since you are so keen on Hessa knowing every bit of my life, you can tell her."

Shilla led Hessa to the bench, then sat beside her. Lorev could see her going into story-teller mode.

"The great war between the Isle of Pigs and the Isle of the Eagles had raged for thirty years," she said. "Some say it was the fault of a spirit messenger called Albyn, who stole sacred artefacts. The last raids of the war left both sides ruined. They laid warriors to rest and rebuilt homes, but nothing would bring back the lost men. A spirit apprentice called Lorev brokered the peace. With great courage, he went to the Isle of the Eagles to speak to the chief.

"Chief Jath and her mate were also rebuilding their village but, unknown to Lorev, the chief had borne his son after a brief liaison that lasted a few moons. They agreed his tribe would never attack his son's home and that her tribe would never raid the home of the boy's father. Lorev returned to the Drogga people a hero. Nevertheless, there were not enough men to father the next generation.

"A widow by the name of Joreen came to Lorev and asked him to father a child for her. She understood he would never bond with her, but she wished to do her duty to her tribe and bear children. Lorev agreed, and the widow became pregnant.

"Soon, other widows heard of the arrangement and also asked Lorev for his aid. He helped them all to fulfil their duty. So the Bridge Clan of the Drogga people grows, despite the savage war that took many of their menfolk."

Hessa looked at Lorev, her face unreadable, then turned back to Shilla. "A hero, eh?"

"Undoubtedly."

"How many?" Hessa asked.

Shilla smiled. "Five."

"You!" Hessa said, rounding on Lorev. "You father children for five women and expect that none will ask for your promise of bonding?"

"That is our arrangement. The tribe and the village are prosperous. They are well provided for."

"So you have six children?" Hessa said, palming her face.

"Five were pregnant when we left. I cannot foretell the outcome," he said. Hessa sat, shaking her head.

"Now you," said Shilla, nodding to Hessa.

"What?"

"Tell him your news," Mai said from beside her sister.

"What is your news?" Lorev asked.

"If I tell you, you'll just say that the Hill Clan is prosperous, and I will be well provided for," she muttered.

"You're going to have our child?" Lorev asked. Hessa nodded. "Then, I would not say that. I would say that I've waited for you most of my life, but my life took one path, and yours another. Now those paths cross again. I would say, Hessa, will you give me your promise of bonding?"

Hessa stood, shaking. Her glistening eyes fixed on Lorev.

"Um, it's a yes or no question, Hessa," he said. "I might settle for 'maybe' if that's the best I'm going to get."

Hessa flung herself at him, arms around his neck, face buried in his chest. "Maybe," she said.

"What might make that maybe a yes?" he asked.

"Get me some bread and cheese," she sniffed, "I'm starving."

Lorev ran into the house, grabbing half a loaf and a lump of cheese from the basket on the shelf.

"Is everything alright, Lorev," said Col.

"Yes. Hessa has just agreed to be my mate, and you're going to be a grandfather again," he said, making for the door.

"What? So two grand-babies?" Talla asked.

"Perhaps seven," Lorev said, running outside.

"Seven?" Talla asked. "Lorev? Lorev!"

* * *

"Do you want me to stay here?" Lorev asked. Hessa's head was on his chest, his arm wrapped around her.

"No. I want to return with you," she said. "You are the star master of the Drogga people, your son is there. Even Shilla wants to return."

"I want you to be happy," Lorev said.

"The ancestors gave me a prophecy, long ago," Hessa said. "I would be bonded, but not at Classac. I would bear a son and would live far away. My second child would be a girl, and in time, I would be happy. So, it seems that if I move far away with you, once our daughter is born, happiness will follow."

"A girl?" Lorev said.

"So the ancestors said." Hessa turned to look up into Lorev's eyes. "These children of yours, the five women that were pregnant, I want to know who they are, I want them to know that I know about them."

"There is no need for jealousy…"

Hessa's finger sealed his lips again. "I want them to know I support them, and I want you to acknowledge all of your children. Will you do that?"

"I would like that," he said.

***

The ropes creaked as the massive stone reached the balance point.

"Strain on the back ropes," Lorev shouted, hoping to stop the slab toppling forward. He ran to the pit, dropping rocks in to brace the new megalith. Col and Gren joined him, pounding the rocks to secure the first of the 'Albyn stones'. The bank of earth stood redundant now, and Lorev got the men to shift it alongside the second hole.

The process began again, raising the smaller stone for the south by south-west. They levered the rock up with long poles, packing the earth under it. The base of it hovered over the prepared hole until the angle got just steep enough, and it slid down into its socket. Again they attached ropes and pulled it upright. The filling took less time for this smaller stone, and they soon secured it.

"Pack the earth around the bases," Lorev said, directing the labour. "Fill in the gaps to make it all secure."

"It is an excellent job, Lorev," Col said.

"Thank you, Father. Will you dedicate them at the solstice?"

"Yes, our celebration will be bigger this year. New spirit masters, new keepers and apprentices. These stones to be consecrated, and your bonding."

"I look forward to it," Lorev smiled.

***

Mai sat with Saren on her lap, while Shilla spooned beef stew into his mouth. She wiped away the dribbled gravy as the boy chewed and swallowed.

"Will Hessa be back tonight," Mai asked.

"I doubt it," Shilla said, filling the spoon again. "She's doing a master's ceremony."

"Walking spirits?" Mai asked.

Shilla laughed. "That has got to be the worst kept secret amongst the protected-of-spirit, ever."

"Well, you have one, and I know Lorev does, and you're not even messengers yet. Do you think I have one too?"

Shilla shrugged. "You'll find out one day, I suppose. Come on, let's get him to bed," she said, wiping the boy's face again.

* * *

Hessa drank the last of the bitter tea and lay down beside the other messengers. She closed her eyes and waited as Zoola set a steady drumbeat.

Her body lifted, floating up into the roof timbers, through the smoke hole and high into the night sky. She emerged into bright light, shielding her eyes against the glare.

"Greetings again, Messenger Hessa," said a voice.

Hessa waited for her eyes to adjust, then looked around. The old woman stepped forward, arms outstretched. "Geth? Is it you?" Hessa asked. "You came to me before, but I didn't know about walking spirits then."

"Yes, I will be your spirit guide, Hessa. Is there anything you want from me?"

"Your prophecy is coming true now, isn't it?" Hessa said. "The bonding, my son, moving far away." Her hand stroked her belly, just showing now. "When she is born, perhaps I may find happiness."

Geth smiled. "Perhaps you already have," she said.

* * *

Hessa was glad of Shilla's and Mai's help the next day. They fed, changed, and amused Saren until her head stopped pounding. She was delighted that they would all be together on the Isle of Pigs.

Lorev was almost finished with the new stones, 'The Albyn Stones' they were calling them, and summer solstice was only two days away. Hessa spotted him coming down from the circle on the hilltop, his hair white with rock dust, his hands and forearms caked in dirt.

"Wash in the stream," she said. "I'll make you some food and tea."

Lorev returned, squeezing water from his hair as he sat at the hearth. "So, you have your walking spirit now?" he asked.

"Yes, and I hope not to use the mushrooms too often. They made my head hurt so much," Hessa said.

"They are a tool, but a dangerous one," Lorev said. "I had my fill of mushrooms when I learned the star teachings."

"One day," Hessa said, "Will you tell me about your year with the star master?"

"One day," he said.

* * *

The village at Classac had been busy for close to two moons, with apprentices and messengers coming for training, some even travelling from the Great Island. Now the work was done. It was the solstice, the longest day. All the protected-of-spirit were awake at dawn, making preparations for the ceremonies.

"How will we awaken Albyn's stones?" Lorev asked.

"We must summon his spirit to do it. There we have a problem," Col said. "Fetch Shilla."

The girls arrived, hands clasped. Col looked at Mai. "Should I assume that you and Shilla share everything now?" he asked.

"Yes, Spirit Master," she said.

"Call him father," Shilla said, "He's Lorev's father, and you're Lorev's sister."

Col smiled. "I would consider it an honour," he said. "So Shilla has told you about walking spirits?"

"Yes — Father."

"Very well, sit down, both of you. We must summon Albyn to bless the new stones. I know he is your walking spirit, Shilla, so I need you to call him in the ceremony."

"I can do that," Shilla said.

"The problem is your status. You should be a messenger to attend a rite such as this, but you are too young though I'm sure you could pass. The lore prohibits the status of messenger until you are an adult. In a girl, first moon blood, in a boy, his first hunting kill."

"That's not fair," Shilla said. "I made my first kill already. I took down a hare, on our journey, with Lorev's bow."

Col ruffled her hair. "I do not make the lore," he said, "But I may stretch it a little. If you were a master, you could attend. I think you are ready for plant and lore master status. Will you accept them and have your tattoo's changed?"

"Now?" she asked, braiding her hair away from her face. "I want Lorev to do it."

Lorev fetched his tool pouch and stood Shilla on a bench. "Ready?" She nodded.

He took the fine blade and cut the intricate spirals ends to her plant and lore marks. She hissed as he rubbed in the lamp-black, then stood facing Col.

"Well, Father?"

"Perfect."

"Shall we update Mai's tattoos now?" Lorev asked, glancing at his father.

Col looked baffled, then smiled. "What a marvellous idea. Do you agree Mai is ready for plant and lore keeper marks, Shilla?"

She turned to Mai, aware that her friend, her sister, lived in her shadow a little. "I think it is past time," she said. "And at the celebration tonight, we will walk the fire together. Agreed?"

Mai grinned and hopped onto the bench, presenting her face to Lorev. He took a fresh blade and began the incisions. Tears streamed from Mai's eyes, but she never flinched until Lorev applied the black to the cuts. As soon as he put down the blade, Shilla hugged her friend close.

"There, you're catching me up, Mai," she whispered. "Come on, let's show mother and Zoola."

Forty-one.

Hessa stood at the northern gateway of the Classac circle. Zoola came first. Dipping her fingers into a pot, she drew lines of red ochre down both Hessa's cheeks.

"I align you with the spirit of earth," she said, "bringing you grounding and courage."

Talla came next, wafting smoking herbs over her. "I align you with the spirit of air to cleanse you and bring a clear mind."

Gren stepped up, lifting a cup of water to her lips. "I align you with the spirit of water and give you a thirst for knowledge."

Col came to her last, his face stained red, Kark, his raven on his shoulder. His palm went to Hessa's forehead, pressing.

"I align you with the element of fire," he said, "To give you passion for life, and for teaching those who come after us. Welcome, Spirit Master Hessa."

Hessa almost stumbled as she stepped into the circle of stones, making her way to the other masters. The last graduate stepped up to the gateway. Rolva held her head high as Zoola, Talla, Gren and Col inducted her as a spirit master, then she joined Hessa.

"Nervous?" Rolva asked.

"No, that was the part I was dreading," Hessa said. "Being bonded to Lorev is the fun part. Come on, they're starting."

Zoola and Gren stood outside the sacred circle at the head of the north avenue. Hessa walked to them, facing them with a smile. Lorev came and joined her, taking her hand.

Gren smiled. "Lorev, Star Master of the Bridge Clan of the Drogga people. Do you choose this woman to be your mate?"

"Yes, I do."

Zoola stepped forward. "Hessa, Spirit Master of the Hill Clan of the Tribe of the West. Do you choose this man to be your mate?"

Hessa turned to Lorev. "I do."

"Will you honour each other as companions, friends and lovers through the years to come?" Zoola asked.

"Yes," Lorev said.

Hessa smiled. "I will."

Zoola lifted their clasped hands, and Gren tied a ribbon around their wrists, joining them together. "I bind you, each as mate to the other. All the tribes, the ancestors and the spirits have witnessed this," Zoola proclaimed.

Lorev leant over to kiss Hessa, and the crowd cheered, shouting congratulations to the young couple. Shilla, Mai and Jeeha brought over a small bundle.

Mai passed it to Hessa. "It's a birthing cloth for our new niece."

"We all worked on it for you," Shilla said.

"Everyone added at least a stitch," said Jeeha, "Even little Isla."

There was a lump in Lorev's throat as he realised that all his siblings, and all Zoola and Gren's children, had gathered to give the gift. He unfolded it, spreading the cloth for the tribes to admire. Hessa pointed out the embroidered patterns as each child told her how they'd helped create the blanket. Isla, the youngest, chattered to herself.

"It is time to speak with the ancestors for this solstice," Col said, stepping to the front. "We will also call to our ancestor, Albyn, to bless our new stones. Because of her close bond with him, I call on Lore Master Shilla to join us in this ceremony."

There were a few whispers, and nods of approval amongst those gathered as Shilla stepped forward. Col escorted her into the stone circle.

Col, Talla, Gren and Zoola sat facing the north, Rolva and Hessa sat behind as drummers.

"Shilla, Lorev, join us please," Col said.

Shilla sat beside her brother, a nervous smile on her face. Lorev took her hand. "You've done this before. It'll be fine," he said.

The drums started, and the protected-of-spirit closed their eyes.

The four spirit masters stood along the bank of the death river, each calling to their ancestors. Lorev and Shilla stood a little further downstream. Lorev raised his arms, calling out across the water.

"Ancestors that love us come. We ask for your advice and your help in our ceremony."

Two shapes materialised opposite. Albyn was dressed in his swan's feather cloak. Holding his hand was Verra. They stepped into the water, wading through the shallows until they climbed onto the bank beside Lorev and Shilla.

"Hello, little one," Albyn said. "I see you are a plant and lore master now. You make me very proud."

Shilla bowed her head. "It is because of your skill as a teacher that I have fresh marks, Messenger."

"It is because of your love of stories and your dedication to learning. I was only there to guide you," Albyn said.

"Should I ask you about the fortunes of the tribe for the coming seasons?" Shilla asked.

Albyn glanced at the four spirit masters. "They have all the help they need," he said. *"And I'm sure Verra will tell Lorev anything I may have forgotten. Come, let's look at your new stones."*

Shilla looked up and found a replica of the Classac stones stood ahead of them. She could see the people of the villages gathered around them, but they looked ghostly and transparent here. She wondered if any of them could see her and Albyn. As she watched, some older masters followed them with their eyes.

Albyn patted the great slab by the north gateway, then walked across the circle to the second stone. He stood behind the southerly stone and looked along the edge, lining them up.

"Perfect," he said.

The spirit masters drifted over to the stones as they finished their conversations with their ancestors. Lorev followed, Verra still at his side.

"Spirit Messenger Albyn," Col said. *"Please honour us by blessing our new stones. They have replaced the posts you left to mark the full moon rise at the low of the moon."*

Albyn stood tall. "We, the ancestors, have watched the erecting of these stones. They will be a permanent marker of the moonrise, and a credit to Lorev and the Hill Clan for generations to come." He stepped up to the stone and placed his hands on the rough surface. *"I bless this stone, awakened from the earth to mark the movement of our heavens for us."*

Albyn walked to the second stone, again touching the surface. He repeated the prayer, then turned back to the spirit masters. "You have transformed your landscape to honour the moon, and Lorev has come forward to carry on the teachings of the stars. The tribes of men are back on course to harmony with nature they should never have lost. Guard your ways well and do not forget your lore." He turned to Shilla. "A new generation springs up to carry the teachings forth. I must return now, but never forget that I, and my kind, are here for you always."

Albyn strode off towards the river, Shilla keeping pace. They reached the bank and Shilla took the old man's hand, stepping into the water.

"No!" screamed Talla. "Shilla, you cannot touch him, you cannot cross."

Lorev ran towards his sister. Then he was flying. He swooped down as the couple stopped at the mid-point of the river. Albyn patted Shilla's head and set off for the far bank. Lorev skimmed down, snatching Shilla from the water and dropping to the ground on the bank. Talla ran to them, just as Col called out.

"Back."

Lorev opened his eyes, still gripping Shilla in his arms in this reality. His sister smiled up at him.

"What's wrong?" she asked.

Talla snatched her from Lorev's arms, clutching her tight. "What did you do? You cannot touch the dead, you cannot cross the death river."

Shilla wriggled from her mother's grip and smoothed her dress. "You can cross the river unscathed, as can father," she said. "I am the daughter of Fire and Air, did you not think I was the same?"

"But how did you know?" Talla asked.

"Albyn would never allow me to come to any harm. I walked him home, as I used to do when he lived. He said half-way across was enough. That I should never fear the land of the dead."

Col placed his hand on his daughter's back. "I am glad that you are safe," he said. "I suppose we should have expected that our firstborn would have some of our magic. Thank you for bringing Albyn to bless our stones."

Shilla took Lorev's hand as Col turned to address the people. "Tell me more about the flying," she said, leading him from the circle of stones. "I want to learn how to do that."

Lorev stood with all the young ones, watching as Col and Gren raked the cooking fires out to build the fire-walk. Shilla and Mai stood ready and behind them Gart and Jeeha, Gren and Zoola's oldest children. Lorev considered them all siblings. If he added the younger ones, his birth mother's three, and Gianna, his step-sister, that made eleven in total. A magical number. He wondered if they would ever all meet.

"Will you walk with me?" Hessa asked. "The fire-walk is all I need to complete fire keeper status."

"I have never done it," Lorev said. "But I will go with you."

Col and Talla stepped off first, followed by Zoola and Gren. The new masters walked, singly or in pairs. Then it was Lorev and Hessa's turn. He gripped her hand tight as they stepped onto the coals. The heat was bearable as he trod down and lifted his other foot. He glanced at Hessa, grinning as she paced along beside him.

"Almost there," she said.

They stepped onto cool grass, and Hessa's arms wrapped around his shoulders. "Thank you," she said.

Shilla and Mai were next, rushing a little, but they made it with only a tiny burn to Mai's foot. Jeeha and Gart had both walked the fire before and strolled over the embers.

Lorev led Hessa aside and sat them down on the grass.

"We must think about moving back to the Isle of Pigs soon," he said, rubbing her baby bump. "The year is half done, and their harvest will need taking in soon."

"I am ready when you are," Hessa said. "As long as we are together, I will be happy."

"You are taking on Shilla and Mai too. Do you mind?"

Hessa smiled. "You are taking on Saren. I am glad to have a big family. Mine was taken from me when I was young, so I'm looking forward to it."

* * *

"You'd better come and visit us," shouted Shilla from the back of the boat.

Jeeha grasped Gren's hand. "I'll get father to bring me," she called.

Lorev checked the pile of belongings in Folon's boat, then pushed off from the beach, leaping aboard at the last moment.

Folon chuckled, pointing to Trav, standing at the bow, head into the wind. "It bodes well to have our tribe's totem aboard," he said, "Better still to have so many of the spirits' favoured ones with him."

"Did the wolf skin bring you a good price?" Lorev asked.

"I gave it to our Tribe's leader as a gift," he said. "He made me chief trader, and gave me the labour to build this vessel so, yes, I got a good price."

"You are sure we cannot pay you for this trip?"

Folon smiled, pointing to the second hull, loaded with a layer of rock. "I have schist, bloodstone and flint," he said,

"I will be loaded on my return, but for now, you are no impediment to my trading."

Lorev sat next to Hessa, taking Saren from her and holding the boy up to see the waves. Shilla and Mai chattered behind him, excited to be at sea. The journey took a few days, with a stop to trade stone for leather and dried meat. Folon made another stop the following day, offloading the meat in exchange for beautiful pots.

"You know your route well," Hessa said.

"I know who needs what, and when," he said. "These pots will be of value on the Isle of Pigs, as will be the leather. Any surplus will go to the Isle of the Eagles, then I'll head down the east coast."

The third day they came to the place that Lorev called home. As they sailed up the sea-lake, Lorev gasped. Coming from the village, in the distance, was a plume of black smoke.

Forty-two.

The figure rushed along the shore, towards them, as the boat crunched into the shingle. The lone woman reached them just as Lorev jumped into the shallow water, rope in hand. He looked up into the tear-streaked face of Kimmi.

"What has happened, are the Drogga under attack again?" he asked.

Kimmi flung her arms around Lorev. "No, it is a mourning fire. You know of our tradition."

"Mourning who? Who has died, Kimmi?"

"Today," she said, wiping her eyes. "I found Spirit Master Gelyn dead."

"I am sorry," Lorev said. "He was your mentor, your friend."

"I've never had to conduct a funeral, Lorev. I don't know if I can do it," she whispered.

Lorev beckoned to Hessa, who jumped over the bow, landing beside the grieving girl. "I will help you," she said. "Come, help us get our things ashore, then we can talk."

Kimmi took in the tattoos of the woman and bowed. "Spirit Master," she said.

"My name is Hessa, and I am bonded to Lorev now." She glanced back at the boat. "Shilla, you will recognise, and the other girl is Lorev's sister Mai."

A streak of grey flew through the air. Then Trav was standing with his forepaws on Kimmi's shoulders, licking her chin.

"I see you know him too," Hessa smiled.

* * *

Though the clan was in mourning, Lorev received nods of acknowledgement from many people as he entered the village. He led his new family to the house he and Shilla had shared. Dreena, Kimmi's mother, was kindling a fire as they came through the door.

"Lorev, it's so good to see you," she said, hugging him. "I thought it was you when I saw the wolf." Shilla made introductions to Hessa, Mai and Saren, while Lorev placed the star charts on the table. He looked around, taking in the home he remembered.

"You have kept the house well for us in our absence," he said to Dreena.

"Ready for you to return," she smiled, "And with such a family too."

"We had best make our presence known to Chief Norlyn," Lorev said, taking Hessa's hand. Shilla picked up Saren, and she and Mai followed on.

* * *

Norlyn looked so much older. Lorev had been gone more than a year, but the leader seemed to have aged far more in that time. He struggled to his feet as Lorev knocked on the door frame and entered.

"Greetings, Chief Norlyn," Lorev said.

"Greetings," he said, shuffling over and taking Lorev's hand. "You have a star master's mark now. We will be pleased to have the temple in use again." The old man thought for a moment. "You will stay, won't you?"

"We will stay," he said. "Let me introduce my mate, Spirit Master Hessa, and her son, Saren. Shilla, you know, and this is another sister of mine, Spirit Apprentice Mai."

Norlyn bowed. "It is an honour. You will have heard our sad news today. I hope you will take on the care of our community, Spirit Master. Kimmi has been panicking all day at the thought of being the only protected-of-spirit here."

"I would be happy to call the Bridge Clan of the Drogga people my home," Hessa said, "As would Mai."

Mai came forward and bowed to Norlyn, then took Shilla's hand. Norlyn eyed the two girls. "These two come as a pair?" he asked.

"They are inseparable," Lorev laughed.

Norlyn made his way to the hearth and sat on a bench. "Spirits help us," he said, smiling and shaking his head. "Get your home organised. We will talk another time."

Hessa soon made herself at home, storing their few possessions and allocating a bed for her and Lorev and one for the girls. They found a basket for Saren, though he would soon need his own bed. She had just thought what to make for their meal when Dreena appeared with a steaming pot wrapped in a thick cloth.

"I have made a simple stew, Spirit Master," she said. "May Kimmi and I join you to eat?"

"You may and please call me Hessa. There are bowls on the dresser there. Let me help you serve."

They sat to a delicious meal, then Hessa and Dreena bonded over the baby. Lorev went with Kimmi to view Gelyn's body.

"Have you said the prayer for the dead?" he asked.

"Yes, but I'm so unsure, Lorev. Did I do it right?"

Lorev placed a hand on the old man's head, and one over his heart. "He has gone. You did well," he said. "Hessa will work with you tomorrow to send him across the river. The girls may observe, Shilla at least knows lower world journeys." He looked at the spirit master's lined face. "Was he ill for long?"

"Many moons," Kimmi said. "I was giving him spirit mushrooms for the pain at the end. Yesterday, his lips were so blue. Then this morning…" She broke down in tears again, and Lorev held her until her grief passed a little.

"He is out of pain now," Lorev said. "Tomorrow he will be with the ancestors."

* * *

Hessa conducted the ceremony, with Kimmi's help, the next morning. Shilla and Mai drummed while Kimmi accompanied Hessa to guide Gelyn across the river. Lorev stood back, letting Hessa find her place in the clan. He walked over to the temple. The building was spotless, despite being unused for a year and a half. He got out Brode's old star charts, laying them out beside those from Bron's cave, comparing the two.

When the light failed, Lorev realised he had not eaten all day. He rolled up the charts and headed out of the door.

"Star Master Lorev," came a voice. Joreen stepped out, a small child in her arms. "I wanted to tell you I have a daughter."

"This is our daughter?" Lorev asked, tickling the girl's nose. "You must come to the house. I want you to meet Hessa." Joreen followed him across the square, eyes wide as she entered Lorev's home. Hessa looked up from serving food to Mai and Shilla. "Oh, a visitor. Will you join us for dinner?" she asked.

Joreen hung her head. "I am sorry, Spirit Master. The child will have no claim on your mate. I had no idea he was to be bonded to you."

Hessa walked over and lifted the woman's chin. "You must be Joreen. What are you sorry for? Was Lorev bonded when you asked him for a child?"

Joreen shook her head.

"Did you think he was promised?"

"No, Spirit Master."

"Then you did nothing wrong. He was single, and you are a widow, as I understand it. Now, what is your daughter's name?"

"I have called her Urva."

"Well, Urva will know her father, and I would like to be your friend," Hessa said. "I believe there are more of you who asked Lorev for his services?"

Lorev was blushing now as Joreen realised she was not in trouble for having the star master's child. "Four more women," Joreen grinned. "Five more babies."

"Twins?" Lorev asked.

"Yes, Sona had two boys. They were a hard birth, but they are well now," she said.

"Well, bring them all to meet me tomorrow," Hessa said, rubbing her belly. "I will have another before winter is over."

They sat to a simple meal of cooked meat, bread and cheese. Hessa chatted with Joreen while Saren and Urva played on the floor. Lorev looked around him and realised that he had a family of his own, at last.

* * *

Lorev swallowed the potion, screwing up his face at the bitter, earthy taste. He lay back on the small bed in the temple and waited. He'd left the family sleeping and mixed flying mushrooms and spirit mushrooms to make an infusion. The blood rushed through his veins, heart pumping as his vision blurred a little. There was movement beside him, and he looked up to see Shilla standing over him.

"I'll watch over you," she whispered, stroking his sweating brow. "Don't worry, go to your stars, Lorev."

His eyes closed, and his body lifted up through the temple roof, into the night sky. Soaring among the stars, he recognised the star-patterns' shapes as they flew by, bull, goat, fishes, wildcat. He smiled, happy to be back in his element. The evening star was rising, brighter than all the others. There was the red star, glittering higher than usual tonight. The sensation lessened as he dropped to the village again, soaring across the moonlit fields. Over the cattle, over the crops. The water shimmered the stars' reflections as he skimmed across the sea. Then he was back at the village, dropping through the roof of the temple, settling into his body once more as sleep took him.

* * *

The first thing he saw was the tattoo. Spirit apprentice under the left eye. Mastery of plants and lore.

"Hello, Shilla. How long was I out?" he asked.

She stirred and stretched, rising from the bed beside him. There was light as she pulled aside the door curtain.

"It's morning, but no one's about yet," she mumbled. "Early."

Lorev climbed out of bed. "We'd better get home. Hessa will worry," he said.

When they arrived at the house, Hessa was pulling stones from the fire. She smiled as she dropped them into the water pot. Shilla stumbled to the bed and crawled in beside Mai, while Lorev sat at the hearth.

"Were you up all night?" Hessa asked.

"No," he said. "We slept. I tried a new flying potion. Shilla must have seen me go out. She came to watch over me as I flew."

"She will want to learn from you," Hessa said.

Hessa served breakfast, even Shilla getting up before all the porridge was gone. Mai was clearing the bowls and platters when there was a shout.

"A sail on the lake!"

Lorev wandered out to see if another trader was arriving, but saw, instead, the small square sail of an Eagle

Tribe vessel. He set off for the beach, making the water's edge just as the boat ploughed into the shingle.

"Hello, Jath."

"Hello," she called, running down the sail. "We heard you were back. Loryn wanted to see his father."

"Nuru. It's good to see you," he said as Jath's mate leapt off the bow and handed him a rope. She hugged him and smiled at his tattoo.

"Is that a star master mark?" she asked.

"It is," Lorev said. "Now, do you have goods, or is this a family visit?"

"Family," Jath said, handing her son to Nuru, while she climbed out of the vessel. "I believe we have to meet your new mate?"

Lorev and Nuru hauled the boat above the high tide mark. "Come on, there are lots of people to meet," he said.

The village had gathered to watch Jath arrive. Many had heard talk of Nuru, her mate from far to the south, but few had ever seen black skin. Norlyn had donned his cape and carried his ceremonial mace as he stepped out to meet them.

"Chief Jath. Chief Nuru. It is an honour," he said, bowing to each. "Will you visit with me?"

Jath handed Loryn to his father. "Look after him, Lorev. He will need to get to know you again. We'll come to your house soon."

The lad struggled in Lorev's arms, and he set him on the ground, taking his hand as he toddled across the square.

"Who was it?" Hessa asked, as he entered.

"Jath and Nuru. They are with Norlyn," he said. "And this is my son, Loryn."

"He looks like you," Hessa said. "Now, let him meet Saren while I make introductions. Kimmi, Shilla, Mai, come on."

Lorev watched the women leave, then looked down at the two toddlers at play together. He poured the dregs of the morning tea into a cup and sat to watch them.

* * *

Lorev had just laid the tired boys down for a sleep when the women returned. Jath and Nuru were chatting with Hessa and the girls, but his eyes widened when more women arrived. He recognised Joreen, Loria and Sona, then realised what Hessa had done. The mothers of all his children were in the same house together.

Hessa smiled at his embarrassment as they all introduced him to his offspring.

Nuru wandered over all smiles. "Seven?" she asked, patting Hessa's belly, "And one on the way."

"Don't forget one to adopt," Hessa said, lifting Saren from the bed. "My mate doesn't do things by halves."

* * *

The celebrations of the winter solstice were only days past when Hessa's waters broke. Her apprentices fussed around her, and they sent Lorev to the temple with Saren for the day.

They played until the boy became sleepy, then Lorev studied the star charts while he dozed. The sun was setting when Shilla came in with an enormous grin on her face.

"We have birthed your daughter," she said, hugging her brother. "She is strong and healthy."

"How is Hessa?" Lorev asked.

"Tired. She's asking for you." Shilla looked around at the stark furnishings of the star temple. "Do you think Albyn studied here once, long ago?" she asked, taking his hand.

"It seems likely. Have you asked his spirit?"

"He will not speak of it."

Lorev lifted Saren and led Shilla from the building. "Then we may never know," he said. "Come on, introduce me to my daughter."

The End.

Get your free book!

A prequel in the Guardians of the Circles series.

Albyn and Layne run away to avoid an arranged bonding with a man Layne doesn't love.

Heading for a new life on the Great Island, they are captured by the hostile Eagle Tribe and forced into slavery.

When their escape is thwarted, Albyn takes brutal revenge, and steals an artefact of great power, but how will he control the wrath of the spirit it holds?

Go to www.apprenticetattoo.co.uk for more details.

Printed in Great Britain
by Amazon